THE SOURCE OF MAGIC

ACADEMY OF FALLING KINGDOMS 1

MARISA MILLS

DRAKE MASON

URBAN
EPICS

Printed in the United States of America

First Printing, 2019

ISBN: 9781072947509

New York, NY
www.UrbanEpics.com

URBAN EPICS

DISCOVER YOUR NEXT

READING ADDICTION

Sign up for new release updates and get a sneak peek of our upcoming projects. You'll also get exclusive previews of our most popular series starters.

ONE

I DUCKED UNDER THE MASSIVE, rusted fence that separated the Scraps from the Dregs, keeping my head low, looking out towards the piles of junk that stretched in every direction. It was refuse to the sky dwellers – everything from half-empty containers of high-end cosmetics and old clothing to malfunctioned mage tech – but that didn't mean it was worthless. Even their garbage was often finer quality than the stuff we were used to. Dig long enough and you could find something really valuable. Only problem was, the Dregs was forbidden, though that hadn't stopped me before. There was no sound except for the wind whipping through the barren earth and the crumbling ruins of long-forgotten buildings. I clenched my jaw to keep my teeth from chattering. My threadbare jacket did nothing against the sharp, winter wind. Sterling settled beside me, and for a few seconds, we listened.

"If we die of hypothermia, I'm gonna come back as a ghost and haunt your uncle for the rest of his life," Sterling hissed. "It's too cold for us to be doing this crap, Wynter."

It would be even colder in the Dregs. Darker, too. Looking

up, I could see the rocky underside of the Floats above us, casting a deep, perennial shadow over their protected refuse piles. Just around the ledge I could see the bright tips of the floating city in the sky, an impenetrable fortress to those without a magical means of reaching its towers. While the Scraps got some shade depending on the time of day, the Dregs were always dark, and at night, the inky blackness was especially ominous.

"If you die of hypothermia, you've got my full support in haunting my uncle," I said.

"Good. I was worried about having your approval," Sterling said. "I *totally* wouldn't have haunted your uncle anyway."

"We both know that's a lie," I replied. "How many times have I had to talk you outta something dangerous?"

"A lot."

"And how many times have you listened?" I asked.

"Never," Sterling replied, "But I do it for you. See. That makes it okay."

I stifled a laugh. "How is ignoring my legitimately good advice doing *anything* for me?" I asked.

"You get a lot of pleasure from saying, *I told you so,*" Sterling joked.

I shook my head and drew my attention back to the fence. Normally, it had wards magicked into it that would prevent intruders, but those wards had been down for years. They weren't really needed. Mage tech could be dangerous, and few had both the courage to brave the Dregs, as well as the skills to repair it into something useful. I had neither, but I was more afraid of my uncle's belt than the Dregs, and his connections knew enough about magic to use it without blowing up half the town. Usually. Gold and silver were nothing next to the value of magic.

I crept slowly forward towards a small hole at the base of the fence. I dropped onto my belly and squirmed beneath the fence, careful not to catch my hair or clothes. When I emerged on the other side, I edged along, leaving room for Sterling.

As he crawled in, I reached into the pocket of my coat, my cold fingers fumbling with the match and candle I carried. It took me three tries to light it. The candle's flame did little to fill the darkness, but that also meant we'd be harder to find. I knew there was a security tower near the main entrance, but it was sporadically manned by underpaid and lazy human guards. They weren't the ones I was worried about. The fire danced over the trash before us, illuminating jagged shards of metal and broken glass. We got to work, taking turns between holding the candle and digging through the dump with long sticks.

I carefully pulled aside a warped piece of metal—potentially a frame of some sort—and nudged it aside. Leaning forward, I gingerly pulled on the thin, silvery-blue piece of metal out of a tall mound of garbage. When it came free, I breathed a sigh in relief. More than once I'd inadvertently collapsed an entire mountain of metal on my head. Even if I'd emerged unscathed, the noise would have attracted unwanted attention from other scavengers, if not worse. Dark things bred among the mages' discarded garbage.

The item was some kind of broken rod. I turned it, and a weak blue glow shone through the cracks on its otherwise dark surface. Definitely mage tech of some sort. Sterling held the candle closer; the blue seemed to brighten and flicker in the firelight. "I've never seen anything like that before," he said.

"Me neither," I replied, turning the item around in my hands, "But it didn't blow up in my face."

"It's a good day, then," Sterling said.

He'd been on the receiving end of an explosive piece of mage tech more than once. By sheer luck, neither of us had ever gotten more than a minor burn or scrape from a piece of mage tech. Others weren't so lucky. I'd seen people with missing limbs and blackened skin after having an accident in the Scraps, which is why jobs like this were left to stupid kids. Like us.

I unshouldered my backpack, an old and heavily patched find from five years before. After carefully wrapping the tech up with a rough strip of cloth, I slipped it into the front pocket and kept looking. My uncle wouldn't be pleased with one piece of mage tech, even one as unique as this one, and the last thing I wanted to do was anger Gabriel. He was a volatile man even in his best of moods.

Sterling and I spent most of the night rummaging through the trash, looking for the diamonds in the rough. I had never seen a diamond before in my life, but I'd heard of them. In my mind, diamonds were shimmering bits of metal. They were a good length of steel or copper wiring. When the moon was at her fullest, after filling our bags with treasures, we sneaked back through the trash heaps and crawled through the fence surrounding the dump.

This was the dangerous part; some gangs preferred to wait in town and jump scavengers just when they thought they were safe. We kept to the shadows, eyes tense and watchful as we snuck through the dark streets. We passed tight alleyways glowing from the yellow oil lamps, and soft moans from ladies of the night as they entertained in the shadows. I jumped at the sound of a broken bottle, followed by bursts of raucous laughter. I sighed in relief when the entrance to the old subway appeared. Gabriel said it had once housed a form of transportation that could carry a thousand people great distances, but that was before the mages first appeared.

"Well, looks like that's a wrap, Wynter," Sterling said, furrowing his brow.

"I guess," I said.

Sterling pulled his pack off his shoulder and handed it to me with a wry smile.

"Make sure old man Gabriel doesn't cheat me, huh?"

"He wouldn't," I replied.

Not enough to get caught anyway.

Sterling grinned. "Yeah, sure."

"*You* are the one who decided to do business with him," I pointed out. "I told you it was a bad idea."

"I thought we'd already established that I never listen to you," Sterling replied.

"Rude," I said.

Sterling laughed.

"You know," I said, "You could stay the night and make sure Gabriel doesn't cheat you."

Sterling's easy smiled fell. "I need to get back home, so I can sleep. I'm heading out to the forests in the morning. Mom needs medicine."

I nodded. Sterling's mom, Claribel, had always been good to me. When I'd been very little, she'd set me by her, with Briar and Sterling, and read from this old book of fairy tales she had. I'd loved visiting her, until Gabriel said Briar and I were too old for children's tales. Claribel been sick for a while, and she relied on the forests outside the Northern area of the Scraps for medicine. Gabriel never let me go to the forests, but Sterling had learned to gather herbs and plants for his mother.

"No problem. I'll make sure you get paid," I replied. "Be careful."

He punched me lightly in the shoulder. "I'm always careful. It's everyone else you gotta worry about."

He was careful, but that didn't mean I didn't worry about him walking home alone in the dark. Although he was probably safer than me, now that I was lugging two bags full of loot. I'd been carrying a short dagger since last year, but my hands were too full to reach it. Still, they'd have to be stupid to rob me on Gabriel's front doorstep. My uncle and his connections practically owned the full expanse of the subway tunnel.

I waited until Sterling's footsteps faded, then walked quietly down the stairs, ducking into the darkness of the tunnel. Bits of metal poked my back through the thin fabric of my backpack as I trod down the broken steps and stepped into the shadows to wait for my brother. He was younger than me and less experienced, so he usually scavenged in the Scraps, never venturing close to the Dregs. There were safer places to search, places without fences or dangerous mage tech, but those places didn't usually offer rewards as good as the ones I found. This was my inheritance, all the trash held behind locked places and high fences.

Soon, I heard the slap of boots, and Briar descended the stairs. No one would have guessed we were brother and sister; we looked nothing alike. While I was short and dark-haired, Briar was tall and blond with hair that stuck out in every direction, like the briars on a scraggly rosebush. The only similarity between us was our blue eyes, and even then, it wasn't the same shade of blue.

"How'd it go?" I asked.

He shrugged. "The usual," he said, sighing, "Which won't be good enough for Gabriel."

It never was, and it probably never would be.

I forced a smile and threw an arm over his shoulders. "Someday," I said, "We're gonna find our own place on the outskirts of the Scraps, and then, we won't have to deal with Gabriel anymore."

Wishful thinking, and I knew Briar was too old for bedtime stories. Our uncle was too powerful to run from. Spiteful, too. Every time I tried to save up some money, or even fence a valuable piece I'd discovered on my own, Gabriel found out and left a permanent mark on my skin, so I wouldn't forget the betrayal. I had a small collection of them now: a row of burn marks and scars running up my arm.

"Yeah?" Briar asked. "Are we doing that before or after you discover you're a long-lost princess?" He was teasing, trying to make light of our situation like I was, but I could see the jaded skepticism in his eyes, and along with a darkness that hadn't been there a year ago. We both knew there was nowhere to run.

"Obviously, we'd run away first, peasant," I replied, with an exaggerated sniff.

"You'll have to change your name to something really pretentious," Briar joked. "I've never heard of any princess being called *Wynter*. You'd have to be Kristiana or something."

I gasped, as if irreversibly offended by the name Kristiana. "Wrong. When I'm a princess, I can have any name I want," I said smugly. "If anyone is getting their name changed, it's you. I hope you don't mind being called Chanticleer."

He laughed. "That's horrifying!"

"So is your face," I joked.

Briar nudged me with his elbow. "We have the same parents!" he protested. "If my face is horrifying, yours is, too!"

"Maybe I got all the good looks," I replied. "Sorry. I don't make the rules."

Briar sighed. "You're so mean to me," he said. But the spark of humor stayed in his eyes, and for a moment, we were ourselves again. Then we grabbed our bags and headed into the tunnel.

***

"So how's Sterling?" Briar asked.

"The usual. His mom's really sick."

"She's been sick for months," Briar said.

"I know."

"Do you think she's…?" Briar trailed off.

"I dunno," I replied. "Maybe. I hope not."

We'd reached an old part of the subway; Gabriel said it used to be called a station. Gabriel himself was there, waiting on a dark leather couch under the glow of a lamp. While most of the people in the Scraps were gaunt and bore the scars left by starvation, my uncle never had. He remained handsome, but it was a strange, frightening sort of beauty. His star-pale skin stood in stark contrast to his thick, black hair.

He smiled at us, revealing his unnervingly sharp teeth. "Children," he said.

"Hello, Gabriel," I said.

Briar's greeting was quieter.

Gabriel hummed and clicked his tongue loudly against the roof of his mouth. He didn't look at us; he'd already turned back to the book he was reading. "I'm sorry. Did you say something? I can't hear you."

Briar audibly swallowed. "I said hello."

Gabriel sighed. "You should be more careful. When people sense weakness, they go for the throat. You know I won't tolerate weakness in my family."

"I know, Uncle," Briar said. "I'm sorry."

"It's always *I'm sorry* with you, ain't it?" Gabriel asked. He tugged at the collar of his fitted shirt. He tried to dress like a gentleman, because it inspired trust, but I knew it was the only fine suit he owned and his rough speech gave him away immediately. "You wouldn't need to apologize nearly as much if you'd just do things right the first time. I don't know how I managed to raise such a useless child, but here we are."

"Is this really something you need to make a big deal out of?" I asked.

Of course it was. Gabriel pounced on every mistake, no matter how small. Arguing with him was pointless. Gabriel couldn't be reasoned with, only distracted. And over the years, I'd become very good at diverting my uncle's anger before it boiled over.

I walked past him and set my backpacks on a nearby table. When I looked over my shoulder, my brother hadn't moved. But Gabriel had. He tilted his head, his green eyes considering me over the cover of his book. Gabriel was reading about gemstones again.

"Sterling went home," I said, "But I brought his pack in with mine."

"Briar," Uncle said slowly, "Hand me your wares. You can go for now."

He stuck out his hand, expecting his command to be obeyed. My brother's pale eyes darted between our uncle and me. I nodded, and Briar handed over his backpack. Before my brother could leave, Gabriel pulled him close and hissed something in his ear. Briar's eyes widened in alarm. He glanced once to me, before leaving quickly. My stomach lurched, but I still forced myself to turn away. As I unzipped my backpack and emptied my wares, my hands trembled.

I felt my uncle before I saw him. The man moved with a predatory quietness, and as hard as I'd tried over the years, I never heard him coming. "I don't think your brother's been beaten enough," Gabriel said. "That would explain his cowardice. But with you, I can't quite tell. Maybe I was too harsh. I've read you make the most mistakes on the eldest child."

"I'm not your child."

"No, but as I recall, I did raise you."

Yes, but only because my parents weren't around and never had been.

"I didn't ask you to take care of me, so don't act like it's my fault you're stuck with me."

"Someday soon, this defiance will be your undoing," he said.

"Will it?"

Gabriel grasped my chin without warning and pulled my face around, so I met his gaze. "Do you recall Sterling's little sister?"

When I was a little girl, Gabriel used to tell me scary stories about how Sterling had a little sister, who liked to misbehave. One day, a mage lady came from the Floats. She couldn't have children of her own, so she went around stealing little kids out of jealousy. After she found Sterling's sister, the mage lady took her away and ate her. And if I misbehaved, Gabriel always said, the mage lady would come and take me, too. Stories about cruel and powerful mages were common in the Scraps, but I was too old to believe in such tales.

"Everyone knows Sterling doesn't have a sister," I said, "And he never did."

Gabriel smiled thinly. "Come with me."

I began to gather up the items I'd just scavenged, but Gabriel was already at the door.

"Leave them," he said. "I'll collect them later. I've got something else in mind."

I frowned. Gabriel usually opened my backpack like a present on Christmas morning, but tonight he didn't even want to look at what I'd discovered. *Something was wrong.*

Gabriel beckoned for me, and after a second's hesitation, I followed. We entered his study. It wasn't anything special—just a room of concrete with mismatched chairs and a metal drum that was sometimes filled with fire. There was a smattering of old psychology, business, and geology books, which Gabriel read often and forbid anyone else from touching.

Gabriel had a guest, an elegant-looking man, dressed all in black and wearing a sword, who lounged across an old, worn loveseat. Seeing us, he rose to his feet. When he moved, the light rippled across the purple trim on his coat, gleaming in the dim light.

"Here you are, Dorian," Gabriel said, sinking into a chair.

As Dorian approached, my blood turned to ice. Like my uncle, this man bore no traces of the hard living that had plagued the rest of us in the Scraps. But my uncle didn't look so...so unnaturally beautiful. There was something uncanny about how *healthy* Dorian looked and how his skin seemed to hold a faint, golden glow just beneath the surface. And Gabriel's implications about Sterling's sister suddenly sank in. I was staring at a mage, and he was here for me. Even if I didn't know why.

Dorian put a finger beneath my chin and coaxed my attention back to him. I tried to take him in pieces, to make him less terrifying. His hair was a warm autumn-brown, probably only a little darker than Sterling's was. Very ordinary, even if I'd never seen anyone have hair that looked so sleek and healthy before. And Dorian's eyes were steel-blue rather than the fierce red Gabriel said the mage-lady had. But even those observations didn't help much. I'd heard too many stories of mage wars not to be afraid. Sorcerers who could slice through a hundred humans in one blow; who could melt the stones of a fortress or pass straight through its walls; who could whisper to the trees and have them destroy their enemies.

"And who do I have the pleasure of meeting?" he asked.

"Wynter," I said.

"That's very...unusual."

"If you don't like it, you're welcome to change it," Gabriel replied.

Change it?

Dorian circled me and then, swept back into his seat. He awkwardly edged his sword around and glared at the loveseat as if it was its fault he couldn't sit properly. When he moved, I caught the glimpse of something blue along his wrist; it looked like a drawing. It was probably magic of some kind.

Dorian winked before casting a mischievous look towards my uncle. "How did a plain man like you have such a beautiful niece?"

It was clear Dorian was trying to be charming. Maybe if I didn't act charmed, he'd decide he didn't like me and abandon whatever this was.

"I ain't all that pretty," I said, picking up my uncle's diction. "There's lots of prettier—"

"Beauty is in the eye of the beholder," Dorian interrupted, "And if you're as smart as Gabriel says, we should be able to make this work. Of course, it'll take a little polishing to make anyone believe you're a lady, but this seems doable. Are you literate?"

Gabriel scoffed. "Do you really think I wouldn't teach my kids how to *read*?"

"Potentially," Dorian said.

"Why would people need to think I'm a lady?" I asked.

Gabriel looked absolutely gleeful, steepling his fingers. His lips curved into a smile, and his teeth shone in the light of the flickering fire.

"We're considering a business venture. Dorian wanted to see you before we negotiated a price."

I felt faint. Would Gabriel really go this far? I didn't want to believe it, but with a cold jolt of fear, I realized that he absolutely would.

"You're selling me?" I asked, nearly choking on the question.

It hurt more than I expected. My uncle was terrible and

quick-tempered. Impossible to please. But he was still my family, the only family I had aside from my brother. And now he was done with me. My stomach twisted painfully.

"It's more like…" Gabriel trailed off and waved a hand. "…indentured servitude. A contract. I ain't *actually* selling you anytime soon. Your brother, however…"

"You wouldn't," I said.

I needed to throw up. I rested my palm against the cool stone wall for support.

"Do you really think that?" Gabriel asked.

Not for a second. Gabriel didn't make empty threats. My mind whirled as I pictured being separated from Briar. I couldn't let that happen. If I did this job, whatever it was, maybe I'd be allowed to come home. As long as I didn't get caught. I didn't know Dorian or what he wanted, but good, honest men didn't do business with my uncle.

"What do you want me to do?" I asked, stalling for time.

"Dorian is a mage," Gabriel said.

I'd already guessed that, but hearing my fears confirmed was so much worse.

"I want you to enter in the Academy as a student. It's a school for mages."

Were they both out of their minds?

"I can't," I said. "There's no way anyone would mistake me for a mage. I—I don't have any magic!"

"For your sake, I hope you can fake it," Gabriel said.

"We aren't going to have you stay very long," Dorian said. "I just need you to steal something for me. Our plan is to have you pose as a student, enter the Academy, and help me find what I'm looking for. Then, we'll pull you out and bring you home.

It's a relatively simple task. Low risks involved, too."

Thieves in the Scraps lost fingers for stealing, one digit for each offense; I couldn't even imagine what horrible things might happen to thieves in the Floats. Maybe this had low risks for Gabriel and Dorian, but definitely not for me.

"Sell this well, and you ain't gotta worry," Gabriel said. "We've got a few weeks to get you ready. Tomorrow, we'll take you to the Market and buy some things to help you look the part."

Dorian nodded. "It'll be great," he said, sounding genuinely thrilled with the prospect.

I looked at Gabriel, hoping he might relent or reveal that this had been some horrible joke to teach me my place, but my uncle's smug smile never faltered. Whatever Dorian was paying him, it was worth a lot more than what I dug up in the Dregs. This was really happening. My pulse raced. There had to be some way out. I just had to find it.

TWO

MY STEPS WERE HEAVY AS I walked back to the room I shared with my brother. How was I supposed to tell Briar about all this? I have to go away for a while. Where? Oh, to a mage school in the Floats. I promise I'll come back. Probably.

And then, I'd have to tell Sterling. If my uncle even allowed that. My heart twisted when I thought of just leaving without saying goodbye; him having to hear second-hand that I was gone. I shivered and rubbed my forearms in a half-hearted attempt to warm myself. I wasn't ready for this conversation.

I paused and leaned against the wall. The cold, rough stone felt reassuring beneath my fingertips. Slowly, I sank to the ground. I felt like I might throw up, and I lowered my head between my knees, taking deep breaths to help with the nausea. I needed to think logically about this.

One. My uncle had sold me for an incredibly dangerous scheme. There was no way anyone would ever think that I was a mage. I'd been average my whole life, and mages were anything but average.

Two. Arguing would be pointless. Once my uncle settled

on something, he did it without any hesitation or pause. Dorian likely wouldn't be sympathetic either, considering this whole scheme had been his idea to begin with.

Which meant, the only way to get out of this suicide mission was to run. Surviving in the Scraps was already hard, but with my uncle, at least we had protection, shelter, and a meager supply of food. That was more than I'd have on my own.

Maybe I could go to the Dregs again, fill my pack, and instead of returning to the subway, I could just leave. Walk away just like that and take Briar with me. Sterling, too, maybe. My heart twisted. No, taking Sterling would be impossible. Sterling would never leave, not with his mother sick. It would have to be just Briar and me.

Would my uncle even let me scavenge after this, though? He was more likely to keep me under careful watch, expecting that I'd try and run. I grimaced. He might not be watching Briar as much, but I couldn't send Briar to the Dregs alone. Maybe I could ask Sterling to go with him, but then, I'd have to get a message to Sterling about everything without my uncle's goons intercepting it.

I leaned my head back against the wall and gazed upward. The stone above my head was cracked, and through the cracks, I saw slivers of the full moon; bright and silver in the dark sky. As a kid, I'd heard that the moon was the mother of the world, and I remembered being comforted by that once. When I was upset, I'd look at the moon and think of her as the mother I never knew. Any mom was better than none. But the moon had ceased to comfort me long ago. Tonight, her presence was cold and distant.

I stood slowly and pushed open the door to our room.

Briar sat on his bed, little more than a mattress and a couple of sheets. "I'm sorry," he said.

I shrugged and sat on my bed. "It's not your fault our uncle's a monster," I said.

After kicking my shoes off, I fell backward onto my bed and kneaded the blanket beneath my fingers. I let my eyes shift from the cracked ceiling to the bare stone walls. We'd put a patch of torn fabric over the small window to keep mosquitos out, so there was fresh air at least. During the winter we left is open, despite the cold. When we were small, we collected baubles to craft into dolls and toys which we hid under the bed, but that was years ago. Neither of us felt like playing make-believe anymore.

I had to tell Briar. I was working up to it.

"Maybe he wouldn't be so bad if I didn't mess up so much."

I shook my head. "Some men are just bad. Our uncle's one of them."

"Yeah?" Briar asked.

"Yeah. Even if you did everything perfectly, he'd still be awful. Nothing is gonna change that," I said. "That's the way Gabriel is and probably how he's always been."

Briar sighed. "I think I maybe know that deep down," he said. "I just hate that I always make him angry, and then, sometimes, he takes it out on you."

"I'm your big sister. It's my job to take care of you. I can handle our uncle."

"Better than I can," he said. "That's for sure."

I hesitated, mulling over my words. How did I want to break this to him? It didn't seem like the kind of situation that I could really soften. "Briar," I said slowly, "I might be going away for a while."

"What do you mean?" he asked.

"Gabriel has hired me to do some things," I said. "That's all. He has a friend who is hoping to have me steal a few pieces of mage tech. Nothing that dangerous."

"Stealing?" Briar asked. "But thieves are—"

"I know," I replied. "But this is what he wants me to do."

"Why can't Gabriel just steal them?" Briar asked. "Or have one of his men bully their way into getting whatever he wants? He's done that before."

"I guess he's just trying to...get me to branch out or something. You know Gabriel is weird sometimes. Besides, we steal all the time."

"Not from people," Briar said. "Nobody cares if we scavenge. Thieves get punished. For real. It's too dangerous."

"It's not like I have a choice," I said. "Also, there's something else."

"More?" he asked.

"It's not just anyone that Gabriel wants me to steal from. He wants me to steal from mages."

"*Actual* mages? In person?" Briar asked. "But there aren't any mages in the Scraps."

"No," I said carefully. "There aren't."

I let the words sink between us. Briar inhaled sharply, then I knew he'd gotten it.

"You can't be serious. You'd have to go to the Floats."

"That's exactly where he wants me to go," I replied, sitting upright.

My brother's face was horrified. With a twinge of guilt, I

wondered if I should've lied to him and downplayed the potential danger. But he needed to know what was at stake.

"Say something," I said.

"I don't know what to say!" Briar exclaimed, running his hands through his hair. "I—Wynter, you can't! How does he even expect this to work?"

"He wants me to pose as a mage."

"A mage that comes from the *Scraps*?" Briar asked.

"I dunno," I replied. "It's something that Gabriel and his contact are planning together. I'm sure they've thought about that already."

"It's ridiculous," Briar said. "You'll never pass as a mage. Can't you just…?"

"Just what?" I asked. "Threaten to sabotage them? Turn them over to the mages? I can imagine how well that would go over."

Briar crossed the room and plopped onto my bed with me.

"Let's be realistic," I said. "Our uncle would be furious. There's no telling what he'd do to us if I tried to sabotage this plan of his."

"But you can't go through with it. If you go up there… you won't come back."

I reached over and ruffled his hair. "I know," I said. "I'm trying to figure it out."

"What if you run away?" Briar asked quietly, his eyes darting to the door.

"If *we* run away," I replied. "I'm not leaving you here with him."

Briar slowly curled his hands into fists. "I'll only slow you down," he said. "I'd just be an extra thing to worry about."

"You don't think I'd worry about you either way?" I asked. "With me or not, it doesn't matter. Besides, if you're with me, I don't have to worry about what Gabriel might do to you."

"I don't guess he'd let me go instead of you?"

I didn't know, but I wasn't going to ask. "No," I said.

Briar scowled.

"His contact is a mage, too," I said.

"Yeah?"

I nodded.

"Did he look like the mages from the stories?"

"Some," I said slowly. "He didn't have the red eyes. He was…impressive."

"Did he use any magic? Are you sure he's even a real mage?"

"No magic," I replied, "But I definitely think he's the real thing. At least, he's clearly a man from money."

"What was he doing in the Scraps? Mages never come here."

"I don't know," I said. "Looking for a street urchin to pose as a mage lady, I guess. He didn't seem to like it down here." Maybe I could convince Dorian that I wasn't the deal he thought I was. Then he'd have to find someone else. That wouldn't be without repercussions, though, unless I could also convince Gabriel that I'd done nothing wrong. At least not on purpose.

"Nobody *chooses* to be in the Scraps," Briar murmured. "I wonder how they met."

"No idea. Maybe they have some sort of secret society for frauds," I joked, trying to make my brother feel better.

"I'll bet Gabriel is their founder," Briar said.

"Definitely."

"It's strange, though," Briar said. "Why would a mage want *you* to steal anything? He's a mage. Can't he just do it himself? Or hire another mage to do it?"

"I dunno," I said, "But I agree it's a little weird."

Briar slowly nodded. "So you're gonna run, then," he said.

"If I can," I replied. "There's a lot that I have to figure out first. I don't really like the idea of starving in the Scraps either, and it's not like we can hide out with anyone here. Gabriel would tear the place apart to find us, and he'd probably start with Sterling's place."

And could I really deal with the guilt of having brought Gabriel to *Sterling*? Sterling with his sick mother. With a sigh, I buried my face between my hands. Briar leaned his head against my shoulder. "I'll do what I can to help," Briar said. "Maybe when I go scavenging tomorrow, I can manage to slip some things past Gabriel."

I doubted it. Even if Briar did manage to slip a few things past our uncle, they wouldn't amount to much. We might be able to buy a couple days worth of food, but even that would be a risky venture. People who bought mage tech usually had dealings with our uncle, and even selling something could put Briar and me in danger. But I didn't want to dash my brother's hopes. Not when we were dealing with something so serious.

"Maybe," I said, mustering up as much optimism as I could. "I might try doing the same. I could even snatch a couple of things at the Market."

"You're going to the Market?"

"Yeah. Gabriel's contact is going to fancy me up, so I look like some a lady or something. I'll look so ridiculous. They'll probably have me dressed up in lace," I said, pausing while I tried to remember what mage-women were supposed to wear, "And corsets."

"Those *huge* skirts," Briar said.

I groaned and swatted his shoulder. We'd uncovered a mage's skirt once in the trash, and it had been made of yards and yards of once shining fabric that was softer to the touch than anything I'd ever felt. It weighed a ton, and my arms had literally ached by the time we'd dragged the thing back to the subway. Once there, we'd hacked it apart and found enough fabric to cover half of the Scraps. I wrinkled my nose at the thought of trying to sneak around in something so heavy. "Don't even talk to me about the skirts," I said.

The comment brought a smile to Briar's face. "If you fall from the Floats, you'd be able to use it to cushion your fall."

I groaned and fell backward onto my bed. "Maybe Gabriel will let me wear pants instead. Or Dorian. I dunno who's actually going to decide that."

Briar squeezed my hand. "It doesn't matter. We're going to figure this out, right? And then, it'll be on our uncle to pick up the pieces when we're gone. Maybe he should dress up in skirts and try to steal from the mages himself." I laughed out loud at the image, until I realized they'd just find someone else. Another disposable patsy; someone nobody would miss. My stomach lurched when I thought of another innocent girl being thrown into this because I'd refused. But that wasn't my problem. I closed my eyes and breathed in the stale, still air. Running was the only option. Anyone would run from this.

THREE

THE MARKET WAS OPEN FROM sunrise to sunset every day, and served both as a place for trappers and craftsmen to sell their wares, and an informal division between the Scraps and the nicer areas of town that surrounded the gated community called the Gardens. The tables and booths stretched for nearly a mile, though I'd never walked the full length of it. I had no need, since the last quarter-mile of the market was filled with expensive wares I would never be able to afford. Or so I'd always thought. Gabriel and Dorian, flanked by a handful of my uncle's cronies and me, headed right into the heart of the market's most exclusive traders.

Bright fabrics, exotic spices, perfumes, exotic pets and vibrant jewelry dazzled my eyes. I wanted to ogle and touch everything, but Gabriel pushed me along so quickly I practically stumbled over my own two feet. It was all so overwhelming and beautiful, I wished Sterling and Briar had been invited along for this as well. I'd just have to describe it for them later. Dorian talked loudly about needing me to be prepared for my first semester, and for just a few minutes I slipped into the roleplay, pretending that I really was a mage heading to the Academy to learn magic. I imagined returning to the Scraps years later, so powerful that even my uncle couldn't stop me. How wonderful would that be? I imagined carving out a space for myself in the Floats and living on a sprawling estate with Briar and Sterling, far from my uncle's reach.

Gabriel tapped a long, slender finger against a bolt of white fabric. "What do you think, Dorian?" he asked.

It was beautiful material, but it seemed so impractical. People in the Scraps didn't wear *white*. Most of us only had a few items of clothing. We dressed practically, and anything white would have been quickly ruined by the cloud of filth that seemed to cling to every surface. This seemed like such an expensive, absurd thing to even consider spending money on. But maybe Dorian's plan was to buy all these nice things for me and then sell them once I'd stolen what he wanted. If so it would all even out for him.

"Do you like it, Wynter?" Dorian asked, fixing me with an unnerving stare.

"It doesn't matter if she likes it," Gabriel said. "I think it's appropriate."

"And your opinion only matters if you're going to wear it," Dorian replied cheerily. "What do you think, Wynter?"

I looked between Dorian and Gabriel. "If it's appropriate, it's fine," I said, hoping the answer would be good enough for both of them.

"But you must prefer some colors over others," Dorian said. "I'll buy you any color you like. Except for black. I'm half-sick of it."

And yet black was all Dorian seemed to wear.

I looked uncertainly over the fabrics. "I like blue," I said finally.

He nodded and began comparing bolts of blue fabric. I hadn't figured out how Dorian worked yet. He seemed too friendly to be engaged in this kind of business. What was he hiding? There had to be something. As I looked over the market, an idea began turning over in my head. Everything was so busy and bustling, if I ran now, could I manage to escape? My uncle, perhaps. I was younger and faster than him. That was assuming one of his goons didn't catch me. But what about Dorian, the mage? What powers did he have?

Without warning, my uncle grasped my bicep. "Come along," he said, his command edged with warning.

I stared wistfully towards a dark alley, and he dug his fingers in more harshly. Running wasn't an option. Not right at the second. There was no way I was going along demurely with this scheme of his, though. The mages wouldn't take kindly to being infiltrated, or sharing secrets with a mere human. They might even execute me if I was caught, while my uncle would probably manage to escape the whole mess unscathed. Who would protect Briar, then? Sterling would try, but how could he possibly be enough? My pulse raced, even as my uncle pulled me along behind him.

Suddenly, everything in the market was too much. Too loud, too hot, too crowded, too colorful. My skin prickled uncomfortably as I bounced between the shoulders of a dozen strangers. I felt like I was being asked to choose my funeral shroud.

"Dark blue or light blue?" Dorian asked, at a booth with more selection.

I awkwardly picked out colors, and after I'd chosen them, Dorian paid. He then placed the armful of wrapped packages into my arms. They felt cool against my cheek. Dyed fabric of this quality was very expensive. *Could I sell these?* My mind whirled with the possibility. Maybe this was the chance I'd been looking for. Let Dorian buy me these very expensive things. I could sell them, plan my escape with Briar, and start a new life somewhere far away. It wouldn't be easy, but it sounded possible. It was worth a try.

I followed Gabriel and Dorian, conscious of the way my uncle's eyes kept drifting towards me. He would expect an escape, so it was in my best interest to act like I had given in and was going along with his plans. For now.

Although Dorian looked like a wealthy man, he haggled cheerfully over every single item. Perhaps, he did it out of principle; he could get a better deal by haggling. And yet I couldn't help but wonder if there was something more it. Gabriel probably knew. He stood back and watched most of the bargains pass with a smirk on his lips.

And the items added up. I tried to memorize how much each had cost, but soon, it became difficult to keep track. Dorian purchased things I hadn't even known existed. Silken gloves, sweet-smelling perfume and heavy necklaces were bought and wrapped. Mercifully, these items were distributed to my uncle's underlings, so I wasn't left to carry them all. There were discussions of future trips to fittings for dresses and corsets, fittings that Dorian said someone named Francisca would handle.

We arrived at the last section of the market, and it was the strangest of all. The alley was tight and tented canvas stretched between the rooftops, filling the space with a deep shadow. The table Dorian finally paused at looked like a junk booth, overflowing with devices made of shining metal, that I didn't recognize and couldn't fathom their use. I drifted closer, my fingertips hovering above them, as if I could sense their function. The objects were in a variety of sizes, and some emitted flickering lights or ghostly flames. A faint, blue sheen lingered over the whole table. Probably an enchantment of some sort.

"Don't touch anything," my uncle whispered.

I nodded. Something tugged at the edge of my consciousness as I looked over the mage tech. It was as if someone was speaking just out of earshot, so softly that I couldn't make out the words. The result was a dull, consistent buzzing. Strange. I'd never had that reaction to mage tech before, but the tech I'd scavenged before had never looked this new or clean either. Selling enchanted objects below the Floats was probably illegal, but tinkering with cobbled-together junk and repurposed mage tech might not be. After all, they'd chosen to throw it out.

Out of the corner of my eye, I saw a woman tapping her long, slender fingers on the table. I glanced towards my uncle. His head was leaned in towards Dorian, and the men were speaking together softly. Seeing that Gabriel's attention wasn't on me, I reached forward with a finger and tipped a mirror towards me. The item caught my reflection along with the woman's. She was tall with red, curly hair and wore a dark blue coat with silver star-like embroidery. She was as nicely dressed as my uncle but not Dorian, and the bright red lipstick didn't seem appropriate for a real lady. An escort dressed above her means, probably. I wondered if her clients were wealthy humans or lower ranking mages.

Her hazel eyes snapped towards me. I gave her a small smile.

"Morning," I murmured.

"Good morning to you," she said.

I leaned forward, pretending to be engrossed in some of the wares. Really, I was trying to block the merchant's view of his table. Maybe I'd be able to pocket something to sell later.

"I'm Wynter," I said conversationally.

A small laugh. "What are the chances? I'm Autumn."

"That's pretty," I said.

My uncle cleared his throat. I shot Autumn an apologetic smile.

"Ain't I told you not to talk to strangers?" Gabriel whispered in my ear.

"I was wishing her a good morning," I replied. "She spoke to me first."

"Focus on the task at hand," Gabriel said lowly, "Or I'll beat you within an inch of your life when we get back home."

I tilted my head towards him, my attention still half on Autumn beside me. The woman's fingers were inching forward towards a small, metal box. She was clearly trying to steal something. The box looked vaguely familiar, and I realized it was a piece of something Sterling found last month in the Dregs. Anger filled my veins. We'd done all the work, Gabriel's contacts had hacked the device into something useful, and this man was selling it for a huge markup. People like this, who dealt in mage tech, earned their money through threats and blood, depending on kids like us. Why should I care if someone swiped a few of their goods? Plus, I thought desperately, maybe if I helped her, she'd seek me out and share the profit. I didn't even know her and she probably thought I was some servant girl, but people in the Scraps were resourceful, and most were familiar with debts and honor.

"What are these?" I asked, pointing to a group of objects on the far end of the table.

Dorian picked up one of the square objects and turned it over in his hand. He flicked his thumb down on it, unleashing a burst of blue flame. The flames hissed and crackled above his outstretched hand. I stepped back quickly, and the fire evaporated.

"Don't worry," Dorian said, a smile playing on his lips. "It's just an illusion."

Dorian passed the item to me. I pretended to inspect it, sneaking a glance down into the mirror in time to see Autumn slip another piece beneath her hand. She turned nonchalantly away. For a few seconds, it seemed as though she'd get away with it. I held my breath as Gabriel and Dorian went to pay for my mage tech. Then, a shout split the air. "Stop her!" The merchant shouted, pointing in my direction. Autumn took off running, and the merchant's security man charged straight towards me.

He was at least a foot taller than me and his arms rippled with muscle. A long scar, likely from a knife wound, ran down the length of his cheek. He'd easily overtake Autumn, even if she was tearing her way through the crowd. He was going to run right past me. Maybe even shove me out of the way to get to Autumn. Unless I stopped him.

My heart pounded so loudly that I heard it reverberating

against my chest, but I stepped back at just the right moment, blocking his path. I let out a sharp scream as he practically threw me sideways, but I kept my feet planted long enough to slow him down. The man's face twisted in fury as he stumbled.

"My uncle is paying for this!" I snapped. "How *dare* you?"

At my raised voice, one of uncle's men wedged himself between us, inadvertently aiding Autumn's escape. Perfect. I widened my eyes and rubbed my shoulder, the fabric nearly falling from my grasp. "He just came right at me!" I exclaimed.

My uncle and Dorian both turned to look at me. The merchant's face was bright red. "He wasn't going after you, you idiot!" he snapped.

The security guard scowled and stormed past us. I knew without looking that Autumn was already gone, lost in the crowd. It was too late to pursue her now. She probably had friends in the market, too, ones who would hide her.

"Well, maybe you ought to give better orders!" my uncle snapped, sweeping an arm towards me. "Even if your man was going after another woman, he should've known better than to charge right at my niece!"

The merchant glared at me. He might suspect that I'd helped the other woman flee, but he couldn't prove it. If I was all alone, he might have punished anyway for aiding a thief. He could've had one of his followers grab me in place of Autumn. It wasn't like there was anyone to intervene if a punishment for petty theft got out of hand. The mages didn't care, and no one in the Market would be willing to risk getting involved. But I was with my uncle, and he needed me for this scheme of his. If I was branded as a thief, it would make it *much* harder to steal from the mages. He couldn't have me losing my fingers.

"She made me lose that," the merchant told Gabriel. "I suggest you pay for it."

"Do you?" my uncle sneered.

"Yeah," the merchant said. "I think your girl did it on purpose. Pay up, or you'll regret it."

Gabriel glanced at me, his face furious.

"Wynter," he said, "Do you know what this man's first mistake is?"

"I dunno," I said.

"Our merchant here only appears to have *one* man hired to protect him, and that one man has run off. And now, he has the nerve to ask *me* for money?"

The merchant took a step back. "I only want what's owed to me," he said.

"And you're gonna get it," Gabriel hissed, leaning forward with his teeth bared.

"There's no need for that today, Gabriel," Dorian cut in. "I'm sure this is just a misunderstanding. This merchant's man ran at your poor, terrified niece, who was obviously traumatized by the brute, and everyone is *very sorry* for the inconvenience."

Gabriel's fingers pinched my skin as he steered me away from the merchant. "This will *not* happen again," he hissed.

"It won't," I said.

The merchant didn't pursue us as we moved quickly away from the stall and back into the crowded street of the main market.

"It had better not," Gabriel whispered. "Dorian paid good money for you, and I expect him to get everything I promised."

Dorian cleared his throat. "There's no need to be cruel to her, Gabriel. She didn't do anything wrong, other than being in the wrong place at the wrong time."

"It ain't your place to tell me how to handle my niece!" Gabriel snapped.

"Isn't it? I'm paying for her services, aren't I?" Dorian asked.

"You're welcome to find someone else's kid if you can afford it," Gabriel said.

Dorian smiled, but with an edge to it. "Be careful how many insults you send my way," Dorian said. "I may not be the most powerful of mages, but I'm still quite confident I could destroy you if the need arose."

I frowned and wondered if Dorian's faith in me was misplaced. Was he really so easy to fool? If so, I could play to Dorian's sympathy. Unless he knew the truth, and was just trying to endear me to him. Maybe that was how *he* got people to do things for him. I wondered which was better, my uncle's brute force and threats, or Dorian's smooth manipulation? I wasn't sure I wanted to find out.

FOUR

I crossed my legs and sat on the bed, practicing. With a flick of my thumb, blue flames burst from the piece of mage tech. I closed my eyes and breathed in deeply, trying to focus on the hisses just at the edge of my hearing.

For the merest of moments, it almost sounded like whispers in a language I couldn't understand. But that was silly. Maybe mage tech always made noises like that. I opened my eyes and looked over the device again, passing my fingers through the rippling blue light. Then with a flick of my wrist, I put the flames out. It was a pity they weren't real. I would be dangerous if I could actually summon fire.

Briar peeked into our room and smiled wryly. "Time for work," he said.

I held my hand out. "Don't freak out," I said.

I flicked the flames back on. Briar jumped back and swore. A small, sharp laugh escaped me. "Don't worry. They aren't real," I said.

He stepped closer, considering the fire. Then, he stuck his hand right in it, watching as the blue flames flickered harmlessly over his hand. "That's cool," he said, his voice awed.

"Kind of," I said.

Briar furrowed his brow. "Is this how you're gonna convince people you're a mage?" he asked.

"Yes," I replied. "At least, that's the plan."

Briar nodded knowingly. "Are you gonna tell Sterling?" he asked.

"I have to," I said, grabbing my pack off the floor.

If Briar and I ran away, Gabriel would likely go to Sterling first, and I couldn't let Sterling face Gabriel without at least a warning that the man might be coming.

"He won't take it well," Briar said.

No, probably not.

"Well, that's for me to worry about. Not you."

Sterling was waiting at the subway entrance, like usual. For him, it was just another night. But when I got closer, Gabriel stepped out of the shadows next to him. My first instinct was to freeze in horror at the sight of them together, but I forced myself to keep walking. Beside me, Briar clenched his hands so tightly around his backpack straps that his knuckles were white like moonlight.

"Wynter," Gabriel said. "Heading out?"

Obviously. Why was he asking?

"Yes," I said.

"Wonderful," Gabriel said. "I think Briar should stay here with me, though."

"With you?" I repeated slowly. This was a trap somehow.

Gabriel swept around me and roughly grabbed Briar's arm. "Yeah," Gabriel said. "You and Sterling have a good night. I need Briar here to help me with some things."

Warmth flooded my face. I hadn't planned on escaping during this scavenging trip, but I still felt a hot flash of anger. How dare Gabriel make my brother a pawn in this scheme of his? I clenched my jaw. "Sure," I said.

As if I could stop him.

I trudged out after Sterling. Once we were out of earshot, Sterling whistled between his teeth. "Old man Gabriel's being a real jerk today," he asked.

"What did he tell you?"

Sterling shrugged. "Nothing. He paid me for the last trip and asked how my mom was doing. The usual."

At least, Gabriel hadn't told Sterling what he had planned for me. I took a deep breath, steeling my nerves until we were a few blocks away.

"I might have to go away for a while," I said, once I was sure we were alone.

"Where to?" Sterling asked.

"My uncle is sending me to steal something for one of his connections," I said, "But I don't know if I'm going to go through with it."

A thick silence settled between us. "What's the alternative?" Sterling asked.

"Running away."

"Wynter—"

"I know it's a bad idea," I said, "But this plan of Gabriel's could get me killed. I'm not just gonna wait around for that to happen."

Sterling swore under his breath. "He wouldn't let you die," Sterling insisted. "He may be a terrible person, but he's not gonna let *you* get killed. You're his niece!"

Sterling didn't get it. He knew that Gabriel was a terrible person, but he didn't understand just *how* terrible.

"He would if the payout was high enough," I replied, fishing through my pockets.

"Okay, so you steal from some—" Sterling waved a vague hand "some crook or some wannabe aristocrat. We steal from the Dregs and the Scraps all the time. It shouldn't be any different."

I pulled the device from my pocket and rubbed my thumb over it. Sterling's eyes widened as the flames burst forth, hissing. I held Sterling's eyes as I reached a hand into the flames. "He wants me to pretend to be a lady," I said quietly, "So I can steal from mages."

"He's out of his mind," Sterling said with dawning comprehension. The blue flames flickered in his eyes. I let the flames fade away and tucked the device safely into my coat. "Possibly," I said. "The good news is that this will make scavenging much easier. At least for tonight."

"No, back up," Sterling said. "He wants you to steal from *mages*? You can't!"

"I know," I replied, "But Gabriel thinks I can. I have two options. I can either stay and do what he wants, or I can run away."

"Wynter, I—I'll volunteer to go in your place," Sterling said.

I shook my head. "It's too late for that. Gabriel's connection already went and bought all the dresses for me."

"Well, he can return them," Sterling replied. "You can't go!"

"Sterling," I said quietly. "I don't plan on going."

Sterling shoved his hands into his pockets and stormed ahead. I pinched the bridge of my nose. Sterling just didn't handle things like this well. I hastened to keep pace with him.

"We have to talk him out of it," Sterling said.

"It won't do any good."

"It has to! It's too hard to survive in the Scraps on your own, and you know Gabriel would just hunt you down anyway," Sterling argued. "Running is too dangerous."

"You think I don't know the dangers?" I asked. "But I'd rather risk starvation than—than being found out by the mages! If you think justice is harsh in the Scraps, can you even imagine what they do to thieves up there?" I let my eyes flicker up towards the dark shape of the Floats above, a massive piece of rocky land blocking out the stars, rimmed with glowing lights.

Sterling shook his head, stomping forward again.

"I'm gonna give your uncle a piece of my mind," he muttered, clenching his fists.

"No, you aren't!" I hissed, grabbing his arm.

"Why shouldn't I?" Sterling asked.

"Because he's dangerous," I said. "I don't want you to get hurt. I'm just telling you so you'll be prepared. Besides, you're probably right. He said it was temporary. He wouldn't put me in real danger. I'll be back before you know it." I was lying through my teeth now, trying to calm Sterling down, but he knew me too well.

"That's before I realized he was going to have you steal from *mages*!" Sterling protested, flapping his arms like a clumsy duckling.

"I know. That's why—"

"And you can't run away either! So he's just going to have

to change his mind! We—there has to be some way to convince Gabriel that this is a bad idea. You just haven't tried all the options."

A sharp flash of anger shot through me. "You don't think I've thought *this* through?" I asked. "Really, Sterling? I've been thinking about this nonstop since I found out."

Sterling turned back towards the subway, hiding his face. I'd seen him angry before, but never this worked up. He was taking deep breaths, and kept glancing up at the Floats with a combination of fear and malice, like he thought it might fall from the sky and crush us. The mages had always seemed so distant up there. It was like an alternate reality. A world full of magic and wonder, maybe, but it had nothing to do with us. Until now. Even from so far away, they'd managed to tear our world apart.

Sterling kicked a bottle and we watched it shatter against a wall. I moved closer and put my hands against his chest.

"Stop," I said.

Sterling scowled and curled his hand over mine.

"And what?" he asked. "I'm just supposed to let you do this, without even trying to stop it? No matter how much it hurts?"

Beneath my fingertips, Sterling's chest rose and fell, each movement quick and sharp. I swallowed the lump in my throat and rocked onto the balls of my feet. I planted a quick kiss on his cheek. "What choice do we have? Please, just…"

"Just what?"

"Wish me well," I said. "Tell me it's gonna be all right."

"It ain't," Sterling replied coldly. Then he stormed away, into the shadows.

***

I froze, unsure whether or not to pursue him. I'd expected anger and disappointment, but he'd never just walked away from me like that.

"Sterling," I rasped, my voice too quiet for him to hear.

I waited for a few minutes to see if he'd return, then tightened the straps of my backpack and headed to the Dregs alone. With a sigh, I crawled beneath the fence and emerged on the other side. I rubbed my thumb over the device, casting the blue flames over the darkness. If Sterling had come with me, we would've had a great score. The device lit everything so much better than a candle did. The argument settled like an apricot pit in my stomach. What was I supposed to do? I could talk to my uncle until I was blue in the face, and it wouldn't change anything.

I sat in the garbage, looking upwards to the pink glow of the Floats. It seemed like a dream. It was probably beautiful and terrible, like Dorian. I imagined that everything was colorful and bright, like the expensive dresses he had bought for me. There would be no dark shadows to hide in. I'd be utterly exposed. How was I supposed to survive that?

After an hour had ticked by, I started digging. The chill was sinking into my bones, and I knew the movement would help the blood reach my veins. Plus, Gabriel wouldn't be happy if I returned with an empty bag. After a few minutes of digging one-handed, I carefully placed the device on the ground. The flames faded when my skin broke contact with the smooth metal. With a frown, I groped around in the pitch darkness until my fingertips landed on the device again. "I don't guess," I said slowly, "That there's a way to make you stay on without me touching you, is there?"

The flames burst forth. I started, nearly falling back into the trash. I hadn't even touched the device that time. I gulped and leaned forward. "Um, thanks," I said awkwardly. Clearly, this device had been enchanted to answer commands. I had no way of knowing if it could register something like being thanked as well, but better safe than sorry.

While I sifted through the metal, the flames continued burning, accompanied as always by the faint sound of hisses. But the more I dug, the less I noticed the faint buzzing at the edge of my awareness. I crammed my pack full of anything remotely valuable, though the enthusiasm of discovery was gone, leaving my heart empty and heavy. Searching with Sterling was almost fun sometimes, and returning home I'd be filled with trepidation. If I had an especially good haul, Gabriel would smile and pour me a thimble full of spiced brandy. I always felt that someday, if I brought him enough treasure, if I earned him enough money, he'd accept me and my brother and we'd be a real family. I scowled at myself in the dark. What a stupid, childish dream.

Once my pack was full, I slipped a few things into the pockets of my coat and pants. I planned on running away with my dresses and the device, but more to barter and sell was always good. I filled my pockets as much as I could without them bulging. Then, I picked up the device. I swiped my thumb over it, and the flames faded away. I tucked it into my pocket and headed back towards the fence.

I was so busy feeling sorry for myself, I didn't see the

monster until it was just in front of me. Movement against the perimeter fence caught my eye, and I froze, slowly reaching for the knife tucked into my boot. The scraggly black silhouette seemed to emit coils of steam, that diffused the light of the buildings behind it. Its face was feline, but its limbs were long and spindly, like a spider's. No one really knew what monsters were. Some said the spirits of people who'd fallen from the Floats. Others said the result of a mage's curse. Sterling thought they were just animals and bugs that had absorbed too much magic from the broken tech, and mutated into something terrible.

Slowly, I crept around the edge of the fence. Monsters could be unpredictable. While some were distant and skittish, others were vicious and bold. They were all poisonous, though not always fatal. This one arched its back and hissed, lashing the air with its tail. It was about waist-high on me, I tightened my grip on the knife and waited. The monster considered me for a long moment, and I turned the blade slowly so the edge glinted in the moonlight. Finally, it fled into the darkness. I let out the breath I'd been holding and ducked quickly through the hole in the fence. As I walked home, I clutched the polished handle of dagger in my sweaty palm until I reached the station.

When I entered the subway entrance, it was quiet. I hurried down the steps and pushed into the vaulted center room, where my uncle waited as always.

"Where's Briar?" I asked, setting my pack on the table.

My uncle didn't move from his chair. "His room," he replied. "He was good this evening, don't worry."

I clenched my teeth together. He talked about my brother like he was six rather than sixteen. "I'm glad," I said.

"Where's Sterling's pack?" Gabriel asked.

"He didn't scavenge with me tonight. He wasn't thrilled to hear about this scheme of yours. Probably blowing off steam."

"His loss," Gabriel said, shrugging. "And I'd prefer you not tell anyone else about this venture of mine. The last thing I need is some blabbermouth cutting into my profits."

I didn't even know who I *could* tell about this situation. None of my uncle's men would help me, and I didn't have any friends besides Sterling. There was no one else to tell. And even if we told half the Scraps, I doubted anyone would be willing to mess with Gabriel over it.

"How did you meet the mage?" I asked. Maybe I could learn more about Dorian, and find out what I was really up against.

"Awful curious tonight, aren't you?"

My uncle waved me away, turning back to the open book on his desk. I took the hint and headed to my room to find Briar.

"Hey," I said, leaning against the doorframe.

"How'd it go?" Briar asked.

"Sterling is mad at me," I said.

Not that it mattered. I wouldn't be around to see him get over it. I just hoped he didn't beat himself up over this. Sterling was quick to anger, prone to saying things he didn't mean and then agonizing over them afterward.

"It ain't your fault, though," Briar said.

I glanced outside the room to see if Gabriel had thought to keep people listening nearby. But there wasn't a soul to be found. "I know," I replied, walking into our room and plopping onto my bed, "But I can't really blame him. I'd be mad if he was doing this to me."

I sank onto my bed and sighed. My gaze drifted to the fabrics, still wrapped in thick, brown paper and tied up with thin, blue ribbon. At least, Gabriel had left those and the device with me. That meant I wouldn't have to sneak around and find them before this all went down. And he'd been too distracted to check my pockets. I pulled them out carefully and lined them up on the windowsill, trying to estimate their value.

I scribbled some numbers on a pad of paper and frowned.

"Is it enough?" Briar asked timidly.

"It has to be," I said. Then I tore the piece of paper into tiny pieces and swallowed them down whole, so my uncle could never find them.

FIVE

A WEEK LATER, IT WAS time to leave. I'd scavenged away what little supplies I could, living in terror that Gabriel would discover my cache of stolen goods. Sterling hadn't reappeared, and I was worried about him, but he was probably off sulking in the woods or taking care of his mother. I toyed with the device, unleashing sparks of blue flame. It was a pity that it wasn't real. I had the irrational impulse to burn this place down and cover my escape.

It was late and quiet, save for my brother's snores. I pocketed the device and climbed out of my bed. The mattress and blanket were both thin, but I knew it was still more than most people in the Scraps had. I wondered when I'd be able to sleep in a real bed again. I padded across the room, grabbed my pack, and tossed it over my shoulder. Then, I returned to Briar's bed and shook his shoulder.

My brother stirred and mumbled sleepily.

"We're leaving," I said quietly.

He sat upright and rubbed his eyes with the back of his hand. I gathered the rest of my gear, giving him time to wake.

We had time, and this plan would require both of us to be alert. While our uncle had never really cared if we went out at our leisure, I wouldn't have put it past him to have something planned in the event I decided to run. My uncle was smart; I would have to be smarter.

Briar put on his coat and threw his pack over his shoulder. We split the wrapped fabrics and dresses between us. I checked to make sure that the device was within reach in my jacket pocket; while I knew the flames weren't real, they might be enough to fool somebody else.

"You ready?" I asked.

Briar nodded. "Let's do this."

I pushed open the door and peeked down the subway. It was empty and dark. I took a deep breath and crept out, keeping close to the walls and shadows. Briar followed my lead, and together, we inched along in silence. This was too easy. My heartbeat quickened.

Gabriel knew me well. He'd surely set a trap somewhere. Something skittered across the floor. I froze and waited, my eyes straining against the darkness. A shadow moved. It was just a rat. I swallowed back a sigh of relief.

We reached the top of the stairs without difficulty and stepped out into the Scraps. I shivered as a cool wind tore through my jacket. The moon overhead, bright and full, provided enough light to see by, but that same light would make it easier for the guards to see us. The city guards rarely patrolled this far south however, and my years of scavenging had taught me how to hide. The challenge would come once we reached the outskirts of the Scraps; I had no idea what existed beyond its borders.

Metal clinked, halting me in my tracks. Briar and I crouched low. I fumbled with the device in my pocket. Hopefully, if it was a threat, I could scare it away with a bit of fire.

"I know I heard something."

I flinched. That voice was familiar; it was one of Gabriel's underlings. I glanced at Briar, his eyes wide and terrified in the dim light. I gulped. What should I do? Run? Hide? I strained, listening hard for another sound, anything that might tell me where exactly my uncle's thugs were. Or even how many there were. When Gabriel needed to threaten or hurt someone, he sent his men in packs.

Metal shrieked. I jumped as a pile of rusty metal pipes clattered right behind us. Briar must have knocked them over. A shout, and a figure grasping in the darkness. Without thinking, I burst into motion, trusting Briar to follow. I ran, my feet pounding against the broken and cracked concrete.

"Stop!"

There were men in front of me, and I heard more closing the distance behind us. I darted down an alleyway between the ruins of two crumbled buildings. How long could I run? Longer than them? I had no way of knowing. Adrenaline was making everything too sharp and too distant all at once. Light blared before my eyes, and I halted, stumbling back and tripping over my own feet. Black spots obscured my vision, making it impossible to keep running. I backed into Briar, who swore quietly under his breath.

My heart pounded so loudly I heard it in my ears. We were trapped. I had to think fast. I reached into my pocket and pulled out the device, rubbing my thumb over the metal. The blue flames burst forth obediently. Some of uncle's men gasped and fell back.

"I would back up if I were you!" I snarled. "You don't know what I'm capable of. I can cover this whole area in fire if I want to!"

The device responded. Flames leaped from my hands and spread onto the ground, growing higher and higher. The whispers sounded frantic, hissing and snapping. My uncle's men scrambled back, wide-eyed before my power.

"A mage," one of them whispered.

My pulse raced. I had no idea how I'd done that.

"That's right!" I shouted. "I am a mage! I can summon fire from the sky itself!"

Could the device really do that? The hisses grew louder, and blue fire rained down from the clouds, whistling like shooting stars. There were shouts, then, and cries of surprise as the men dove for cover.

I backed away and grabbed Briar's arm. "Run!"

We ran, the flames still crackling and snapping behind us. Everything was covered in brilliant, blue light. Gabriel's men would figure out it was an illusion the second one of them noticed that my flames carried no heat with them. More men rounded before us. I shoved my brother behind me and held the device before me once more.

Flames burst forth from my hand.

"Stand back!" I shouted. "Or I will burn you!"

Once more, the men stumbled back. My heartbeat quickened. This was going better than I'd planned. I had no idea the device was capable of so many different effects.

"Go ahead, Wynter."

Gabriel's voice cut through the air like a knife. My heart

plummeted as my uncle stepped forward, right through my flaming defenses. Emboldened, a few of his men followed. Just like that, all the power I'd held over them was gone.

***

Gabriel sighed. "What *am* I gonna do with you?" he asked.

My eyes were glued to the oak crossbow in his hands. I swallowed the lump in my throat and raised the dresses against my chest with one hand, as if those layers of fine, expensive fabric could halt a crossbow bolt. My other hand curled around the device.

"Go ahead," I said, my voice wavering more than I liked, "Shoot me."

"Oh, I'd *love* to," Gabriel drawled, "But I don't wanna lose my sale."

I caught the implication behind his words immediately.

"That isn't fair. This was my idea!"

"I know it was," he replied.

He leveled his crossbow at my brother. I threw aside the dresses and lunged at my uncle. But I never reached him. One of his goons wrapped his arms around my waist, with nearly enough force to lift me off the ground.

"Don't!" I screamed.

I thrashed and kicked, trying to break free, but there was a reason my uncle used these men to bully people. They were strong, much stronger than me. I fought, but it wasn't enough. The twang of my uncle's crossbow split the air, followed by my brother's pained shout.

"No!" I screamed. My brother fell to the ground, his hands

pressing hard against his knee. Blood spattered against the brown paper covering the fabric. There wasn't much of it. He wasn't going to die. It wasn't a killing shot, and with a sick jolt, I realized Gabriel hadn't missed. Even the worst shot in the world couldn't have botched it so much at point-blank range. He knew if he killed Briar, he'd have nothing left to hold over me. But cripple him, and I'd never leave. Without warning, Gabriel's muscled minion released me. I scrambled to my brother's side. His breath came in sharp, shaky pants.

"I'm sorry," I said. "I'm sorry, I'm sorry."

Briar was breathing too hard to answer. His face was pale, and a sheen of sweat covered his skin. A crater of blood and torn flesh surrounded the wooden bolt. My stomach lurched. What should I do? I didn't know how to treat a wound like this.

"I wouldn't pull it out if I was you," Gabriel said. "That'll make the bleeding worse."

I clenched my fists together. I sprang to my feet and spun around. "I *hate* you!" I shouted. I clawed at his face, but he dodged and slapped my cheek with a blow that left my ear ringing.

"I'm sure you do," he replied. "What are you gonna do about it? You realize that your brother needs me, don't you? And if you don't cooperate, well, I'm sure you realize that there are so many things that could go wrong."

He was right. Absolutely right. My breath caught in my throat. I shook my head, holding the device so tightly that my knuckles ached.

"And I must say, I had my doubts about Dorian's whole scheme. But after your little display tonight I have much more confidence in this little plan of ours. You even had some of my men fooled. Who would have guessed you'd play such a convincing mage. Maybe after you return, I'll rent you out to entertain for birthday parties. So what is it going to be?" Gabriel asked. "Are you in?" He stepped forward, pressing his boot into Briar's knee until he squealed with pain, "or out?"

I shoved his leg away and pulled my brother's limp body closer, cradling him against my chest. "I'm in," I said, a tear sliding down my cheek. "I'll go through with it. Just don't hurt him."

"Good girl," Gabriel said, seizing my arm. I craned my neck to see Gabriel's men lift my brother's body and carry it between them. This was my fault. I shouldn't have tried to run. I shouldn't have brought him with me. My uncle pulled me along, forcing me over the broken pavement and back to his subway headquarters. There wouldn't be another escape attempt. There couldn't be. It would take at least a month for that wound to heal, and who knew whether Briar would even walk properly again.

How could I have been so stupid. I'd given Gabriel exactly what he needed to control me. He would hold Briar as collateral until I finished my mission and got Dorian what he wanted from the Academy.

If I failed there…

My stomach lurched, and my breath shuddered. I was terrified of the Floats, but I had to do everything I could to keep my brother safe. He was the only thing I had.

There was nowhere left to go, but up.

Six

"SMILE, WYNTER. YOU LOOK PRETTIER that way," Gabriel said.

Dorian was having a whispered conversation with the auburn-haired woman seated beside him. This was evidently Francisca, who'd found and sent the seamstress and corsetmaker. I fought the urge to fidget with my new, blue dress and picked at the bandages on my injured hand instead. I'd never worn anything with sleeves that fell off my shoulders or anything with crinolines underneath. I'd never even worn a *dress* before. And although the corset had—according to Francisca—not been laced very tightly, it still felt uncomfortable.

Francisca remained seated, but Dorian stood and considered me. "I think you're almost there," he said. "We just need a little refinement before judging."

"I think I should go to the judging with you," Gabriel said.

"No," Dorian said. "Wynter, do you have the device with you?"

"I got it," Gabriel said, retrieving the item from his jacket pocket. He was wearing a different suit today; charcoal black with purple trim and a gold clip that seemed to have no other function but to broadcast wealth. It would have been stupid to dress like this in the Scraps, but he blended in here in the Gardens. Everything seemed cleaner and brighter here. Gabriel, meanwhile, looked rumpled and dirty like he'd just crawled out from under a bridge.

Dorian took the device in his hand, coaxing the blue flames into appearing. The hisses sounded angry. I knew I was probably just imagining that the mage tech sounded different when he held it, but I liked to think that—maybe—the device liked me more. Dorian had used his thumb to activate it. I wondered if he knew he could just speak to the device. Probably. He was a mage, after all.

"You must keep this hidden during the exam," Dorian said. "Magical objects aren't explicitly forbidden, but something like this is."

"What if I'm not good enough? What if someone sees it?" More importantly, if I was caught cheating, who would take the fall for it? I could throw myself at the judges' mercy and tell them that Dorian had blackmailed me into it, had made me lie to them. But no, he'd deny it, and the mages would believe him. Getting caught wasn't an option.

Gabriel glared at me in warning. He hadn't told Dorian about my escape attempt. Instead we'd pretended I cut my hands scavenging the Dregs, and assured Dorian I'd take better care of myself from now on. Truthfully, the bandages on my hands were comforting; they were the only familiar thing on my body. A reminder of who I really was, and the pain I'd endured. They made me think of Briar, and I winced remembering his injured knee. Even though he didn't blame me for what had happened, it was hard not to feel guilty. I'd been the one who planned our escape, and he was the one suffering for it.

"You'll be fine," Dorian said. "It's not unheard of for a mage to be taken from the Lower Realms."

"If you do anything like that display the other night," Gabriel said crudely, "they'll shit their fancy britches." My cheeks burned at the way Gabriel smirked. He knew he'd really gotten to me, and he was just going to keep rubbing salt into the wound. I clenched my jaw. Someday, I was going to find a way to escape him. Really escape him. And when I did, I would take Briar with me. Sterling, too, if I could. It would be my way of making this up to them.

"What display?" Dorian asked.

"I had her practice with it," Gabriel said. "She's very good."

Dorian narrowed his eyes suspiciously.

"It isn't that hard to use," I said.

Dorian grabbed my hands as if noticing the bandages for the first time. He whipped a silver pen out of the inside pocket of his jacket, and scrawled a row of small symbols across my palm. The pain faded immediately, and when Dorian removed the bandages, the skin beneath was smooth and pink.

"There," he said. "That's better."

I was too stunned to respond. I twisted my fingers, marveling at the unbroken skin where cuts and scrapes had been seconds before. It was the first I'd seen of *real* magic.

"You'll also need a story chronicling how you discovered your powers," Dorian said, moving on. "And it must be convincing. A good story and a little posturing will go a long way with this."

"Right," I said. "So what's my story?"

"The most common time for humans to discover their magical powers is during puberty," Dorian said, "But not always. Sometimes, it takes a little coercion for them to be discovered. Magic can be incredibly fickle, unfortunately. We'll say that you discovered it by accident."

"How do you accidentally make fire?"

"Any number of ways. Maybe you were really angry or really scared, and it just happened. Maybe you woke up, and your room was ablaze. And word spread, so I decided to investigate rumors of this mage in Plumba."

"Won't the judges find it strange that no one else has heard of me?" I asked.

"No," Dorian replied, "Because I've already sent them a letter informing them of my discovery. Now, they have heard of you."

"Besides, the mages don't care enough about us to pay attention," Gabriel said. "I wouldn't be surprised if there are a few legitimate mages in the Scraps that ain't been found."

"He's right," Dorian said. "When they read my letter, the selection committee was probably deeply amused."

Somehow, that didn't make me feel any better about the situation.

"You don't need to be flawless," Dorian said. "You just need an average score, and that's what we'll aim for. The better you do, the harder they're going to inspect you. They'll let a human pass with just a pinch of magic, but a really powerful one…"

"But how do I know where I should be falling?" I asked. "I can't actually perform magic."

"Try three times to make fire appear. Accomplish it on the

third," Dorian said. "I'm going as your sponsor, so I may be able to keep them from looking too deeply into things."

I bit the inside of my cheek as Dorian pocketed the device. A surge of anger rose inside me at the way he folded his fingers over the device. That was *mine*. Or it felt like it ought to be mine. I thought about asking for fire, just to see the surprised look on his face when flames erupted. But I couldn't. Not with Briar's health on the line. Not when I knew he'd be at my uncle's mercy if I really messed up.

"Now," Dorian said, "Because we're going to say that I discovered your talents and brought you to the test, it will be my reputation on the line for you, so I need you to deliver."

"But what if something really unexpected happens?" I asked. "What if the device malfunctions or something?"

"He'll lose a ton of money," Gabriel said.

"I would worry about your own finances," Dorian replied.

"But you…" I trailed off, my eyes lingering on his gold pin. "You look like you have money."

"He enjoys the table a little too much," Gabriel said smugly.

"Gambling?" I asked.

"The odds should have been in my favor," Dorian said.

"Caught cheating with the wrong people," Gabriel added.

Maybe we were more alike than I thought.

"Nevertheless, you've been paid," Dorian said, "So if you would let *me* handle this, that would be excellent. I'm confident Wynter will get in without any difficulty. Then, comes the hard part."

Right. Stealing from the floating mage school.

"But do I really need to do all this?" I asked, gesturing to the dress.

"Yes," Dorian replied. "Considering what *I* am, it's much better if I'm sponsoring a cultured young woman. You might come from Plumba, but we'd prefer that people think it's Argent. Besides, the more genteel people believe you are, the more likely they are to trust you."

"Plumba? Argent?" He's mentioned the term earlier but I'd been too embarrassed to ask.

Dorian paused. "You call them the Scraps and the Gardens, but Plumba and Argent are their proper names," he said. "You didn't know that?"

I shook my head.

"Do you know where Reverie is?"

"Sorry," I replied.

"Do you know *anything* about geography?" Dorian asked.

"She knows the Scraps," Gabriel said, "Because that's what she *needs* to know."

"In that case, I think she should stay with me until the testing," Dorian said slowly.

That meant I'd be away from Briar, and although that seemed inevitable, my heart ached at the thought of being away from him so soon.

"Absolutely not," Gabriel said.

"Well, given her apparent ignorance of *basic geography*—"

"You're welcome to find someone else if you've got a problem with the way I do things!" Gabriel snapped.

Dorian placed a hand on the hilt of his silver sword. "I bought her services," he said, "so she'll go where I want her to. Right now, I want her in Argent. And *her* magic may be an illusion, but mine is very real. Don't test me, Gabriel. I've slain worthier men than you."

Francisca shifted in her seat. There was something dark and eager in her brown eyes.

"I think you're all talk," Gabriel sneered. "So far all you've done is fix a minor injury. I ain't all that impressed."

Dorian's sword rang as he unsheathed it. He swung the blade once, quickly and sharply. The hisses emerged, the world crackled, and jagged ice skidded across the floor towards Gabriel. My uncle darted from his chair, tipping it over. Abruptly, the ice halted. "I froze a man's blood in his veins once," Dorian said. "You can't even imagine how exquisitely painful it was, Gabriel, but I'd be *delighted* to demonstrate. Wynter, bid your uncle farewell."

Those spires of ice looked sharp enough to draw blood. I swallowed the lump in my throat. "Bye, Gabriel," I said.

***

Days turned to weeks, and I still hadn't figured out how I was going to escape all of this. I thought about Sterling and Briar constantly. Was Briar up and walking around yet, or was he still confined to bed? How was Sterling's mom doing? Hopefully, my uncle wasn't pushing Sterling and Briar harder to make up for me being gone.

Francisca returned to the Floats to manage the estate, leaving Dorian with molding me into a lady. He didn't live like Gabriel, in some old, decrepit place underground and dressed up like a gentleman. Instead, Dorian and I stayed in a beautiful set of rooms that took up the whole second floor of our building, just across from the central square. I wore the finest of clothing. All my clothes were made of soft and colorful fabrics that I'd never heard of before. I never knew how comfortable clothing could be, and I even got used to the liberating dresses that left most of my skin bare. I bathed in warm water every evening and morning, and Dorian had so much food. There were fresh, exotic fruits—firm oranges, sweet apples, and plump strawberries. The only fruit I'd ever eaten was browning and bruised. And freshly baked breads and meat! I practically moaned through every meal, until Dorian kicked me under the table and said I couldn't react to everything like I'd never tried it before.

I hated that I was enjoying myself so much. Briar and Sterling were scavenging and eating scraps, while I was dining like a wealthy mage. It wasn't fair. So many people were starving, just a few miles away. I agonized over a thousand different plans for how I might be able to bring this luxurious food to them.

My days were carefully scheduled, every minute filled with learning etiquette, but as I sat across from Dorian on the way up to the Floats for the exam, everything I'd learned flew from my head. We were aboard a cable car, being lifted up to Reverie— as Dorian insisted I call it. Outside the car's windows, the lower realms stretched before me. All the lovely salons and business halls of the Gardens, which was called Argent. The decaying gray of the Dregs, the yellowish Scraps and the long colorful stretch of the market. Together they made up Plumba. I recited the names to myself nervously. Above everything, pink clouds stretched all the way to the mountains on the horizon. I had never realized the world was so vast. I folded my fingers in my lap, twisting them into the folds of my fabric.

"It won't be that arduous," Dorian said, gesturing with a

glass of red wine. "They'll ask you a few questions. You'll answer them to the best of your ability, and then, they'll ask to see what you can do. You'll show them, and if something goes wrong, I'll step in."

"Step in how?"

"Depends on how badly you fail," Dorian said. "Only tell them what they ask for. Don't try to overcomplicate things."

As if their whole plan wasn't overly complicated already. It was dependent on so many different variables aligning exactly right, and if even one thing went wrong, everything could fall apart. My heartbeat quickened. What would happen if I went to the exam and just blurted everything out? Would the mages help me? Sure, they'd never helped anyone from the Scraps before, but the mages had also never encountered a deception like this. Maybe the mages would believe me and punish Dorian and Gabriel for their crimes. Maybe the mages would take them far away. I could return home and resume scavenging with Sterling and Briar. With Gabriel gone, we might even manage make things better. We could be powerful and build the sort of empire my uncle had! But—

But could I do it? I had no idea how the mages would punish such a crime. As horrible as Gabriel had been to me, he was still my uncle. He'd known my parents, and if he was locked away somewhere or executed, I'd never learn anything else about them.

And what if it didn't all go as nicely as I planned? What if Gabriel's absence only made things worse? It was too easy to imagine one of his underlings rising instead and taking his position. I drew in a sharp breath and glanced at Dorian, so beautiful and terrible all at once. Just like the ice he'd summoned to threaten my uncle. My eyes darted towards his sword. "Are all mages as threatening as you and Francisca?" I asked.

"Francisca isn't a mage."

But she was so beautiful! "What does she do for you, then?" I asked.

"I tell everyone she's my apothecary," Dorian said.

There was clearly an implication there, but I couldn't quite grasp what it was. "Why is your apothecary involved in all this, then?" I asked.

"Francisca knows deception well," Dorian replied.

I tightened my grip on the device, drawing comfort from the quiet hum of the magic. "What's to keep me from spilling everything at this exam?" I asked. It was a stupid question, but it seemed like Dorian was placing far too much faith and trust in me. Gabriel would have unleashed a dozen different threats by now, making sure I'd act according to his plans. He anticipated betrayal, while Dorian had the quiet confidence of someone who never doubted his peers. Which made him naïve, or very dangerous.

"I would insist it was only a bit of mischief," Dorian replied, "Which means I would pay a small fine for wasting everyone's time and return you to Gabriel. And after collecting my fee from your uncle, I would take my leave."

I nodded and absentmindedly reached beneath a sleeve of my blue, velvet dress and brushed the device over the scars spanning up my arm. The coolness of metal met the heat and bumps of my skin. If I failed, I'd end up back in the Scraps, with my uncle. There would be a punishment, for sure, but eventually things would just go back to normal. I could live with that.

"And what happens if we succeed?" I asked.

Dorian seemed to mull something over for a few seconds before finally offering an ambivalent shrug of his shoulders. "It depends on how this plays out," he said.

That wasn't really an answer that inspired confidence.

"Do you enjoy living in Plumba?" Dorian asked.

"That's where my brother and my best friend are."

"And your uncle," Dorian replied.

"Yes, he's there, too."

"Need some wine?" he asked.

I tried not to smile. Sure, my uncle would probably drive anyone to drinking, but the joke wasn't really that funny. And Dorian was terrifying. I was suddenly aware that we were trapped together in a glass box, hundreds of feet above the ground.

"No, thanks," I replied.

"*No, thank you.* And suit yourself," he replied breezily.

I bit the inside of my cheek. "Why me?" I asked.

Dorian arched an eyebrow.

"Why did you choose me for this?" I asked. "My uncle doesn't usually deal in human trafficking."

Dorian hummed and stirred his wine glass. Well," he said, "I've had dealings with your uncle in the past. That's all. I told him I had a plan, and he agreed to provide a girl."

"But why not a lady? Or a call girl. I've heard there are some girls that even cater to mages in the Gard—in Argent."

"That would work brilliantly, unless—of course—a former client saw us. Citizens from Reverie occasionally go to Argent. Plumba, on the other hand, remains a very unpopular destination."

"If I pass the test, will you let me say good-bye?" I asked, the question coming out softer than I really wanted it to.

"Of course, I will," Dorian said. "I'm not a monster, Wynter."

Oh, but he was. Something told me he was far more dangerous than my uncle, despite his fancy clothes and easy smile. He sighed at my expression, and turned away to look out the window. I followed his gaze and gasped as we cusped the edge of the cliff, revealing the Floats for the first time. The whole city seemed to be made out of gleaming metal and crystal, reflecting the pink sky in an array of dazzling lights. Dorian finished his wine glass and set it down on the small table.

"Do what you're supposed to do and to the best of your ability, and everything will be fine," he said, as the car slowly came to a stop.

I gripped the handles of the cable car tightly, like they were an anchor linking me to the ground. The door opened, and Dorian gestured for me to get out. A footman was waiting in a silver uniform to take my hand and help me down the steps. I held the hem of my dress and cautiously stepped onto the paved surface, as if the floating city would shatter into a thousand pieces.

 SEVEN

WE WALKED FROM THE STATION to the recruitment center. To my disappointment, the tall buildings were right beside one another, separated by narrow alleys, which meant I only caught tantalizing glimpses of everything else. Quick flashes of people and buildings, carved statues and decorative gardens, elegant shopfronts and restaurants. These buildings were even nicer than the ones I'd seen in the Gardens. Tall, silvery gates opened as we entered a sprawling courtyard, with patches of snow clumped between unnaturally precise bushes that framed the entrance with green columns. I spun around, trying to take it all in at once. The building before us was as white as starlight and shimmered in the sun.

I started when Dorian linked his arm with mine. I knew this was how proper ladies were escorted to proper places. But still, it took my mind a few minutes to catch up with the gesture.

"Overwhelming?" Dorian asked. "This is only the recruitment center."

We walked up a flight of gilded stairs and into a massive room. My throat felt dry. Never before had I felt like my uncle's section of a decaying subway was *small*, but this single room looked more massive than the entire system. The walls and floor were white and trimmed with glistening gold. A large, crystal-laden chandelier sparkled overhead. Across the room, there was another massive staircase with elegantly carved banisters made of polished and gilded wood. Everything was bright and perfect.

I was wearing my best blue dress, but suddenly felt every ounce of deception and fraudulence weigh down upon me, as if they were physical weights upon my shoulders. I didn't belong here. That was going to be obvious the second I went into the exam.

I was so distracted I didn't see the woman approach until she was right in front of us. She was wearing a white dress trimmed with gold, and a choker lined with bright, circular crystals. Her long, white hair was pulled back and styled in elegant coils. She had a warm face with fine lines around her eyes and over her forehead, and when she smiled at me, I instinctively smiled back. Even if her skin glowed in a distinctively magical way, there was something friendly about her. She would've been old enough to be my mother, I thought suddenly, if I'd had one. Her arms, bare from her elbows down, were lined with shimmering, silver symbols I didn't recognize. I remembered that Dorian had something drawn on his wrist, although I'd forgotten to ask what it was.

"Your Lordship," the woman said, dropping into a curtsey.

Lordship?

Dorian offered a bow that seemed either absurdly overdone or facetious. "Good morning, Celeste," he said. "It's been a long time."

Celeste's face softened. "How are you getting along

without Amelia?"

"As well as I can be, considering the circumstances."

Amelia?

"I'm glad," Celeste said. "And I assume this is Wynter?"

"Yes," Dorian said. "This is, indeed, the luminous, young lady."

The woman smiled. "Welcome," she said, "I am Celeste, headmistress of the Academy. Lord Rosewood has told me so much about you."

"Pleasing, I hope," I said.

That *sounded* like the right thing to say.

Celeste's laughter was very sweet and delicate. "Of course," she said. "Why, the committee has been so eager to meet you! We haven't taken a mage from Argent in decades! If you'll follow me, I can start the preliminary questioning. Following that, I will report my findings to my colleague, and then, we will continue with the magical examination, where we measure your skills and your magical potential."

We walked through several hallways, all gold and white. Each was more lavish than the last. Maybe if infiltrating the Academy didn't work out, I could steal a couple of things from here. My eyes darted to the heavy, shining curtains and the gilded, crystal mirrors hanging on the wall. The frames alone must be worth a fortune.

We entered a room—a parlor, my studies had taught me. I'd expected something bare and formal, but this room was bright and airy. Celeste seated herself on a tapestry-backed chair before a polished, elegantly carved table and gathered a stack of papers in her hand. She gestured to the loveseat across from her. I seated myself beside Dorian, nervously shifting my feet, clad in silk slippers, on the beautiful woven rug beneath me. I didn't belong here, and that was becoming more and more obvious by the second. I wondered if Celeste already knew, and was just playing along. I squeezed the device, as if it was a lifeline, the only thing keeping me together through all of this.

"Now," Celeste said brightly, "Tell me about yourself, Wynter…Wilcox?"

I flushed, acutely aware of how little my first name matched my family name. "My uncle was very bad at naming children," I said.

"He's bad at many things," Dorian said.

I laughed, more from nerves than amusement. Celeste's smile grew indulgent; I wondered if she thought I was stupid, or if she looked down on the lower realms like everyone else. Warmth rushed to my face. I wasn't some sheltered little girl, and I was sure that there was some lurking ugliness beneath the pristine cities in the Floats, too.

"I grew up like anyone else," I said. "I had my uncle and my brother Briar. My best friend."

Celeste scribbled down a note. I wondered what exactly she'd taken from the phrase "like anyone else." I paused and shrugged. "I…um…" I trailed off, trying to remember my rehearsed past. "I survived by working in a shop."

"And what did you sell?" Celeste asked.

"Embroidery," I said.

Hopefully, Celeste wouldn't ask for a demonstration.

"Oh!" Celeste exclaimed. "Tell me about your education, then."

"My—uh—the merchant I worked for made sure I had a good one. I learned to read. I learned manners, algebra, geography…" I trailed off. "Accounting."

"Any singing or dancing?" Celeste asked.

"No," I replied, "Unfortunately. But of course, I'd be very eager to learn."

Celeste nodded. "Swordplay?"

I had slashed at a few monsters. Clubbed a couple of others with a rusty blade.

"Not really," I said.

"So tell me about your magic," Celeste said, without looking up from her papers.

Her pen moved quickly across the page. Hopefully, that was a sign of eagerness, rather than suspicion.

"A man tried to steal from the merchant I was working for," I said, "And I panicked. I mean, it was a lot of merchandise and worth a lot of money. So I just kind of—um—I dunno. I had this really overwhelming feeling, and I thought I'd set him on fire—"

The pen stopped. Celeste's eyes, a stunning shade of violet, met mine with a look of intensity that took my breath away. "You *thought* you set him on fire?"

"It was an illusion," I said awkwardly. "It looked like flames, so I thought I'd set him on fire. But then, I realized it wasn't real. I still got the wares back, though."

I gulped and clasped my hands together in my lap.

"I have seen Wynter's powers," Dorian said, "And I will personally vouch for them."

Celeste put her pen against her lips. "And I assume you're going to continue to sponsor her, Your Lordship?"

"Of course," Dorian said, winking, "I'm not going to abandon my little mage *now*."

Little mage?

"Noted. I think that's all I need for now," Celeste replied. "Feel free to wander the grounds. We'll make an announcement when it's time for the next round of testing."

"Thank you," Dorian said.

He bowed again and sauntered from the room. I offered Celeste an awkward smile before lifting my skirts and following. "You didn't tell me you were royalty," I said, once we were out of Celeste's hearing.

"Nobility," he replied. "I'm a count."

That meant nothing to me. Sure, it was a title, but I had no idea where exactly that title fell or what it meant.

"Am I…" I trailed off. "Am I allowed to ask about Amelia?"

"She's my mother."

And Celeste had asked how he was getting along with her. Now, I knew what she meant. "I'm so sorry," I said.

"Don't be. My mother did two good things her entire life. One was having my sisters and me. The other was dying, and even then, she left me with quite a mess," Dorian replied.

I stared at him, unsure what to make of his clear disdain for his mother. Maybe he felt about her the way I felt about Gabriel, but even then, I felt like I'd have been a *little* sad to see him die. He was still my family.

"Should I call you *Your Lordship* now?" I asked.

I probably owed him a few curtsies, too.

"Call me whatever you wish," he said dismissively.

We passed a tapestry, featuring six clouds, formed with intricate stitches of silvery-white thread, and beneath them, six green areas. A map. I located Reverie and let my gaze drift down to my home. Dorian had shown me maps, but those were only of the Lower Realms or of Reverie. I'd never seen a two-layered version like this, one above the other. "Is this really what the world looks like?" I asked. "Reverie looks smaller than I'd imagined."

Dorian paused and glanced at it. "Reverie is relatively small, compared with the other kingdoms," he replied. "Most of the people you meet will be from Reverie or Aubade, our neighboring kingdom. Celeste, herself, is from Aubade."

"How do you know her?" I asked.

"She taught my sisters and me at the Academy," Dorian said.

"But Celeste looks the same age as you," I said.

"By that, I hope you mean Celeste looks like she's forty and not that I look like I'm sixty-five," Dorian said dryly, "And of course, she doesn't look as old as she is. She uses magic to give her a younger appearance. Most of us do."

Not my mother's age, then. Celeste was old enough to be my *grandmother*. "So is the drawing some sort of magic she taught you?" I asked.

"Drawing?"

"You both have those drawings on you," I said.

"They're tattoos," Dorian said, rolling up his sleeve.

The design looked something like a blue flower, or maybe a snowflake. "One of the skills mages can learn is how to draw sigils. You can have them permanently marked on you, and they grant you certain powers. Mine prevents demonic possession."

"Is that something that happens a lot?" I asked.

"Not for most people."

Most people?

"Hello, Uncle," a delicate, feminine voice cut in.

I spun around. The speaker was a girl about my age, with long, black hair and green, cat-like eyes. She wore a long navy dress fringed with pink, which seemed designed to emphasize her small waist, definitely the result of her corsets. Around her neck, she wore a magnificent necklace of white gemstones. She hung on the arm of a boy who was dressed in bright green and gold. His hair was the palest blond I'd ever seen, nearly the color of sunlight. I felt warmth rush to my face as I realized I was staring. I don't think I'd ever been this close to someone so handsome.

"Hello, Viviane. Alexander." Dorian paused, seemingly contemplating something. "This is Wynter of Argent, my charge."

"Your charge?" Viviane asked, arching an eyebrow. "Are you getting lonely in your old age, Uncle?"

"No," Dorian replied, "But thank you for your concern. Are Frederick and Eleanor here?"

"They aren't," Viviane said. "Thankfully. I won't have to spend the rest of the day worrying you and Eleanor are going to kill each other."

"I've been to Argent," Alexander said, looking me over. "It's not terrible."

Not terrible? What sort of praise was *that*? Argent was beautiful, more beautiful than any other place I'd seen in the Scraps. "It is," I replied. "Thank you. The Fl—Reverie is nice, too. From what I've seen of it so far."

Alexander stared at me like I'd just said the stupidest thing in the world. "As if any place could compare to Reverie," he said.

Well, then.

"I assume you just completed the preliminary testing?" I asked, trying to match his level of obnoxiousness.

"We did," Alexander said. "Not that either of us needed it."

"Yes," Viviane replied. "We passed with ease, but of course, that isn't a surprise. I do wish you good luck, though, Wynter. It's unfortunate what happened to the *last* mage from the Lower Realms."

"What happened to him?" I asked.

Dorian shook his head and looked at Viviane with a sort of fond exasperation. "Aren't you a little old for ghost stories, Viv?"

Viviane shrugged. "I'm just warning Wynter, so she isn't disappointed if something goes wrong. I wouldn't want her to be in over her head. I mean…Argent isn't the worst place ever, but it's still the Lower Realms."

My face grew hot, and I bit back a snide remark. If I was going to pull this off, I needed to work as hard possible not to be noticed. It was clear Viviane and I would never be friends, but I couldn't afford to make enemies on my first day.

"I've known some exceptional men from the Lower Realms," Dorian said.

I *really* hoped he didn't consider Gabriel an "exceptional man." If so, Dorian was clearly lacking in taste.

"I dunno—I mean, I'll do fine," I replied.

Viviane narrowed her eyes. I hoped she hadn't noticed my slip of the tongue. I really was trying to speak properly, but it was so *hard*. I'd never had to worry about the way I talked before.

"I suppose we'll see," Dorian said.

"If she passes, will you bring her to the opening gala?" Viviane asked.

"Why shouldn't I?" Dorian asked.

A gala? I felt the color drain from my face. I didn't know anything about galas, but this seemed like an easy way to get caught. Viviane clearly only wanted me to go because she thought I'd botch it up somehow.

"Because Eleanor will *kill* you," Viviane said, smirking.

I looked at Alexander, whose face revealed nothing. Maybe he was privy to these sorts of conversations all the time, but it seemed strange to imagine people joking so easily about killing one another.

"Eleanor can *try* to kill me," Dorian said, sounding as if he might genuinely enjoy the attempt. "Many people have before. Perhaps, she'll get lucky."

"Well, we'll see you later, Uncle," Viviane said. "And—what was it? Summer?"

Hilarious.

"Yes," Alexander said, looking away like he was already bored with the conversation. "We'll see you later."

I watched them for a while as they walked away, eventually leaving through a tall, gilded door. "Your niece, huh?" I asked. "Your family seems…lovely."

"Viviane is really a nice girl. Most of the spiteful things she says are things she's learned from Eleanor. I expect she'll grow out of them someday," Dorian said, "And if it wasn't for Viviane, Eleanor and I probably would have killed one another by now. I know if my sister sends one more spy into my household, I'm going to return a corpse."

Was he serious?

"But for now…" Dorian trailed off. "Did you see the necklace Viviane was wearing?"

"I did."

"If Viviane is still wearing it at the gala, I want you to steal it," Dorian said.

My blood froze in my veins. I'd be too concerned with tripping over my own feet to worry about stealing a necklace right off someone's neck.

"And then what?" I asked, stalling for time.

"I'll take it home," Dorian replied. "This task doesn't have anything to do with what I've hired you for. I just want to see if you're as good as I've been told, and this has the added benefit of angering my sister."

I wondered how good exactly Gabriel had said I was. No doubt he'd laid it on thick.

"And if I'm not as good as you've been told?" I asked.

"Then, I'll take you back." He dropped the threat easily, like it was no big deal. He must know Gabriel would torture me for failing, or worse.

A servant, clad in a knee-length, modest dress walked past. I guessed she was human, like me. Mages had a certain glowing confidence about them. But she looked better than I ever had. Her face wasn't thin like mine. She probably didn't have scars either. I swallowed hard. I'd always known the world was unfair, but that realization had never struck me so strongly before. I wondered if things would have been better if I'd been born here, like this servant. Would serving the mages be better than scavenging all day?

Realistically, I knew the answer was yes. It was cleaner and richer here. That woman looked well-fed. But I childishly clung to the Scraps. Sure, they weren't like this, but they were my home. They were familiar in a way that this place wasn't. And I'd already seen enough casual cruelty from the mages to know I could never lower my guard up here.

"I wonder where they keep the wine," Dorian said.

"I'm sure they'd tell you if you asked," I said.

I didn't want to talk about wine, especially with the realization that even if I *could* trick these mages, Dorian might still send me back to my uncle if I didn't pass his arbitrary and pointless test.

Dorian strode onwards, seemingly oblivious. "Should you ever get the inclination to purchase a fine wine, you should be aware that cheap and expensive wines both taste the same," he said.

"Do they?" I asked.

He nodded. "I've been serving cheap wine for months, and despite the many rumors that have spread about me, no one has ever criticized my wine."

"That seems…distasteful," I said, "After your mother…"

"The rumors began long before Mother died. My sister Guinevere killed herself," he said, "And time doesn't erase a scandal like that."

I shuddered at Dorian's latest revelation. Why would a rich, powerful mage even think about killing herself? Despite the situation, it was hard not to feel a *little* sympathetic towards him. He'd lost both his sister and his mother.

"Why would that be scandalous? That's—that's terrible. I can't even imagine how…" I trailed off. "I'm so sorry."

"In Reverie, most consider suicide shameful," Dorian said. "But mastering magic isn't without its dangers. Sometimes, young mages can't control their powers, or are driven to madness. Accidents are fairly common. But suicide is treated as a sort of a… weakness in your bloodline. People are wary of marrying into a family that they think is marked by a failure to master magic."

Was magic even worth all of that? It seemed like it'd be easier not to have it at all.

"But don't worry over the magic. You're just pretending, after all," Dorian said.

Easy for him to say. Dorian was only serving as the middleman. I was the one perpetrating the fraud. I was the one who would be breaking into a school filled with mages. All Dorian had to do was dance and drink wine, while I risked my life stealing a journals and jewelry. Viviane was just a student, like me, but I wondered how much magic she already knew, and what she'd do to me if I were caught. Something told me she wasn't the forgiving type.

EIGHT

THE BELLS RANG, WHICH ACCORDING to Dorian, was the sign that we were meant to reconvene. We gathered into a ballroom with a small crowd of people. I picked out Alexander and Viviane, still clinging to his arm. Above us, there was a balcony. Two mages stood there, overlooking the crowd. One of them was Celeste, in her white and gold dress. Beside her was a man with a cleanly shaven face and long, dark hair. His skin was so pale it looked like he'd been carved from marble. It stood out against his dark suit and gray cloak.

The air shimmered and Celeste's voice filled the room.

"Welcome, everyone," she said. "I am Celeste, headmistress of the Academy. With me is Markus, serving as this year's Council representative. The preliminary testing is now complete, so we'll have everyone move to the main testing hall."

"Well, here we go," Dorian whispered.

"Please, continue to the testing room," Celeste said.

Markus took over, giving directions to the room, but Dorian needed none. He grasped my arm, firmly but not roughly, and led me out of the ballroom.

"Now, comes the hard part. Remember what I said about this," Dorian said.

Third try, summon my fire. Pass but don't draw too much attention to myself. I slipped the device further up my sleeve. It needed to be close at hand, but also completely hidden.

"Right," I said, taking a deep breath. I'd been practicing for weeks but hadn't managed to replicate any of the effects I'd displayed the night I'd tried to run away, no matter how much I begged the device. Still, I could produce a burst of cold flame easily, and I'd always been decent at basic sleight-of-hand. I'd just never done a magic trick for mages before.

Dorian and I were the first to arrive. We emerged in a massive auditorium. At the front of the room, there was a long table; the rest of the room contained velvet-covered seats. Servants ushered us into them. Dorian ignored the instructions to sit where directed and instead, chose to sit as far away from everyone else as possible. No one seemed to care enough to stop him. Then, we waited. Alexander and Viviane walked in and headed straight for the front row. A few more people filed in, taking seats closer to the front. Celeste and Markus arrived shortly after. "The benefit of your last name is that you'll get to see the others go," Dorian said.

But that didn't mean I would do any better. These people had *actual* magical powers, and I had a device that was probably illegal.

Viviane was first. She moved onto the stage with a bold sort of confidence. A small stool was placed before her and a large stone of some sort placed in the center. I wished Dorian had moved us closer. Celeste handed Viviane a card.

"What will happen," Dorian said lowly, "is you'll be handed

a card with an incantation. If you're a mage, the object before you should respond to your powers."

Viviane began chanting, her words so soft that I couldn't make them out. Nothing happened. I shifted in my seat, watching. Celeste said something I didn't catch.

"Sometimes, even the most powerful of us don't get it on the first try," Dorian said.

"Did you?"

"Yes."

I was supposed to get it on the third try, which meant I'd have to pretend to fail twice, and I'd never been great at acting. Viviane was still trying, with a look of concentration on her pretty face. Suddenly, the world hissed and shifted. Flowers blossomed from the stone before her. Bright green leaves and delicate purple petals tumbled over the stool and down onto the floor. Viviane laughed loudly, the sound edged with relief. She bowed and exited, amongst the smattering of applause.

"Is she good?" I asked.

"It's hard to say," Dorian replied. "The stones are enchanted to react to magic and indicate which elements you would most easily align yourself with. They don't show how powerful you are."

"Do you only get one power?"

"No, it's just that you learn some things easier than others. Most of us are really good at a few different things."

"What are you really good at?" I asked warily.

"Allow a man some mystery, won't you?" Dorian asked.

Like he needed any more mystery.

Alexander went next. The stool remained in place, but a new object was placed upon it. He was handed his card.

Alexander read it over a few times. Unlike Viviane, who had stood back, Alexander scooped up his object and held it in the palm of his hand. That was a good idea, it would make my deception easier. Hopefully. He spoke softly, too, and after a few moments, a gentle breeze blew through the room. The heavy purple curtains flickered and rippled like water, letting in shards of bright light from outside.

Alexander returned the object to its place and bowed. Then, he returned to his seat. There were a few more, each of them managing to perform magic, but none of them on the first try. But still, they all made it look so easy. What if my device didn't work at all? A cold chill of panic crept under my skin, and a tremor ran down my spine when they called my name.

"Wynter Wilcox!"

My knees shook as I stood. I thought I might vomit or pass out as I made my way to the stage. I curled my fingers into the palm of my hand, ignoring the stares and whispers. The device was nestled in my sleeve. Now, it really *was* my lifeline. I had to make this work.

As I climbed onto the stage and looked at the judges, Celeste smiled encouragingly. There was a flutter of movement as Dorian moved closer, holding his glass of wine out primly as he navigated his way through the seats. I wondered who kept supplying him with alcohol. It didn't seem right that he was so relaxed, when both of us had so much riding on this deception. He sat beside Viviane, who briefly pulled her gaze from Alexander to him.

"Hello," I said lamely, waving my fingers at the several dozen mages in the audience.

Had people fainted from this before? If I passed out now,

would I get another chance to redeem myself? This was it, the big moment I'd spent weeks preparing for, but it didn't feel like I'd had nearly enough time. I'd have needed months to make this work, and even then, I'm still not sure I would have succeeded.

Celeste approached the stage and placed my object before me. It was a blue circle, made of some stone I didn't have a name for. My hand shook as she handed me my card. *Blue stone, full of light, I command you with my might.* Whatever that was supposed to mean. There was no way I could possibly manage this.

"You'll do fine," Celeste said. "Take your time."

Celeste returned to her seat. I reached for the stone, shifting my arm so the device slipped down my sleeve, and caught it deftly in the palm of my hand. I took a deep breath and chanted the poem. Nothing happened. I feigned disappointment and glanced to Dorian, who looked—for the first time all day—genuinely interested. And again. Nothing happened.

Maybe I should've ignored what he said and tried it on the first time. What if nothing at all happened when I got to the third time and tried it for real?

"Just breathe," Celeste said. "Sometimes, it takes a few times. Whatever you're thinking, you do belong here. You've shown powers."

Viviane whispered something and giggled, I saw Alexander smirk. I wondered if they were laughing at me. It was now or never. I tilted my wrist forward, just enough to swipe my thumb across the device. Blue flames burst forth from my hand. *Perfect.*

I raised my hand, and the flames crept forward, forming a semi-circle on the stage around me. I grinned victoriously. Then the ground shook. Faintly at first, and I thought I was just feeling dizzy until I saw the lamps swinging overhead. Then all at once, a rushing howl filled the auditorium, and the stage buckled and shook. My hand shook, and the flames burst across the floor and up the heavy curtains. Someone screamed as a chandelier crashed to the ground. I fell to my hands and knees, and thought I saw a dark shape creeping along the wall. It looked like a monster, but that was impossible. There couldn't be monsters up here. The smell of something burning, the scent of something sharp and chemical, hit my nose.

An ear-splitting crack came from above and I looked up in time to see part of the ceiling, gold and enamel, falling towards me. Before it could land, a bolt of ice crashed into it, sending shattered enamel skittering away. I gasped for air. Everything seemed to be happening too fast and too slow all at once. Celeste and Dorian, sword in hand, thundered onto the stage, Markus close behind.

"Are you all right?" Celeste asked.

The device was still in my hand. I curled my fingers around it and slipped it back into my sleeve quickly. "What happened?" I asked.

"A quake," Dorian said. "They're happening more frequently. More severely, too."

Alexander mumbled something from his seat. I didn't catch the words, but Viviane shot him a warning look.

Celeste helped me to my feet. My mouth tasted like ash, and when I looked over my shoulder, I saw that the heavy velvet curtains were scorched and blackened. But I hadn't done that. I couldn't have done that. The device just cast the *illusion* of shadow. It couldn't make actual flame.

"The curtains," I said.

Dorian laughed. "I suppose I *do* owe them a new set, yes."

"I—I didn't—they've never been real before," I stammered. "I'm sorry. I don't know what happened. I didn't mean—"

"Oh, what's a little damaged fabric?" Celeste asked. "Don't fret about that. It was probably related to the quake."

"The quake?" I asked.

Celeste nodded. "To a small degree, your ability to harness magic is tied to your emotions. Obviously, the quake startled you, resulting in a much stronger reaction from the testing stone."

I nodded, biting my lip. That would make sense, if I were actually a mage. Dorian must have made the flames real, to better sell it. But why did he have to be so dramatic with it?

"I told you she had magic," Dorian said smugly. "Can I take this to mean that Wynter has earned her place at the Academy? Surely, you don't expect her to retake the test after *this*."

The judges exchanged looks with one another.

"I vote," Celeste said slowly, "that we move to admit Wynter."

"I agree," Markus said. Markus's voice betrayed nothing, but there was something predatory in his gaze. I wondered if he suspected some kind of deception, and if he did, why was he letting me in anyway? That's when I realized, I'd actually passed. I'd fooled the judges, and they were going to let me into the Academy of magic.

Nine

TRUE TO HIS WORD, DORIAN did take me back to the
Scraps. Or Plumba, as I was supposed to call them. For the trip,
I'd worn my usual dark pants, blouse, and jacket. Francisca
saved them but had them washed. They were stiff with starch
and smelled like roses. When I caught a glimpse of myself in the
window of the carriage, it was surreal. My face looked too bright
and clean to belong with my old, ragged clothes.

I clasped my hands in my lap and leaned my head against
the cool glass. Outside, rain pounded on the carriage, beating
out an erratic rhythm. Across from me, Dorian was silent and
sprawled over his seat as if it was his personal goal to take up as
much room as possible. At first, he'd been reading a book about
how memories are formed. He promised it was riveting if you
had an in-depth understanding of modern philosophy and a
certain branch of magic, but later discarded the book and
declared it contrived.

I wondered if I ought to ask about it. I was going to the
Academy. It would be beneficial to know as much about the
mages as possible. But I didn't feel like talking. I pulled my knees

up to my chest and let my feet rest on the edge of the seat. Dorian glanced at me, but said nothing about my dirty boots on the lush fabric. Maybe he didn't care.

"Thank you," I said quietly.

I didn't want to thank him for anything. Dorian had torn me from my home and now expected me to risk my life for this scheme of his. And for what? To pay off some gambling debts? It all sounded so stupid. But he was taking me to say good-bye. I knew that he didn't have to do that, and I'd have been heartbroken if I'd had to leave without seeing Briar and Sterling again.

"I see no reason to be needlessly antagonistic," Dorian said. "We're accomplices now. If you want to say your farewells to your family and friends, why shouldn't you?"

Right, accomplices. Even if I hadn't had any say in the matter. I let my head rest against the back of the seat and listened to the rain. It was such a soothing sound.

"So is it just your brother and your uncle?" Dorian asked. "What about your parents?"

I stared at him for a moment before responding. Did he actually care? He seemed like he was being genuinely nice, and I hated that. In my experience, kindness always had ulterior motives. Maybe he was worried about how I might sabotage him, but I knew it was far too late for me to do that now. I just had to find what he wanted as quickly as possible, without getting caught.

"My father died, and my mother didn't want me," I said, "So she left me with Gabriel and ran off with a man she met."

It was the simplest version of the truth. I didn't mention how many times I'd fantasized about my mother changing her mind and coming back for me.

"Do you remember either of them?"

"No, I was too little."

"That's unfortunate," Dorian said. "For what it's worth, I do understand. My father died in a duel when I was five. Sometimes, I still regret that I never knew him. He was said to be a very noble man."

"There's a lot of death in your family," I said.

"So there is."

The carriage jolted to a stop. I stepped out, my boots splashing in the mud. Cold water pounded over my head. There was something almost comforting in the way the rain soaked in, undoing all the careful work that Dorian's servants had put into making my hair presentable. With a scowl, Dorian left his carriage and adjusted his sword. Not a speck of rain touched him, though. Instead, the clear drops bounced right off his black coat.

"Are you doing that with magic, or…?" I asked.

"The fabric is enchanted," Dorian replied. "I don't like rain."

"But isn't your magic tied to water? Because of the ice?"

"I'm just a bit strange, I guess." Dorian paused and looked like he'd been going to say something more, but he seemed to decide against it.

We walked across the road and headed down into the subway. I dashed ahead, leaving Dorian to trail me. I skidded down the stairs and through the front door, nearly plowing into my uncle. "Wynter," he said smoothly. He didn't look surprised to see me, but I guess Dorian had let him know to expect us.

"Where's Briar?" I asked.

Gabriel arched an eyebrow. "I don't get a greeting?" he asked.

"Hello," I said, crossing my arms. "Briar?"

Dorian entered behind me. I glanced to him and saw that his hand was on the hilt of his sword. "Gabriel," Dorian said. "Why don't we talk business while she's saying her farewells?"

"You think you can trust her alone?" Gabriel asked.

"I do," Dorian said.

Gabriel crossed his arms. "You say that because—"

I left them to argue and headed to my room. I was in such a hurry that I nearly ran past it. I clung to the doorframe and peered in, but Briar wasn't there. With a scowl, I returned to my uncle, who was still talking with Dorian.

"Where is my brother?" I asked.

Gabriel's eyes flickered to me. "Out with Sterling, which I would've told you if you hadn't run off."

Out in the rain? In the middle of winter? Neither Sterling nor Briar should be out in weather like this, especially since Briar was still recovering from a crossbow bolt to his leg.

"Where did they go?" I asked.

"Out," Gabriel replied. "They're coming back now."

I heard footsteps echoing through the subway darted outside, back the way I'd come. "Briar!" I shouted. "Sterling!"

I received a loud, excited shout in response. Grinning, I quickened my pace. There they were! I went to hug my brother first. Rain had plastered his blond hair to his head, for once flattening and quelling its usual defiance. I embraced him tightly, rainwater seeping through my coat. "How are you?" I asked, holding him at an arm's length.

Somehow, I'd expected him to have drastically changed,

but he looked the same as he always had. Tall, blond, and malnourished.

"Good," he said, grinning. "You look great. Wow."

"It's all cosmetics," I replied, waving a dismissive hand.

And having enough food. My stomach twisted.

"It's good to see you," Sterling said, clearing his throat.

I smiled and turned to him, my eyes combing over his appearance.

"How is your mom?" I asked.

"The same," Sterling said.

I patted my brother's shoulder and slowly released him.

"How long are you here for?" Briar asked.

"Not long," I said, "Just long enough to say good-bye to everyone. How is your knee?"

"Right as rain," he replied cheerily.

It wasn't. I'd seen him shot. Even as he said that, he shifted his weight from one foot to the other. He was probably having a hard time standing, especially after scavenging all night.

"You're both doing so well without me," I replied. "Better, I think."

Play it off. Act like everything was fine. Act like my brother hadn't been given a likely permanent limp. Act like I hadn't abandoned them and made everything worse.

"We're doing our best," Briar said, "But it ain't the same without you lording your older sibling power over me."

"Don't worry," I said. "When I come back, I'll be sure to make up for lost time."

"You're coming back, then?" Briar asked.

"Of course, I am," I said. "This is going to be easy. I'm prepared for it. I already fooled a bunch of mages into thinking

I'm the real deal, so…"

Briar hugged me again and I tousled his hair.

"Go ahead and meet with our uncle," I said. "I gotta talk to Sterling about a couple of things."

"Okay," Briar said.

He walked a few feet and then turned around and smirked at me. "Try not to fall when you're up there," he said, grinning.

"I'll do my best," I joked, "And if I do fall, I'll make sure it's on top of you."

Briar laughed and continued his way down the subway. I watched him, noting how he favored one leg more than the other. Climbing through the Dregs was going to be tough on him. I knew that Sterling would try to take care of him. But also knew Gabriel would be angry at him if he didn't bring home enough loot. And what about the monsters? Briar barely knew how to protect himself.

I'd messed up so badly. And while they were down here suffering, I'd be up in the Floats, with enough food and nice clothes. It wasn't fair.

Sterling sighed. "Wynter, I feel like I…" he gestured with his hands when he spoke, like always, but this time something was different. The rest of his words faded into the background as I focused on his fingers. The whole world came to a crashing halt when I realized one was missing.

I stifled a gasp and forced my eyes not to linger. I lifted them to meet his green eyes instead. Sterling had never been caught stealing before. But then, we'd always gone places together. There had always been someone to keep lookout. I wanted to throw up. This was my fault. If I'd been there looking out for him, he wouldn't have been caught. I took his hand in mine, curling my fingers over his. I brought it up against my cheek, as a warm tear slid down over my skin.

"So you noticed that, huh?" Sterling asked.

"Of course I noticed. What happened?" I asked.

"What do you think?"

"You stole something, to help your mom?" I asked.

I racked my mind, trying to remember which of the many mob bosses dealt in medicine. The good stuff. Not the shady *maybe*-medicine or *maybe*-poison that was commonly available in the Scraps. We didn't even know what Sterling's mom was sick from. Just that she'd been sick for a very long time.

"No," Sterling said quietly. "I did it for you."

The words felt like a punch to the stomach. They repeated themselves over and over, but I still couldn't make sense of them. He'd lost a finger. For me. Even if I came back, I could never change this. This was permanent.

"Why?" I asked.

He smiled wryly. "I thought that if I managed to get something expensive enough, I might be able to get you out of all this."

"Sterling…" I trailed off. "You shouldn't have done that."

"I couldn't have just sat back and let this happen. I had to do something."

"No," I replied. "No, you—I tried to get out of it, and I couldn't. Did you really think you'd manage to make this work?"

"Not really," Sterling said. "But I had to try."

I hugged him suddenly and lowered my face to his shoulder, trying to hold in my sobs. This could be our last moment together, and I didn't want him to remember me with tears in my eyes. For a few seconds, I was content to just breath him in—the scent of freshly fallen rain and earthiness. Maybe if I held him for long enough, everything could just stay the same forever.

"I missed you so much," I whispered.

"I missed you, too."

Tentatively, I reached for his hand and clasped it between mine. Sterling's breath hitched.

"The worst part is, it's gonna be much harder to flip people off from now on," he said.

"That's unfortunate," I said, letting a smile lift the corners of my mouth. I couldn't remember him ever flipping anyone off before, and it was a bad joke anyway.

"I know. All I've got going for me is my incredible ability to insult people," Sterling said.

I met his gaze, his eyes warm and soft. Seeing him like this was too much.

"Why would you do something so stupid?" I asked, sighing. "You know better."

Sterling took a deep breath. "Wynter… you're the only good thing that's ever happened to me. The only good thing about living in the Scraps. And now, you're leaving, and I dunno for how long. I didn't know if I would ever even see you again. I had to do something."

My breath came out in an uncomfortable hitch. "You're my best friend, Sterling," I said. "You don't…I would never want you to do something so risky."

Sterling furrowed his brow and rubbed his thumb over the back of my hand. "Your best friend?" he asked.

"Of course," I replied. "Who else would it be?"

His laughter sounded hollow. "You're so smart, Wynter,"

he said, cupping my cheek with his other hand. "So smart. How could you have missed this for so long? How're you *still* missing it?"

I frowned and shook my head, unsure what he was getting at. "I'm not missing anything," I said. "I know you care about me, so much that you're willing to risk getting hurt for me. And because you're my friend—"

"Your friend," Sterling echoed.

What did he mean?

"Why're you being so weird?" I asked. "I'm doing the best I can."

"I know you are," he said, running his hand through my hair.

Sterling tilted his head and leaned close to me, so close that I felt his breath, hot and damp, on my cheek.

"I don't understand," I said.

"I know," he replied. "Just promise me that you'll come back."

"Of course, I will. Promise you'll stay out of trouble."

He laughed. "Oh, Wynter, you know I never listen to you," he said.

"Try this time. For me. For Briar," I said. "If I know you're looking after him, I won't worry so much. Just promise me that you'll help take care of him."

"You ain't got to ask that," he replied. "I'll take care of Briar. Always."

"I…" Sterling trailed off and cleared his throat. His eyes darted to my lips. "I wanna kiss you."

I froze, sure I'd misheard. Then, a startled, little laugh tore from my throat. "Fine," I said, turning my cheek towards him.

"Look at you, being all sentimental."

His lips placed a small, quick peck on mine. Then he kissed me harder, crushing me to him. It was unexpected, but not unpleasant.

"I love you," Sterling said slowly. "I'm sorry I waited until last-minute to tell you that. I was working up to it. You ain't gotta do anything. I just wanted you to know. Before you leave again."

"Oh," I replied.

My throat was dry. I finally got it. He *loved* me. Thousands of words shifted through my mind, but I couldn't manage to say any of them. Instead, I stood watching him awkwardly, with a stupid expression on my face. With a soft sigh, Sterling pulled his hand away and walked past me without saying goodbye.

I remained still and quiet for several minutes. Slowly, I forced myself into motion, tracing my hand along the familiar walls of the subway. The cracked tile was cold and familiar. Steadying beneath my fingertips. Sterling loved me.

When had this happened? How had I missed it for so long? I sank onto the steps of the subway and buried my face in my hands. I hadn't known, and I almost wished he hadn't told me. Because I didn't know if I loved him back, and yet I doubted I could ever bear to tell him no. It was really all strange, anyway. I'd thought about being in love once or twice; most people did. Or so I'd been told. But I'd always imagined it to be this wonderful, glorious thing. This thing that broke curses in fairy tales and that always won out in the end. But that wasn't the truth at all. Instead, love was as frightening and uneven and anxious as my first kiss.

Not that pouting over it in the darkness was going to help

me figure it out. And what difference did it make, how we felt about each other? I climbed to my feet and dusted myself off, then walked slowly down the subway. I couldn't believe I was really leaving all of this behind and going to the Floats. To Reverie. I grimaced when I thought of how bright and clean the mages were. I paused by a rain puddle and crouched beside it. Reaching into my jacket pocket, I pulled out the device and swiped my thumb across it. The blue flames flickered out and danced above my waiting hand. I stared into my reflection. With my dark hair soaked and clinging to my shoulders, I looked more like myself. But eating enough food had filled out the thinness of my cheeks. My skin was clearer and brighter. I widened my blue eyes; those, at least, remained unchanged. Those still looked like me.

I wondered if I looked more like Gabriel now, who had always looked a bit healthier than the rest of us, mostly because he hogged all the food. I curled my hand around the device, extinguishing the flames. The hisses lingered for a few seconds after the flames were gone, echoing down the narrow corridor.

I stood and continued walking back down the familiar path. Because no one came looking for me, I didn't hurry.

"*But why do you care?*" Gabriel's voice drifted through the tunnel.

I paused, uneasy. I recognized that tone of voice. He was angry. I didn't hear an answer, and my first thought was that he was arguing with Briar. I quickened my pace, determined to protect my brother as best as I could.

"That's not your concern," Dorian said.

I halted. It wasn't Briar Gabriel was angry at.

"So you're not gonna tell *me* everything, but I'm supposed

to tell you everything?" Gabriel asked. "You got the nerve to come down here and accuse me—"

I leaned against the wall and edged closer. While Dorian's voice remained cold and even, Gabriel sounded ready to rip someone's throat out.

"It's not an accusation," Dorian said. "It's a statement of fact."

"The girl ain't good enough for you, you're welcome to leave her," Gabriel said, "But I ain't giving your money back."

I swallowed. Did I want Dorian to ditch me already? My uncle would be furious if failed. But what had I done wrong? I passed the stupid exam and did everything Dorian wanted!

"This isn't about money," Dorian said, "But your reaction has taught me everything I need to know. I'm capable of finding out the finer details for myself."

Footsteps. I panicked and tried to compose myself, to act like nothing was wrong. When Dorian rounded the corner, he nearly ran right into me. He looked angry, and I waited for him to yell at me. Maybe strike me. He surely realized I'd been eavesdropping.

Gabriel halted a few feet away and glared at me, like this whole situation was my fault.

"I told you she'd come back," Dorian said.

Gabriel scowled. "To think that you'd be so trusting," he said, narrowing his eyes, "With all the things you've done."

Dorian offered his arm. I took it, relieved his anger wasn't directed at me. I guess he wouldn't be abandoning me so soon after all.

"Did you say your farewells?" Dorian asked.

"Yes," I replied, although it wasn't enough. Hours of goodbyes wouldn't have been enough to say farewell to the people I cared about.

"You're gonna lose her," Gabriel said, narrowing his eyes.

"There are better ways to control people than through fear, not that I'd expect you to know that," Dorian said.

Gabriel's face reddened. "You know what happens if you don't do as you're told, Wynter."

"I know," I replied.

"For your brother's sake, I hope you do," Gabriel glowered, before slinking back inside.

My throat was tight as Dorian led me back out and into his waiting carriage. I settled in my seat and looked out the window, my heart growing heavier and heavier as the Scraps flashed before the tinted glass. It wasn't much to look at, but it was the only home I'd ever known, and I was leaving it all behind.

TEN

ONCE WE RODE THE CABLE car up to the Floats, I finally got to see Reverie properly. Large buildings, built of brilliant, faceted crystal stretched into the bright blue sky. The roads, still slick with rain, looked as if they'd been paved of silver and were lined with shops. Bits of clouds, downy and fluffy, drifted by. Men and women walked along the streets, many wearing bright and elaborately decorated clothing. There were large, fur-trimmed cloaks, dresses of brightly hued velvet, elegant suits, and swords with intricately carved hilts. It seemed nearly impossible for all this wealth to exist in one place, and yet here it was. Stranger still, I was dressed as fancy as these mages.

Dorian had made us stop in the Argent so I could change clothes and get cleaned up. I shifted on the seat, trying to find a more comfortable position. The corset didn't hurt, but it made sitting feel weird. I had to perch at the edge of the seat and lean forward, and I still hadn't gotten used to the weight of the skirts or having sleeves that fell off my shoulders.

"What are you thinking?" Dorian asked.

I bit the inside of my cheek and decided against telling him how awkward I felt in the clothes. "Mages really love crystal," I said instead.

"It's a defensive measure," Dorian said. "If Reverie is ever invaded, the plan is to section off the kingdom and hurl fractured gemstone at our attackers."

The crystal was beautiful and dangerous, then. It fit these mages well. Outside the window, a row of brooms swept across the street. "So in the Floats—"

"*Reverie.* Did you bring your dialect back with you?"

"I'm sorry. I just wondered if you have magic brooms sweeping everywhere."

"Sure."

"Wouldn't it be easier to have people sweep?" I asked.

"I suppose it depends on who's doing the sweeping," Dorian said. "It wouldn't particularly affect me either way."

It still seemed strange. We passed a tall fence, made of iron and crystal. Beyond it, there were sprawling gardens, covered in snow, and a red-brown building with elaborate arches and tall glass windows.

"That's Rosewood," Dorian said, pointing. "You'll stay here tonight after the opening gala, then I'll walk you to school in the morning."

"I'd expected it to be white," I said.

"The color is because of when it was built. White was considered old-fashioned at the time," Dorian replied. "You can bring what you've stolen there, and if you require anything while you're at the Academy, don't hesitate to ask. I'm willing to do what it takes to make us succeed."

"Like setting curtains on fire," I said.

Dorian looked at me quizzically, revealing nothing.

"Sure. And for what it's worth, you'll never want for anything while you're here," Dorian said. "I realize the situation isn't ideal, but Reverie isn't a bad place to live."

It still wouldn't be home, though. And no amount of material goods would make up for being away from Sterling and Briar. At the thought of Sterling, my throat tightened. I put a hand over my lips where he'd kissed me. I hadn't even reacted. I'd just stared at him like an idiot.

"You might even make friends," Dorian said.

I stifled a laugh. As if any of these rich mages would want to be my friend. Dorian's continued kindness confused me. Maybe Dorian was trying to justify this all to himself. Maybe he wanted to believe that he wasn't as bad as my uncle.

"But of course, I'll expect you to remember why you're here," Dorian said. "Enjoy yourself, but not too much." And there it was. He was only being nice so I'd steal for him.

"I don't have any intention of enjoying myself," I said.

"I see."

"I do have a question, though," I said. "Maybe it's because I don't understand, but you seem very wealthy for a man who's trying to pay his debts."

"An astute observation."

"Am I wrong?"

"It doesn't matter. Like Gabriel, you are going to receive only the information you *need* to know regarding what I'm trying to do," Dorian said. "I'm surprised you didn't piece that together considering the conversation you overheard."

He really had caught me eavesdropping, then. I winced. "Are you mad?"

"That's not quite the word I would use," he said. "Mind

you. That *isn't* me encouraging you to eavesdrop. I need you to stay out of trouble."

I nodded and looked back outside. Eventually, the carriage stopped, and the doors opened. I stepped out carefully in my long, flowing skirts. A massive building loomed before us. It was white and gold, with columns made of crystal. Seas of silver-flecked stone stretched before us, lined by snow-covered grounds. Elegantly trimmed shrubs curved in long, spiraling rows. Small, blue flowers peeked through the snow.

"Welcome to the Academy," Dorian said.

He offered his arm and led me up the main stairs.

The hallway opened into a lavish salon. Everything was blue and silver. This place looked peaceful, lit by soft light, coming from candles that floated far above my head. One of the servants took my coat, while I gazed upwards, looking in awe at the dark ceiling and the gilded vaults. I'd never seen engineering like this before. I hadn't even realized something like this could exist.

"Wow," I whispered.

Dorian bowed dramatically to the servant before surrendering his coat and hat. He kept his sword.

"Don't worry. It gets old quickly," Dorian said, linking his arm with mine. "Hopefully, we can find Viviane before Eleanor makes an appearance."

Right. Viviane. I wasn't here to enjoy myself. I was here to steal Viviane's necklace. Part of me wished she wasn't wearing it tonight. That way, there'd be nothing to steal.

We walked through the salon into a large ballroom. My jaw dropped as hundreds of people mingled before me. No, not people. *Mages.* I felt suddenly hot, like I might hyperventilate.

"Focus on Viviane," Dorian said quietly. "The rest of them don't matter."

I scanned the crowd, but I didn't see her. "What if she isn't here?"

"I promise she's here, but if we can't find her, Alexander will do for now."

"Because if Viviane sees me with him, she'll challenge me to a duel or something?" I asked. "She seems very attached."

"Of course, she is," Dorian replied. "He's a prince. Viviane hopes he'll become a potential suitor, and I've no doubt Eleanor is encouraging such a pursuit."

"He's a *prince*?"

"The youngest of six children. He's recently become obsessed with proving his worth on his own merits, so he's vowed to spend a year *not* being treated as a prince."

"That's…" I trailed off.

"Noble, if misguided," Dorian said. "He can insist on not being bowed to or addressed properly. He can even insist on not having servants or certain privileges. But he's still a prince, and everyone knows that. Still, it's harmless. I did something similar in my youth."

"That means a lot of people are gonna be watching him, though."

"*Will be,* yes. Fortunately, there are rules to these engagements. If we find Alexander, all you need to do is ask him to dance."

I remembered what Alexander said about the Gardens being *not terrible*.

"So I can be humiliated when he refuses?"

"He won't," Dorian said. "If there's one thing you can

expect from a prince, it's a polite façade in front of crowds. He may dance and loathe every second. He may try to pull you aside, alone, and insult you. He may even do it with a few people around. But an entire crowd of them? Oh, no. He'll stay true to form."

I hoped he was right.

Dorian sighed. "There's Eleanor."

I followed Dorian's nod, my gaze landing on a slender woman. Her thick, brown hair fell in waves over her pale, round shoulders and tumbled over the bodice of her black, satin dress. Somehow, I'd expected something more predatory from Dorian's alleged nemesis, something like my uncle Gabriel's story about the monstrous mage-lady who ate children, but Eleanor was beautiful.

"I see you have similar taste in dyes," I said.

For a few seconds, Dorian looked utterly bewildered. Then, he laughed. "It's not that. In Reverie, when a parent dies, it's proper to observe a year-long mourning period. You wear black for the first ten months, and for the last two, you're allowed to add gray and lilac. My mother isn't worth nearly that level of devotion, but unfortunately, I have a reputation to uphold."

"How did she die?" I asked.

"She fell down the stairs and broke her neck. Or something like that."

He said it as casually as if he'd been discussing the weather.

"You don't believe she fell?" I asked.

"Not entirely."

He didn't sound especially bothered with the possibility that someone might have killed his mother. Maybe he'd done the deed himself. I looked nervously towards Eleanor and wondered how she felt about her mom's death.

"Should I be worried about Eleanor?" I asked.

"She's a very dangerous woman."

"You're dangerous, too," I pointed out.

"So I am. But Eleanor is always looking to stab someone in the back. I'd at least do you the courtesy of stabbing you from the front," Dorian replied.

As if she'd heard him from across the room, Eleanor headed straight to us.

"Don't you have somewhere to be, Wynter?" Dorian asked.

He was right, so I headed away, drifting into the crowd. Viviane or Alexander. Where were they? There were so many people that it was impossible to find anyone. I'd never stolen jewelry off a person before, but I had an idea of how I wanted to do it. Distraction was key. All I had to do was spill a drink down the front of Viviane's dress, draw attention to her reaction and steal the necklace right under everyone's nose. Or if I got lucky, Viviane would go to clean herself up and take it off. But it was still a huge risk. What was so special about *this* necklace? Did Dorian even want it, or was everything just a game to him?

I drifted to the wall and stood there, scanning the crowd. Finally, I found Alexander and headed towards him. My heart raced. Just ask him to dance. It wouldn't be that difficult. Alexander saw me and ended his conversation with a blonde woman wearing a purple gown. I took a deep breath.

"Good evening," I said.

Now that I knew he was a prince, it made talking to him much more awkward.

"Good evening," he said.

"Would you like to—"

"Dance?" he asked. "With you?"

Maybe Dorian had been wrong. Maybe Alexander would humiliate me in front of all these people.

"Yes," I replied.

He put an arm around the small of my back and drew me in closer. "Can I tell you a secret?" he whispered. "I hate dancing."

"Me too," I said.

"Why don't we talk instead?"

"Um…sure," I said.

Without warning, Alexander grabbed my wrist and pulled me along behind him. I stumbled at first, but then followed him out of the ballroom and down a long, dark corridor. This was a trap of some kind, but I didn't know how to avoid it.

"Alex—"

We reached the end. I pulled my wrist away, but Alexander's hand shot out, cornering me against the wall. He was even more handsome from close up, and his blue eyes were staring directly into mine with an intensity that took my breath away. I tried to say something, but all my thoughts scattered and fell apart.

"This is what you wanted, isn't it?" he murmured.

"What are you talking about?" I asked nervously.

"You get all dressed up, attend a fancy ball, and hope to seduce a prince into a dark corner. Don't think you're the first to try."

I sucked in a quick breath. I looked at his broad shoulders and then away.

"Why would I want to seduce you?"

"Why wouldn't you? Unless you honestly think you've got what it takes to become a mage."

"I passed the test, didn't I?"

"Did you?" he asked. My breath hitched. Did he know I'd cheated? Had he seen the device?

"Besides, you're not *that* plain looking, even if you do come from the Lower Realms. I'm surprised, however, you don't *smell* like trash." He leaned in close, sniffing slowly at my neck.

Asshole! I pushed him off, shaking, but he caught my wrist and spun me into his arms.

"Relax," he whispered, "I'm just using you to rile up Viviane. It takes her down a peg, I don't like her getting too sure of herself. Ah, there she is, right on schedule."

I broke free of his embrace, just in time to see Viviane come around the corner in a sparkling yellow dress. I stepped away quickly from Alexander, leaning against the far wall.

"There you are," Viviane's voice drifted to us. My gaze dropped to her throat; the necklace glittered against her skin. I was furious with the way Alexander had treated me, and I wanted nothing more than to run back to the safety of the main gala. But I'd come for the necklace, and it was right in front of me. It would be easier to steal away from the party.

"Whatever are you two whispering about?"

"I was just telling Wynter how dangerous magic is," Alexander replied.

Viviane's green eyes widened. "Why, that reminds me! I never finished telling you what happened to the last mage from Argent. I think it's terribly tragic."

Something bad was coming. I just knew this was going to

be some terrible, morbid story. But I played along anyway.

"What happened?" I asked.

"Well," Viviane said, "He was a prodigy at the Academy, until the day he went mad. Couldn't handle the pressure. He started hearing voices, talking to himself. Finally, he slit a noblewoman's throat. I heard he tossed pieces of her dismembered body off the edge, before leaping to his death. People say you can still hear them calling to each other at night on the outskirts of Reverie."

"That's not true," I said uncertainly.

Viviane sighed and shook her head. "You really don't know *anything*, do you?" she asked. "You're hopeless."

"It doesn't matter how much I know," I said. "It matters only what I'm willing to learn."

"That was almost profound," Viviane replied. "Did you steal it from my uncle? He likes to make people think he's profound."

Hisses struck my ears. At first I thought I'd triggered the device accidentally, but the noise was coming from down the hall.

"We should head back," Alexander said.

"You might be right," Viviane said. "Mother is so overprotective sometimes. Just a moment, I need to finish my drink first."

She stepped closer to me, until we were face to face, and then she slowly emptied her champagne glass down my dress. I gasped as the cold, sparkling liquid dripped beneath my corset.

"There," she smirked. "All done."

I squeezed my hands into fists, blood rushing to my face.

I hated them both.

The hisses grew louder, sweeping down the hall towards us. I turned my head, just before the floor buckled. With a yelp, Viviane fell to the ground and pulled me down with her. Portraits swayed and then clattered to the ground. The overhead lights blinked out, flooding the hall in near darkness. Another quake.

Viviane was clambering and groping in the darkness. Her hand touched my shoulder. Something sparkled in the dim light. *Her necklace!* I shifted, catching the outline of her neck. I took a deep breath and reached forward, feeling for the clasp. She moved away before I could unhook it. Then, abruptly, the lights returned.

Viviane screamed, and there was the familiar ring of steel as Alexander unsheathed his blade. At first I thought I'd been caught red-handed, but they were both looking away from me, down the hall. I sucked in a sharp breath of disbelief when I saw what they were staring at. It was a being of some sort, but I didn't have the words to describe it beyond that. It was tall and inky black. Vaguely humanoid, with long, claw-like fingers. It reached out jerkily and speared one of the portraits, ripping it from the wall. When the creature opened its mouth, it unleashed a roar that pierced my eardrums.

***

"Run!" Alexander shouted, stepping in front of us.

Viviane fled without hesitation. I followed, blindly running down the hall. But then, the lights were gone. All the flickering flames of the candles were extinguished in one fell swoop. I turned around in time to catch Alexander, sword drawn, slash through the monster's middle. The blade passed harmlessly through.

"Alexander!" Viviane screamed.

The prince jumped back, trying to parry the monster's wild swings, but they swept right through the sword's blade. Viviane darted into an open room. I ran after her and let my device slip into my hand. I swiped my thumb over it. Blue flames emerged as Alexander swept in. It may not stop the thing chasing us, but at least we could see where we were going. The room was wide and filled with tables and chairs. A fireplace cast an orange light on half the room. A silver-haired man sat behind a long table, surrounded by stacks of books and notes. He bolted to his feet when he saw us rush in.

"What's happening?" he asked.

"It's a demon," Alexander said. That was the only thing he had time to say before the door exploded inward. The creature entered the room like a black, spiky cloud, but grew upwards towards the ceiling. Its red eyes burned down at us like glowing embers in the dim light. I held up my hand, ablaze with blue flames, and lifted it up towards the being.

"Stop it!" I shouted.

No! Came the response.

I stumbled backward in confusion. Alexander met my eyes, with a look of awe. Had he heard it, too? The monster unleashed a roar that seemed to shake the entire room. Immediately, the older man, who looked like he could all too easily be snapped in half, placed himself between the monster and us.

"Stay back!" he snapped. My blood roared in my ears as the demon surged forward.

I nearly tripped over Viviane as she scrambled to one of

the tables, shoving papers and books to the floor. She grasped a pen just as the floor buckled again, knocking me off balance and sending me sprawling across the room. Wind whirled past my ears, ripping at my face, my hair, and clothes. There was a flash of light, then Alexander was down on one knee, gasping for air. Viviane had fallen on her stomach and was scrawling something directly on the ground. The man had fallen, too, but when he lifted his arm, a burst of bright light shot forth. The monster lunged but struck some sort of invisible barrier. I moved unsteadily to my feet and swept my arm out, shooting blue flames towards the demon, but nothing happened.

"It can't—I don't understand! Why didn't my sigil work?" Viviane shouted.

I backed away as the creature pushed forward, staggering into Viviane and Alexander. The monster was forcing us into the corner of the room. The man went to his knees, drawing dark blue lines over a table. My head hurt so badly that I could barely think. I edged around the wall, drawing my flames with me. A lot of good they were doing me. I quenched the flames and made a run for the door. The monster roared and twisted around. I froze as it blocked my path. My eyes darted to Viviane, her hand shaking as she drew symbol after symbol over her forearm. But it was no use, we were out of tricks.

A hand grabbed my bicep, and I pulled back my fist, ready to fight. But it was Dorian, sword drawn.

The screams became louder, so loud I covered my ears. They pounded inside my head, their screams wordless once more. Alexander ducked his head. I wondered if he was hearing the same thing I was.

"Dorian, make it stop!" I screamed.

The monster roared and turned to face us. Ice shot across the floor, enveloping the monster's feet and crawling up its legs. The monster roared and thrashed, trying to break the ice but to no avail. The screams kept going. I sank to the ground behind, covering my ears. They were in pain, and I heard them, and I just wanted them to stop, stop, stop. And why *wouldn't* they?

Eleanor swept in and went straight to Viviane.

"I need your necklace," she said, unlatching it from Viviane's neck. Vaguely, I remembered I was supposed to steal that, but it was hard to care about anything more than how badly my head hurt.

Eleanor drew a pen from her dress and joined the man making marks on the table. Without a word between them, they seemed to know exactly what to do.

The ice crept up to the creature's waist and rimmed the edge of Dorian's blade. With a sharp, sudden slash, Dorian brought his sword through the creature's middle. The creature screamed and the floor quaked again, sending Viviane sprawling to the floor. She remained down, keeping her weight on her forearms. The screams lessened, finally. I gasped for air, but there didn't seem to be enough of it in the room.

Viviane's necklace glowed a bright silver.

"Ready?" Eleanor yelled.

The creature fell still, as layers of ice continued growing over it. The screams vanished entirely, and all I heard was the crackling of ice encasing the dark smoke. Then, there were whimpers, soft and pleading. My throat was raw.

"Dorian, wait," I rasped.

Without warning, Eleanor and the man flipped the table over. Viviane's necklace fell to the ground. Suddenly, the room was filled with light, so brilliant that it dazzled my eyes. As it faded, I blinked spots out of my vision. The sounds were gone. All of them.

The man moved first and carefully surveyed the necklace. A sharp *crack*! sliced through the air. Immediately, the man dropped the necklace to the ground and backed away. "That isn't going to hold it!" he exclaimed.

"That's impossible!" Eleanor protested.

The gemstones in Viviane's necklace cracked; the metal twisted.

"We tried, and we failed. Let's just kill it and be done!" Dorian snapped.

With a screech, the monster burst free, springing up seemingly from the air itself. But it stumbled. It was already weakened. I winced and covered my ears, trying to block out the terrible sounds. Dorian sliced at the monster again, ice following every movement. The demon screamed and fell to the ground, ice growing quickly along its body.

When I glanced at the silver-haired man, he looked pale and horrified. Then, with a soft, plaintive mewl, the ice shattered and spread across the floor in small chunks.

For a few seconds, I stood still and silent against the wall. Viviane rushed into Eleanor's arms and hugged her tightly. Breathing hard, Alexander sank into a chair. Dorian scooped the shattered necklace off the ground, and stared at it for several seconds with a deepening frown.

Eleanor made her way over to Alexander and coaxed him into lifting his shirt. There was a lot of blood, at least from what I could see. Eleanor began drawing smooth, bold lines over Alexander's skin. I felt strangely detached from everything, like everything and nothing were happening simultaneously, and it just didn't matter.

"I'll alert Celeste," the silver-haired man said. "She'd want to know."

"I'm sure. Thank you for protecting my niece and…" Dorian glanced towards me. "My charge. That's a good first impression of you…?"

"Ah! I'm Nathanial Gareth, visiting professor of enchanted artifacts and sigils. I hope this…performance doesn't cast doubt on my abilities," the man said.

"Not at all," Dorian replied. "My understanding is that it's more difficult to seal a demon directly into an object, anyway. It's certainly beyond my powers. That you and Eleanor nearly did is a clear testament to your great skill."

Gareth's smile was strained. When I looked at Dorian, he jerked his head towards and door and walked out. I followed, and for a while, we walked down the empty halls and then out to the courtyard. The stars were so much brighter in Reverie than in the Scraps.

"Are you all right?" Dorian finally asked.

"Fine," I lied.

Maybe going crazy. That was all.

There was a very long pause, where I had no idea what to say. Or maybe that wasn't quite right. Maybe I *did* know. Maybe I wanted to just talk about how terrified I'd been, how out of control everything felt. But I couldn't tell Dorian. He seemed nice enough, at least, compared to Gabriel, but he wouldn't really care what I felt.

"Are you upset I didn't get the necklace?" I asked.

"No. You couldn't have foreseen a demon attacking, and

the necklace was a fake, anyway."

"A fake?" I asked.

Dorian nodded.

"But how did that happen?"

"I'm not sure. But that necklace belonged to my sister Guinevere, so I know exactly how it was constructed and enchanted," Dorian said. "If that *was* the real necklace, it would have contained that demon without difficulty. It wouldn't have broken like that."

"So someone stole the real necklace and replaced it with a fake one?" I asked.

"Something like that," Dorian said, "But I have no idea why. I can imagine easily enough why someone would steal it. It's expensive, but why bother replacing it with a fake one?"

"So you wouldn't notice it was gone?" I offered.

"Clearly, that was the intent, but that's not typical behavior for a jewel thief," Dorian said. "Their philosophy is to steal and run."

"So how did a demon…end up there?" I asked.

"Well," Dorian said, "I'm sure I can think of more potential causes, but really, there are two options. Either that demon escaped from somewhere, or someone unleashed it."

"You mean, on purpose? But there were so many people at the gala. They must have realized someone would get hurt," I said slowly.

"Exactly," Dorian said, "So if it *didn't* escape on its own, why would someone unleash it? What were they hoping to achieve?"

"Are the demons related to the earthquakes?" I asked. Dorian looked thoughtful. "They do seem to pop up in pairs," he said finally. We'd reached the gates of Rosewood but I lingered by the entrance.

"What happens now?" I asked quietly.

"Tomorrow, you'll start school. There's a journal I want," Dorian said. "It should be on the third floor of the library. I'm also looking for any items you can find related to man named Nicholas Armenia. It should be easy, after tonight's debacle, but you can't *tell* anyone that's what you're looking for."

He was all business, wasn't he? Was it foolish of me for expecting something…else? Some nameless, softer, other reaction than this.

"Why can't you get it?" I asked. "You're a count."

"I won't tell you that."

I nodded, trying to reason out why he would want to steal a journal of all things. I was almost certain this all had nothing to do with paying off gambling debts.

I took a deep breath and followed him into his mansion on the edge of Reverie. Class hadn't even started yet and I was in way over my head. I was sure the prince suspected something, and I'd made an enemy out of Viviane. Even worse, I'd spoken to a demon… *and it spoke back.*

ELEVEN

MY HEAD HURT, AND MY eyes ached. We'd spent the night at Rosewood, but I hadn't seen much besides my room, which was admittedly quite nice. Despite the softest mattress in the world, I hadn't slept well, half-expecting a demon to burst in and try to kill me. I shivered and reached for the device I'd stuffed under my pillow. Having it within reach made me feel safer, even if the flames were just an illusion. I'd always assumed life in the Floats was full of ease and comfort, but between the demons, the earthquakes, and the vengeful mages, there was much more going on up here than I would have ever imagined. Had I really heard a demon speak? If so, what did that mean? Everything was so confusing here. Why couldn't everyone just say what they meant?

I stifled a yawn and shook my head, as if that would help me wake up and put my thoughts into a order. Dorian handed me a mug of coffee and a raspberry scone when I went downstairs, then let Francisca fuss over my hair and uniform until he nodded his approval. I was too nervous about my first day of school to pester him with questions on the early morning ride through Reverie.

The crystals and white stone of the Academy shined in the rising light, reflecting the families and new students gathered for registration. The entryway floor, silver and mirror-like, was covered in brightly colored dots, resulting from the sunlight being refracted through the crystal roof. Beyond that, I could see white pillars and long corridors that made up the rest of the Academy.

"I see they've let Alexander out," Dorian said.

I stiffened and followed the direction of his nod. The prince was with Viviane, who clung to him like a lifeline. Not that I could blame her. He'd been attacked by a monster just the night before. And they looked so perfect together, Viviane's glossy, black curls and smirk. Alexander's crooked grin. I wondered what they could possibly be smiling at, the night after getting attacked. Probably making fun of the new students. Like me.

As they continued their walk, I noticed Alexander limping. I thought of Briar and winced. Maybe it was self-centered of me to blame myself for Alexander's injury, but he had stood to face that monster, while Viviane and I had fled, not that we'd made it far.

We swept past other students and their guardians, some of them chatting eagerly with one another. Most of them probably grew up here and already knew each other. I felt a pang in my chest as an older woman hugged a girl my age, before releasing her to the school. What would it have been like to have parents who loved and cared about me? It had been years since I'd given in to self-pity, but seeing all these doting parents made the years of abandonment burn inside me.

We approached a table where Celeste remained seated. She wore a midnight blue dress, dappled with spots of light from the stained glass windows. She smiled up at me when we reached the front of the table.

Celeste stood to greet us and put a hand to the choker resting in the hollow of her throat. "Your Lordship," she said, curtseying. "And Wynter! How wonderful to see you both again. I couldn't catch you after the gala, and I was very worried. I heard you were involved in that terrible incident."

"We left shortly after," Dorian said.

"Are you all right?" she asked, fixing her gaze on me.

"I'm fine," Dorian answered. "Though I think it frightened Wynter. She's barely said a word to me all morning." I blushed at the surprise reproach. I hadn't realized I'd been any quieter than usual.

Celeste's face softened. "I'm sorry, Wynter," she said. "What a terrible welcome to receive from Reverie!"

"The kingdom is nice otherwise," I said. "I'll be fine."

Celeste's brow furrowed. "I'm glad to hear it," she said, "but I still regret it. Poor thing."

I wasn't used to people being concerned about me, and I ducked my head, embarrassed by the attention. "Are you a teacher here, Celeste?" I asked, hoping to turn attention away from me.

"I'm the headmistress," Celeste replied, grinning, "So I don't get to teach. Fortunately, I *do* get to watch over all the new students coming in. I love how energetic young mages are. They're always so eager to be here!"

At least, she seemed legitimately passionate about her work. Obviously, I wouldn't let myself get close to her or anything, but it would be nice to have someone who *wasn't* actively trying to sabotage me or making my life difficult.

"You'll be watching over me, then," I said, feeling awkward.

Celeste nodded. "I will be!" she exclaimed. "But don't worry. I won't be overbearing or anything like that. I'm just here to ensure everything is going fine and that you're settling in smoothly. Making sure there aren't any fights. That sort of thing. You'll also have an older student act as your mentor to help guide you through your first semester. It looks like you've been paired with Jessa. She seems like a nice girl, and I'm sure you'll have a lot in common."

None of this sounded good. Stealing from the Academy would likely involve a lot of sneaking around, and having someone watching me all the time would only make it harder.

"Great," I said.

"Yes, and you're just in time," Celeste said, pointing. "If you go over there, those are all the new girls in the northern dormitories. That's where you've been assigned. One of your peers will pick you up and show you the rooms, so you can get settled in."

"Perfect," Dorian said, steering me away. Celeste was already greeting the next family in line but I waved a quick goodbye. Viviane joined us in the main hall, walking alongside her uncle. It seemed she'd lost Alexander somewhere along the way.

"Good morning, Uncle," Viviane said. "Wynter."

I raised an eyebrow and wondered if she'd purposefully gotten my name right or if she'd just forgotten to insult me.

"How are you feeling after everything?" Dorian asked.

Viviane glanced at me and I noticed there were dark circles beneath her green eyes, even through the thick concealer. It seemed she'd slept as poorly as I had.

"I'm fine," she said. "A little tired, and angry at myself. I really failed last night."

"How so?"

Viviane cast an awkward look at me. I considered darting away, so she could be alone with her uncle, but I didn't know where else to go. I felt like a third wheel, and it was clear Viviane wanted her privacy.

"Just my sigils," Viviane said finally.

"*That?* You were very brave to try them."

Viviane sighed. "And a lot of good they did me," she muttered.

"Viv—"

"I know, I know," Viviane said. "Don't be upset. Magic takes time. But I've been practicing with Mother and Celeste for months now!

"But it *does* take time. When *I* tried sigils for the first time, I trapped my hand in a sealing circle and couldn't get it out," Dorian said, "And when I first formed ice, I impaled myself on it. It went straight through my knee."

How horrifying. Was being able to control ice really worth all *that?*

Viviane laughed. "Sometimes, I think it's a miracle you're still alive," she said teasingly. Her face relaxed when she smiled, and it was a relief to see such casual banter. I wondered if he knew how cruel she could be.

"So I've heard," he grinned. "Many times."

"Anyway, I just wanted to wish you a good morning,"

Viviane said, "And to thank you for last night."

"You don't need to thank me, Dear. How is Eleanor?"

"She was telling me at breakfast how much she hates you," Viviane said.

"She has good reason to hate me, and I her. What does she think of this necklace business?"

Viviane smiled sweetly. "You'll need to fish elsewhere for that," she said.

"It was worth a try. At any rate, I'll leave you lovely young ladies alone," Dorian said, bowing. "Enjoy yourselves."

I looked away when Viviane went to hug him, then he left us alone together. Viviane crossed her arms and stood by my side, her expression soft and fond as she watched her uncle leave. I thought of Gabriel and grimaced.

"How is Alexander?" I asked, trying to make polite conversation.

"He's limping," she said.

"I saw that."

Viviane huffed, turning suddenly and pointing her finger at my face.

"Look, Wynter. I want to make one thing clear. Alexander is mine, so keep your hands off him and stay out of my way."

Right. Because Alexander was so appealing. How could I *bear* to live without someone who was both vaguely threatening and obnoxious all the time?

"I have absolutely no interest in Alexander," I said, truthfully.

Even though he was so handsome that it made my insides flutter. And the way he'd drawn his sword and stepped between a monster and me had been so...so *noble*. Gallant, even. Of course, one good moment didn't make up for the things he'd said when he trapped me in a hallway.

"Good," Viviane said, "Because it would never work between you two. Alexander is just a tease, and he likes to be the center of attention. That little stunt last night will get him weeks of gossip about him and the new girl. But he'd never seriously date someone like you."

"Someone like me?" I repeated.

"You know what I mean. You don't even belong up here with the rest of us."

"Clearly," I said, crossing my arms.

Celeste walked towards us and waved clipboard to get our attention.

"Great," Viviane said sourly. "As if I don't get enough of her at home." If Celeste didn't teach, why was she giving Viviane private lessons? I didn't get the chance to ask.

"Follow me!" Celeste called out, leading the way.

We rounded the corridor and up a curved flight of stairs. I stayed close to Viviane. She was mean, but she was also the only person I knew. Better the enemy I knew than the one I didn't. And Viviane wasn't really an enemy; she just didn't like me. I could deal with a little jealousy, though I didn't know what she had to be jealous of.

"How do you know Celeste?" I asked.

"She's close to my mother," Viviane replied, "And they talk about my education all the time. And look, I don't know why you suddenly think we're best friends, but we aren't. So you can quit with the act."

"The act?"

"I don't believe you're nearly as innocent and demure as

you act," Viviane said. "You're just another Lower Realms social climber, probably with a bunch of secrets and scandals. I don't even know *what* Uncle was thinking in bringing you here."

"I don't have any secrets or scandals," I lied.

"Sure, Summer."

"It's Wynter."

"Oh, I *know*," Viviane said. "Are you truly so dense you can't tell when you're being insulted?"

I tried to think of something *proper* to say in response, but everything came up blank. "I can tell," I said instead. "I just thought I'd…give you the benefit of the doubt."

Well, if we weren't going to be friends, I'd just have to avoid her. Viviane seemed like the type to actively *look* for secrets, and I didn't want to give her any reason to dig deeper into my story. I guess that meant I'd have to avoid Alexander as well, which surely wouldn't be difficult. He was a prince after all.

"Here are your quarters," Celeste said, as she led us into a long room lined with four-poster beds. "Look for your names, everyone."

I ambled along with the rest. Each bed had a card with a name in elegant script laying upon the sheets. I skimmed them as I went. Finally, I found mine and swiped it off the bed.

"Don't fret!" Celeste called out. "Everyone's things will be brought up shortly!"

That was good. I didn't have any things of my own, but Francisca had packed a thick trunk full of clothes and supplies. I didn't even know all the stuff that was inside it. I glanced around, seeing where everyone else had ended up. The bed to my right belonged to Jessa, who I recalled was my mentor. Jessa seemed not to have found her bed yet. I glanced at the other girls still looking for their places. She was either the tall, willowy brunette or the short, blonde girl.

I looked to my left just in time to see a pale, delicate hand snatch the card from the sheets. I swore under my breath. Avoiding Viviane was going to be *much* harder when she was sleeping right next to me. Viviane caught my eye and groaned. "Seriously?" she asked.

"I didn't pick the sleeping arrangements," I said.

The short, blonde girl brightened and crossed the room to me.

"Celeste said you're Wynter?" she asked.

"That's me," I replied. "Jessa?"

"Hello!" she exclaimed, pulling me into a hug.

I tensed, having never hugged a total stranger before.

Jessa released me and looked me up and down. "You're from Argent, right? I love Argent! I'll bet we even know some of the same people!"

Oh, no.

"Wonderful," Viviane deadpanned, flinging herself back onto her bed. "You'll have so much to talk about."

Jessa twirled a strand of hair around her finger. "There's no need to be rude, Viv."

Viviane rolled her eyes. "Whatever, Jessa. There's a *reason* you got into the Academy with the lowest score in history."

Jessa bit her lip and glanced away. "You can't possibly know that," she said quietly.

Poor Jessa. It seemed I wasn't the only person not good enough to be in the presence of the glorious Viviane. I knew it wasn't a good idea to antagonize Viviane. That would probably only make her more suspicious of me, and Dorian wouldn't like it. But I couldn't stand by and watch someone get bullied.

"Viviane's just in a bad mood because she sucks at sigils," I said. "That reminds me, do you know where the library is? I'd love to see it."

TWELVE

THE ONLY BOOKS I KNEW were the ones I borrowed from Gabriel's bookshelves and the torn pages we sometimes recovered in the Dregs. Nothing could have prepared me for the Academy's library. It spanned four floors, each packed to the brim with thousands of books. Dorian told me the journal he was looking for was on the third floor, so I excused myself from Jessa and went to wander around alone.

But the third floor was mostly just open space—a large reading area with couches and desks and lamps. The walls were lined with shelves so high you needed a ladder to access them. I browsed the heavy leather volumes for an hour, but couldn't find anything about Nicholas Armenia, whoever he was. Then, at the end of the long side alcove, I noticed light coming from behind the bookshelves. I gripped a shelf and it shifted loosely under my touch. The whole wall was on wheels. I took a deep breath, then slid it to one side, revealing a hidden door behind it that said "Restricted Access."

I glanced behind me, then twisted the handle experimentally, but it wouldn't budge. While I had some experience picking locks, I wasn't entirely sure my tools would help me. Mages probably had all sorts of special locks and spells.

But Dorian had been specific. I was supposed to search the third floor of the library. I hadn't found anything yet, which meant whatever he was looking for *must* be behind this door. Why, though? The other books were out in the open and not concealed behind secret doorways. I tapped my foot on the floor and surveyed the lock, trying to find anything unusual about it. There were too many people around to break in now, so I'd just have to come back later and see if I could get it open.

I headed back downstairs, noting that the large spiral staircase appeared to be the only way up and down. It was loud, too, which would be a problem if I had to sneak into the library after it closed, which was at 9pm, according to the sign on the entrance. I couldn't sneak into a restricted area with everyone around, which meant I had all day with nothing to do, since classes didn't officially start until tomorrow.

I reached the first floor, when I heard Celeste calling my name. I panicked at first, thinking she's already caught me trying to access an off-limits area, but I let out a breath when I saw her easy smile. I wasn't doing anything wrong, I reminded myself. There's no reason a new student *wouldn't* check out the library on the first day.

"Hello," I said.

"How are you doing? I hope Jessa has been showing you the facilities?"

"Yes," I said. "She's around here somewhere. I might have gotten a little lost. This place is huge. I've never seen so many books before in my life."

Celeste laughed. "It's really something, isn't it? I'll admit

I've barely read a fraction of the volumes here, but we all have our unique fields. I'm so disappointed that last night was your first impression of our noble institution. I assure you, that kind of thing is exceedingly rare."

"Demons, you mean?" Dorian said the demon had either escaped, or been let out… but from *where?*

Celeste sighed. "They're harmless when properly contained. I assure you, you're entirely safe here." I noticed she hadn't exactly answered my question, but I let it slide.

"I'm sure I'll be fine," I said. It was sweet she was worried about me, but I didn't need protecting. Celeste nodded and smiled gently. "I was going to find you later this evening, but since you're here, why don't I accompany you to your choosing?"

"Choosing?" I asked.

"Yes," Celeste replied. "All the new students are given an amulet or an object to help them channel their magic."

"Oh," I said. Dorian hadn't mentioned this part. I clenched my fists, hoping it wasn't another test. Celeste tapped a finger to her choker. "It's a very important choice," she said. "Many of us keep our objects for life. But you won't be going at it all alone. You'll have Nathanial to help you."

Right. Professor Gareth.

I followed Celeste through a long hallway and down a long, stone staircase. Blue flames flickered along the otherwise dark stone walls, and once we reached the bottom, Gareth greeted us with a smile. "Ah! I remember you," he said, standing up from behind his small table.

"I'll leave you in Nathanial's capable hands," Celeste said. "Don't worry too much, Wynter. This should be an exciting experience!"

Maybe it would be, if I wasn't only pretending to be a mage. How would I even know what to choose? Would Professor Gareth see through me if I made the wrong choice?

"Thank you, Headmistress," I said, the title coming out awkwardly.

Celeste laughed and waved a dismissive hand. "Please, call me Celeste," she said. "I think that's friendlier. Don't you?"

I nodded and smiled. She just had such a warm, enthusiastic personality that I couldn't help it. Then, Celeste went back up the stairs, leaving me along with Gareth.

"I didn't catch your name last night," Gareth said. "Though we were all rather busy, as I recall."

"It's Wynter," I replied. Gareth looked unremarkable in every way, but I'd seen him in action when he tried to bind the demon into Viviane's necklace. Unlike the other mages, his clothes were simple and unadorned. A gray vest, a tweed jacket. His silver hair was pulled loosely behind his ears, but twisted up at the edges.

"Wynter, then," Gareth said. "That's a lovely name. Has anyone explained the choosing to you yet?"

"I get to choose an object, right?" I said, mostly guessing from what Celeste had told me.

"You do," Gareth replied, "And generally, the object you choose will be aligned with your primary area of study. So once you've picked, we'll also help you select your classes."

That sounded sensible. I would have had no idea what subjects to study.

Gareth pushed open a door behind him and gestured in a dark, cavernous room.

"In here you'll find a room filled with enchanted objects. Just choose one and bring it back with you."

"But how do I know what to choose?" I asked.

"That's up to you. Go with your instincts," Gareth said, "And if you choose—say—a pen and learn later that you really dislike drawing sigils, you can change to another area. You should take this seriously but not *too* seriously. If I can offer one suggestion, use your heart, not your head. Pick what feels right."

***

I took a deep breath and stepped past him. I imagined Gareth would close the doors behind me, but thankfully he didn't. As my eyes adjusted to the dim light, I could see the gleaming outlines of metal surfaces. Before me, there was a large room, filled with—for lack of a better word—treasure. There were gems and jewelry, swords and daggers, expensive-looking handkerchiefs and bits of armor. I felt like this was a trap of some sort. I was a thief, and they'd just let me into the vault. Anything in this room would feed Sterling and Briar for three months.

Hisses burst into awareness, their voices scraping and whispering. They sounded like the ones my device made, and my palms started to sweat as I expected to see a burst of flame. My first instinct was to go for a sword. I couldn't use magic, but maybe I could compensate with swordplay. What little I knew. I grimaced. Any of these mages would probably wipe the floor with me when it came to swordplay, but it would be comforting to carry a weapon around.

Then I realized, Celeste said I'd get to keep my object *for life*. Dorian hadn't warned me about the choosing, which meant he either didn't know or didn't care about it. If I picked something ridiculously valuable, would I be able to buy my freedom and get Briar away from my uncle?

I gravitated to the jewelry and trinkets. Everything hissed when I passed it, but the sounds were too soft for me to pick out individual words. I pursed my lips together and picked up a heavy amulet. It was bright silver with a large, faceted stone that shimmered in all the colors of the rainbow. "Would you mind coming with me?" I asked quietly. "I don't really know how this all works."

I paused and trailed my thumb over the gemstone. The hisses grew a little louder, until the gemstone was practically screaming like a tea kettle. I flinched and put the necklace down quickly.

"If you don't want to," I murmured, "It's fine. I understand. I wouldn't want to be chosen by me, either. It's not like I'm going to become some powerful mage."

I wouldn't even *be* a mage. Was I really communicating with these objects, or was I already going crazy, like the mage in Viviane's stories? The hisses increased in pitch, and I could almost pick out words at the edge of my hearing. I spun around, but they were coming from everywhere, whispering accusations at me.

Mage. Thief. Murderer.

"I'm not like the others," I said, raising my voice so it filled the room. "I'm not from Reverie. Or any of the other Floats. Sorry, they aren't called that. Not here."

The hisses stopped abruptly, dissipating to nothingness. Maybe some sort of instinct was supposed to come to me, some instinct I didn't have because I wasn't really a mage. It was like all the objects knew I was a fraud. I considered walking back through the door and telling Gareth I'd failed, or asking him to choose for me, but I couldn't risk exposing myself.

I still had no idea what to choose, but decided I might as well get a weapon. Something flashy, that would fetch a good price when all this was over and protect me in the meantime. I'd be depending on the device to fake my magic, but I knew it would be useless in a real fight.

I'll go with you.

I halted at the sound of the voice. It was, by all accounts, a nice voice. Gentle and soft, like moonlight streaming through a dark sky.

I glanced at Gareth, who was standing outside the room watching me. He hadn't reacted, which meant he was too far away to hear the voice. I wondered what he was thinking. Did he suspect anything? Was I taking too long?

"Where are you?" I whispered, keeping my back to the door and my voice low. I walked through the piles of antiques and collectibles until I found a table with racks of swords, displayed against red velvet. The world shifted around me. The air felt heavy, like I was pushing through an invisible barrier. One sword stood out, practically glowing in the dim light. It was a silver and gold rapier, with an elegant guard and decorative engravings twisting up the blade. Emeralds sparkled as I curled my hand around the hilt of the sword and pulled it free of its scabbard. It looked like the sort of blade Alexander had used, but I didn't think his was magical.

"I don't know anything about swordplay," I muttered.

That can be remedied.

The voice was much louder this time. I was so surprised I practically dropped the sword.

"Yes, but probably not *easily*." Was I speaking to myself, or the voice in the darkness?

I gripped the hilt tighter and held the sword out in front of me, watching the light play down the blade. These voices—they sounded similar to the demon Dorian had killed. Was there a demon trapped in this sword? Were there demons trapped in all of these objects? Did they *know* they were trapped? I sheathed the blade again and cleared my throat.

"I want this one," I said, raising it up as I exited the room.

Gareth hummed. "It's an elegant weapon," he said, "Battle magic is a relatively new discipline, too, so there's a lot of excitement about it."

"Is it?" I asked.

Gareth nodded. "It's…" he trailed off. "Are you from Reverie? You have an accent."

"Argent," I said.

"Ah," Gareth said. "You wouldn't know, then. About…eighty years ago, Reverie began experiencing quakes, so the Council and aristocracy gathered together to fix the problem. I'm simplifying this, but after years of investigation, it was determined that the Kingdom of Aubade had laid a curse upon Reverie."

"Is that possible? To curse an entire kingdom?" I asked.

"Theoretically," Gareth replied, "Although I've never seen a credible account of such a thing. Now, we know that we were wrong. But at the time, it sounded reasonable, so Reverie went to war. And during those years, the Academy was at the forefront of finding innovative ways to use magic in battle. The

Academy was very focused on training students as quickly as possible to fight, so all sorts of different magic emerged. Before that, we relied primarily on sigils, potions, and dancing. But for the war with Aubade, we began exploring other outlets for our powers."

"Oh," I said.

"Most of the magic discovered during that time was eventually outlawed by the Council for being too dangerous," Gareth said, "But battle magic was allowed to stay. It was also around this time that we first allowed admittance from the Lower Realms."

"So what happened?"

"Eventually, we surrendered," Gareth said. "It was, mind you, an honest mistake. Reverie had never experienced quakes before, and we were desperate to understand what was happening. But it was a terrible mistake that cost many people their lives and destroyed swaths of the Lower Realms."

"Oh!" I said, with sudden recognition. Gabriel and some of his lackeys sometimes referred to a mage war, but I'd never met anyone who fought in it. The borders of the Scraps were still pockmarked in places from the fighting. Stirling had pointed them out to me once.

"You've heard of it?" Gareth asked.

"A little. Do you think I should choose something else, then?" I asked.

"I didn't mean that," Gareth replied. "It's a new discipline; that's all."

"So it's battle magic, sigils or potions? That's a hard choice."

Gareth smiled sympathetically. "Sigils is a popular field and one of the oldest, along with potions. There's also dance magic, which shares a lot conceptually with battle magic."

I grimaced. "I don't know anything about dancing."

"We would teach you," Gareth said, "But there are also singing and ritual, which is also a new field. It combines aspects from many of the other disciplines. But pursuing a new discipline can be a good thing. There's more room to learn and grow, especially if you're looking at continuing into advanced types of magic. I don't know what your ambitions are, but it's not easy trying to find an original idea about sigils. Everything has been said already."

It didn't really matter, then. I wouldn't be here long enough for all that, so I might as well choose the talking sword. If all else failed, I could still stab people with it.

"This, then," I said, putting the sword heavily onto the table.

Gareth drew an elegant, silver pen from his pocket and opened a large book. He turned to my name, and wrote down the object I'd taken in small, spidery writing. "You'll need to take introduction to enchanted objects, then. And swordsmanship with professor Delacroix. I saw that your testing stone indicated a preference for fire."

It had, but that was only because I'd used the device. It wasn't because of *me*. "I don't know if I'm ready to control fire," I said, thinking back to the charred, smoking drapes.

"I'm not asking you to," Gareth said with a laugh, "but maybe we'll put you in a basic ritual class to familiarize you with the different elements. Maybe a basic sigils class, too. History of Reverie is one you'll also need."

I nodded, and as he drew up an entire schedule of classes

for me, I buckled the sword belt around my waist. I took a deep breath to calm my nerves. It seemed like I'd passed one more challenge without raising suspicion, at least for now.

"What did you take as your object?" I asked.

Gareth held up his pen. "This," he said, "And she has dictated my life ever since."

"She?" I asked.

Gareth smiled. "It's one of my…eccentricities," he said. "I've always imagined pens as being feminine. Linguistically speaking, pens are female in many languages. Not in Reverie, but in other places."

I nodded, although I didn't really understand. But then, the longer I stayed in the Academy, the less it seemed I knew. Francisca and Dorian had spent weeks trying to prepare me, but they'd focused on silly things like correcting my posture and diction.

"You'll also need a pen for drawing the sigils," Gareth said. "Even if you're going into battle magic, the Academy still likes for you to be aware of other disciplines."

Gareth opened a wooden box filled with an assortment of fancy pens. Soft hisses swept through my ears. Were they enchanted as well? I took a heavy silver one, hoping it would have some street value if I held onto it long enough.

"Thank you," I told Gareth, pocketing the pen. "I'll take good care of them."

"I'm sure you will," he replied, "And I look forward to seeing you in my classes."

I backed away towards the stairs slowly, half expecting him to chase after me and tell me he'd made a mistake. With a silver pen in my pocket and a priceless sword on my hip, I felt more like a mage than ever. Now I just had to learn how to use them.

THIRTEEN

"THERE YOU ARE!" JESSA WAVED as I came back up the stairs and headed towards me. She wore an emerald green, fur-trimmed coat and black boots. Her wild, blonde hair had been made frizzy by the light drizzle that was falling, and with a sharp pang in my chest, I thought of Briar. He had hair like that. Thick and fluffy hair that soaked up water. When Jessa came to a stop before me, her face was flushed, which made her freckles seem brighter.

"I'm sorry," I said, suddenly realizing I'd disappeared on her. "Celeste found me in the library and took me down to the choosing room."

"You picked a sword, huh?" Jessa asked, nodding to my waist. "I've tried battle magic. Unfortunately, I'm just not suited for it."

"I don't know that I'm suited for it either," I said.

"Anyway," Jessa said. "Du Lac is debating at the forum. Some of the students are headed into town to watch. Have you been there yet?"

"No," I replied, "But I haven't been much of anywhere

yet."

Jessa linked her arm with mine. "It's a place where people go to discuss important matters. Presently, there's a good deal of argument revolving around the quakes and what to do about them, but today, I expect he'll be discussing the demon attack."

That sounded like a good reason to go, so I let Jessa lead me past the school grounds and into the busy marketplace. The markets stretched ahead of us, and to my surprise, they really didn't look that different from those in the Scraps, except for the absence of flies and much nicer displays. None of these merchants appeared to have any thugs on hand to thwart potential thieves either. It was cleaner, too, the road before us dusted by small brooms, going *sweep, sweep* across the ground. And it was a paved road, free of cracks and holes. I'd never seen something like that in the Scraps.

Jessa practically skipped when she went through the market, and when she noticed I was behind her, she slowed to accommodate me. She kept her arm linked with mine like we were old friends, and I wasn't sure how to feel about that. I didn't know how to act around girls my age, much less ones that were mages. Gabriel hadn't dealt much with girls, except for me, and that was only because I was his niece.

"It's so exciting being out without an escort," Jessa said, sighing happily.

An escort? Was Jessa someone important? She seemed so…so *normal.* "Does that happen often for you?" I asked.

Jessa shook her head. "No, back home, I had to go with an escort *everywhere.* I come from Aubade."

Like Celeste, I remembered.

"And my family is very wealthy. So any time I wanted to

go somewhere, my parents made me take an escort," Jessa said. "It wasn't proper for a young lady to wander about by herself."

"I don't count as an escort?" I asked.

"I mean, technically," Jessa said, "But you're here because I want you to be here. Not because I had to bring you."

"So we're friends?" I asked.

I'd never really made a friend before. Sure, Sterling was my friend, but I'd known him my whole life.

"Oh! Do we need to make a specific declaration?" Jessa asked. "I'm sorry. My only friends have been—well—paid to be my friends."

This poor girl. I thought of the mean things Viviane had said to her, and my heart ached. I couldn't stop Viviane from being mean, but I could at least try to be Jessa's friend for the short time I was going to be in Reverie.

"That sounds so lonely," I said.

Jessa toyed with the silk purse tied around her waist. "Sometimes," she replied. "I didn't notice it when I was small. Then, I played with my sisters, but when they became older and went away to the Academy, I did. Now, they're finished, and I'm just starting."

We passed a stall full of brightly colored fruit, I self-consciously rubbed my arms. If only I could share all this with Briar and Sterling somehow. There had to be a way to slip them some things from Reverie, but I didn't think Dorian was going to let me go back down again until all this was over.

"Oh, mirrors!" Jessa exclaimed, darting to a small stall and pulling me along behind her.

The shopkeeper smiled at us. She was a tall, round woman with red cheeks and red curls. She lacked the ethereal beauty I'd come to associate with the mages, and with a sudden spark of realization, I realized that she was human. I hadn't realized that there were *humans* here. Not really. Sure, I'd seen a couple of servants, and they'd looked human. But this was different. This was a human woman who made mirrors. I'd assumed, somehow, that humans would only be servants in the Floats, but I guess they let artisans up as well.

Upon the table covered in purple velvet, were mirrors of all shapes and sizes, some in gilded, silver frames. As my face filled them, I gazed uncertainly into the glass. There was something appealing about the mirrors, about their smoothness and sleekness. Their clarity. I lifted a small, silver hand-mirror and looked squarely into my own blue eyes. Those were still the same. Even if my hair and face weren't.

Jessa twisted the mirror and scrolled through a set of options on the frame. Our reflections warped, becoming thinner, then fatter. She made our eyebrows dark and our lips red, then changed our hair color to pink and turquoise. I laughed at the reflection.

"Wait a second, you're just missing one thing," Jessa said. She dug a short black pencil out of her bag and leaned in close. I pulled away at first, but then allowed her to place a small black dot on my cheek. "It's supposed to be the *gallant* mark. You must be very courageous."

I tilted my head and eyed the mark, small and dark against my pale skin. "I don't think so," I replied, "But maybe it's something to work towards, huh? I doubt a mark on your skin says much about you anyway," I said.

"Maybe not," Jessa said, "But I've read books that *swear* by such things."

Books. Jessa wasn't a first-semester student like I was. I mulled that knowledge over, trying to figure out what to do with it. Maybe she could access the upper floors of the library. Would she take me with her if I was just…curious? Was it too soon to ask for a favor like that? I barely knew her, and if she refused, she'd surely be suspicious if I asked again.

Jessa smiled and reached into her coat pocket, drawing out a handful of paper notes. She paid, and with a smile, the shopkeeper wrapped the mirror in thin, white paper and tied it up with a blue ribbon before placing it in a small, paper bag. Jessa hung it on her arm, and after thanking the shopkeeper, she continued on her way. I trailed after her.

"So how are you liking the Academy so far?" Jessa asked. "Have you gotten to look around?"

"A little," I replied. "Say, speaking of books, do you know what's on the third floor of the library? It doesn't look like the other floors."

"Just the archives. They're…sort of like a collection of things. Old books and papers mostly," Jessa replied.

That sounded about right. But it was strange that they would be locked up, if they really weren't anything important. Before I could press further, a piercing whistle split the air. I froze. For an instant, I felt like I was back in the corridor, and voices were hissing and screaming.

"Wynter?" Jessa asked.

"What is that?"

"The whistle?"

Jessa heard it, too. It wasn't whatever the voices were. I let myself relax.

"It's just the forum gathering," Jessa replied. "Come on!

We don't want to be late."

We kept walking, quickly reaching a crowd of people gathered around a raised, circular platform. I recognized Alexander and Viviane, lingering at the edges of the crowd. Alexander gave me a small nod. Viviane followed his gaze and elbowed him in the ribs when she saw me.

"There's Markus," Jessa said, pointing towards the center platform.

"Markus?" I asked.

Jessa nodded. "He prefers to be called Professor Du Lac. You'll have him if you're taking the introductory sigil classes." I recognized him from my testing, but today he was wearing much finer clothes and some kind of wig.

"People of Reverie," Du Lac said, spreading his arms wide, "I've come here today to address the issue of the demon that attacked at the Academy."

A few people shouted. Du Lac waited until the noise abated before continuing, "I realize that this is a very upsetting occurrence. However, the Academy has been protected by the tightest magical security for years, and despite this incident, I assure you that students are entirely safe at the Academy."

"Safe from a demon?" someone shouted. "I heard the prince himself was injured."

"The prince is fine, as is everyone else. I'm sure you can ask him yourself if you prefer," Du Lac said, nodding towards Alexander in the crowd. He frowned deeply, unhappy about being singled out, but rose and gave a small wave.

"Was it an attack?" someone else asked.

Du Lac scowled. I traced my thumb over the scabbard of my sword.

"We are taking the issue seriously. I want to assure you of that. However, we're also not going to jump to conclusions," Du Lac said. "It's far too early to give credence to any theory. However, we believe that the most recent quake may have released the demon from where it was being held, due to some weak wards that should have been replenished earlier. As such, we are already taking precautions to prevent this from happening in the future. The Academy has some of the most brilliant minds in magic working on this issue—"

"What about the quakes?" someone shouted.

"They're getting worse!"

"What is the Council doing about it?"

Du Lac raised his hands and smiled. "Everyone, I know that the quakes can be upsetting. I appreciate your patience as we work to resolve this disturbing issue. In the meantime, it's a change that we will need to adapt to. However, it's not the first time we've seen changes in the environment. We're going to figure this out."

"We're falling from the sky!" someone shouted.

Beside me, Jessa sighed. A smattering of laughter followed.

Du Lac's smile became indulgent. "There is no proof that Reverie is falling from the sky," he said. "In fact, all the evidence indicates the contrary. If Reverie was falling, we'd have noticed a marked difference between the distance of Reverie and the Lower Realms, and thus far, the only differences we've measured fall within the expected level of seasonal variation."

I glanced at Alexander and Viviane; they were whispering together heatedly.

"As for this attack, Celeste and I are working together to increase security measures around the Academy, and many members of the nobility are likewise prepared to tighten security around their estates until the Council can find the cause of this recent attack. I realize this incident is frightening, but I would like to remind everyone that—while rare—demon attacks do happen on occasion. Considering the last one was seventeen years ago, we're doing quite well."

But what about the quake during my testing? I was sure I'd seen something there as well. Was Du Lac lying about it to cover it up? Or was it just another earthquake and I imagined the dark shadows?

"But you never figured out what was causing those either!" someone yelled from the crowd.

"We did," Du Lac said. "We discovered that the attacks could be linked to a rogue mage."

"It doesn't matter because the Council never *caught* that mage!" someone argued.

"What if they've returned?"

Du Lac raised his hands. "Everyone, I think it's a little too early for this sort of speculation. We don't know that a mage is even involved. Overall, Reverie is safe. This is likely just a rare, singular incident that I don't foresee being repeated."

"That's what you said last time!"

"What is the king saying?"

"The king understands that we're doing our best," Du Lac said. "He is understandably upset considering the circumstances, but he has the utmost confidence in the Council and our work."

I glanced at Alexander, who looked angry. I wondered what the king *had* said about the whole thing. He couldn't be happy that Alexander was injured, even if he was the sixth son.

"When we have more information, we will let everyone

know," Du Lac said. "Until then, the Council and the aristocracy need everyone's patience and cooperation."

Du Lac turned away amidst a flurry of questions. There were a few general announcements about guild meetings and upcoming events. Finally, the forum ended, and the crowd slowly began to disperse.

Jessa bit her lip. "I don't really know much about demons. They're scary, though. Which obviously you know. You were there. What was it like?"

At least, I wasn't the only one who was scared. "Terrifying," I said. "And I felt so helpless. But the Council seems to have it handled. Du Lac sounded sure of that, at least."

"Oh, *please*," Viviane cut in. "How naïve are you?"

I hadn't realized she was nearby, but when I looked over my shoulder, there she was with Alexander.

"That's the response *any* politician would give," Viviane said, tossing her hair. "The Council hasn't done anything *useful* in centuries. It's astonishing considering how much you have to do to join the Council. They've certainly gotten us into more problems than they have out of."

"That will change when I join the Council," Alexander said.

"But you're a prince," I said.

"Anyone can be on the Council, provided you can pass their exams," Viviane replied, sounding as if it was the most obvious thing in the world. "You just can't *represent* a noble or royal house *and* be on the Council at the same time."

"I don't think Du Lac's response was that bad," Jessa said.

"What would you know?" Viviane asked. "You aren't even from here."

Hisses pierced my ear sharply. I looked down at my sword,

even though the sound had come from elsewhere. The hisses grew louder.

"Do you hear that?" I asked, practically yelling over the noise.

"Hear what?" Jessa asked.

I looked at Alexander, but his face showed only cold disinterest.

"It must have been my imagination," I replied.

A shiver trailed up my spine, a slight tremor that started in the ground and ran up my legs. I drew my sword, just as a roar thundered from behind us. I had no idea what to do with it. I just knew that something terrible was coming.

"What are you doing?" Jessa asked. She'd taken a step away from me, and Alexander's eyes were fixed on me. He cocked an eyebrow quizzically.

Then Viviane screamed.

***

She pointed down the street, where I could just make out a dark shape tearing towards us. Tables exploded upwards, filling the sky with debris like confetti. A few of the braver mages stood their ground, shooting glowing arcs of offensive spells, but most of the crowd went wild with panic, trampling towards us. I sprang into action, running as fast as I could towards the break between two buildings. Viviane grabbed Alexander and pulled him with her. I didn't know where Jessa was, but there were so many people screaming and running, time seemed to be moving too fast and too slow all at once. The demon's claws shredded through the air and people and buildings. My breath came in sharp, heavy pants.

More screams. I halted suddenly, and a few people stumbled around me in their haste to escape. I glanced back around the corner, looking for Jessa. The street was mostly empty now, except for a few fallen bodies, with blood soaking into their clothes. Viviane halted abruptly as the demon appeared before us. "Alexander!" she shouted, while drawing a pen from her bag.

Alexander began drawing across his arm. Should I try that? I didn't know any sigils yet. Sure, I'd seen a couple, but I didn't even know what they did. I heard crying, and saw a young girl under a table across the street. I took a deep breath and raced across to her, scooping her up with one arm. But when I got up, the demon stepped straight into my path, glaring at me with red, fiery eyes. There was a flash of green, and then Jessa was there beside me. She spun around, doing what looked like the first few steps of a dance, and shouted. Sprigs of bright green grass flowered around the demon's feet, but seemed to have no discernable effect at all. It was enough of a distraction for us to join the others.

"Brilliant!" Viviane snapped. "That'll save us!"

Jessa winced, as the demon kicked out from the tall grass and stalked towards us.

Alexander shoved Viviane behind him. "Run!" he shouted.

Then, the prince moved to meet the demon. Silver light flashed forward from his palm, but the demon swept through it and batted Alexander to the side. He tumbled over a stack of crates and disappeared from view. Jessa spun around again, and a soft breeze flitted through the air, doing nothing. Viviane turned swiftly, extending her arm. The sigil painted on the palm of her hand crackled with golden power.

"Stand down!" she yelled.

The demon swiped at her with its claws and she stumbled back, slamming her elbow into the door of a nearby building. "Open up!" she shouted, pounding desperately on the door behind her.

I didn't have any magic, but I did know how to pick a lock. I pulled a pin from my hair and darted to Viviane's side.

"Cover me!" I shouted.

I leaned close to the door and jabbed at the keyhole, listening for the clicking tumblers. Viviane screamed again, but this time I didn't turn to look. Blood thundered in my ears. I heard the demon behind me, very close, almost whispering in my ear. I glanced behind me, and ducked just as it lunged, covering my head. Vines shot forward from the ground, wrapping around the demon's limbs and bringing it crashing to the ground. It seemed Jessa had finally managed to do what she planned. She stood behind the demon, pale and gasping for air. I grabbed my pin and turned the last tumbler carefully.

Click.

The door burst open. Viviane and I rushed inside.

"Jessa!" Alexander shouted.

Jessa slipped in after us. Seconds later, Alexander closed and locked the door behind him. I looked around the house; the room was mostly empty save for some scattered furniture. My eyes darted towards the one window, but it was barred. There were no other exits.

"Barricade the door!" Alexander ordered. "I'll draw the sigils!"

Without hesitation, I grabbed a table and dragged it across

the floor, being careful to give a wide berth to the silver lines Alexander was making on the floor. Jessa helped me brace the table against the door; her arms shook as she did it. Doing magic must have really worn her out.

Viviane carried over two chairs and wedged them against the table. All the while, the demon screamed outside. Its shouts were punctuated by the sound of limbs thrashing against the door and the splintering of wood.

I felt as though I was being watched, as if someone was watching me from inside my own head.

You…be…

Who was that? Was that voice coming from my head like the hisses had? I glanced down at my sword, before backing away from the door. That was all the furniture. Hopefully, it would hold long enough for someone to come rescue us.

Alexander had finished his sigils. They didn't look like much—a star, a circle, and some scattered symbols. "You need to make sure all the points touch," Viviane said. "If that corner doesn't connect, you might trap the demon *in here* rather than preventing it from entering."

Alexander didn't question her; he crouched down and made a few more lines, drawing the points of the star more firmly together.

Jessa leaned against the wall, breathing hard. The door buckled with a sharp crunching noise and daylight filtered in. I swallowed and drew my sword, unsure what I would even do with it. I'd already seen that an ordinary sword did little against demons, and in my hands, this sword would never be anything other than ordinary.

"What now?" I asked.

"We hope my sigil keeps it out," Alexander replied. "I've never tried this kind before."

Crash!

"It should," Viviane said.

But hers never worked, and she seemed to know *exactly* how to draw them. What if the demon came in anyway? Jessa didn't look well; I doubted she would be able to stop the demon, especially when it had taken her a few tries to begin with. Viviane's sigils weren't working, and I couldn't do magic. If Alexander's sigil failed, we were screwed.

You—

"What about me?" I muttered.

Crash!

"Did you say something?" Alexander asked sharply.

The door split apart, scattering the furniture across the floor. With a burst of sound and light, the demon swept through our makeshift barricade. My heart pounded so loudly that I heard it in my ears. We crouched inside Alexander's sigil as the demon stomped closer.

"How do we know if it works?" I asked, backing away.

"When it steps past exterior lines or not," Alexander said, his voice hoarse. Sweat shone from his brow.

Fire…

I glanced at the fireplace; it was empty and filled with nothing but cinders. I was good at making fires with flint and steel, but I had neither of those with me. Or was the creature trying to tell me it was going to set us ablaze? I could barely hear the voice above the noise, and I wasn't entirely sure whether the words came from my sword or from the approaching demon. The demon placed a foot inside the sigil and halted abruptly.

Smoke curled around its blackened hooves, and it pulled back with a howl of pain. It milled around at the edge of the sigil, swiping and roaring at the air as if it had reached some invisible barrier.

"Oh, good," Jessa rasped.

"Sure," Viviane said, sounding relieved. "Now, someone can just come by and seal it away."

The demon backed away and disappeared through the open doorway.

"We should stay here. It might be waiting for us," Alexander said, holding up his hand. "Demons can be very deceptive. It wouldn't be unheard of for one to feign defeat and attack us when our guards are down."

"That sounds good to me," Jessa said, sinking to the ground.

"Are you all right?" I asked.

"Fine," she said. "Just tired."

Thud!

"What was that?" Viviane asked sharply.

"It sounded like it came from the wall," Alexander said, turning around slowly.

The walls were made of some sort of painted over stone, as best as I could tell. "Do you think it can get in?" I asked.

Probably. They...proper...construction.

"I don't know," Alexander said.

Jessa stood shakily, gripping my arm. I gulped.

Thud!

A brick moved. Alexander crouched to the ground, hastily drawing another sigil.

"Can't you draw that all over the room?" I asked.

"No!" Viviane snapped. "Do you have any idea how much power that would take?"

No, none at all. I didn't even understand how sigils really worked. There had to be *something* besides just the drawings, or Viviane wouldn't be having such trouble. But drawing a sigil in front of one spot of the wall probably wouldn't help.

Sword…you doing…

Was the voice *helping*? I frowned, unsure. I tightened my grip on the sword and raised it in front of us. Bricks collapsed inwards, and a demon claw sprung forth, ripping its way in. Alexander darted back, his sigil incomplete. All at once, the demon burst into the room. Viviane shrieked. Without warning, blue fire erupted along the edge of my sword. I took a deep breath and swiped my blade through the demon. It was a strange feeling, like I'd struck something that wasn't entirely solid. Though my swing was fast, the edge of the blade slowed; it was like trying to cut through water or mist, something that shifted and moved even as I sliced through it. The demon caught fire and roared, tossing its head back in rage. Alexander and Viviane remained frozen before it. Fire licked up my wrist, burning my skin. I dropped the blade, letting it fall to the ground with a sharp clang.

A man with brown-blond hair burst into the house. I recognized him but couldn't put a name to his face. He had to have been one of our professors. Sigils glowed on his arms, their purple light gleaming. "Professor Conrad!" Jessa exclaimed.

"Get back to the Academy!" he barked.

The demon tore away, ripping its way past the mage and darting from the house. Viviane and Alexander looked to me, and I looked blankly back. Then, I dropped my gaze to the sword, still smoldering on the ground. Whatever the voice was, I was probably sure it had just saved us. But why?

I sheathed the blade, its flames now gone. I expected it to be warm, but it felt like ice against my fingertips. When I touched the cold steel, a tiredness swept over me, like the thick fog that sometimes settled in the Scraps. The kind that was heavy and damp.

"Let's go," Alexander said.

I didn't argue.

Jessa looked like she could barely stand. Viviane and Alexander led the way back; I trailed behind them, matching my pace with Jessa's. That way, if she fell over, I could grab her.

"Summer," Viviane said suddenly. "Where did you learn to pick locks?"

I was so tired, I didn't even feel like answering her.

"It's Wynter," I said, hoping she would drop it.

"So where did you learn that?" Viviane asked.

"Um…I knew a locksmith," I said. "He taught me."

Viviane glanced over her shoulder at me and narrowed her eyes. "Your sudden use of fire was very impressive," she said. "Miraculous, even."

Why wouldn't she *stop*? We'd just been attacked by a demon! How could she still have enough energy left to feel like interrogating me?

"Viv, please," Alexander said.

Viviane turned her attention to Alexander and linked his arm with hers.

"I'm glad you could do it," Jessa whispered, her smile weak. "I—I wish I could do that."

But I was pretty sure I *hadn't* done it. The magic, talking

153

sword had just spontaneously decided to help. But I couldn't tell them that, because mages who listened to the voices in their heads went crazy, and I didn't want that to happen to me.

"The vines were really impressive," I said.

Jessa winced. "I was trying something...bigger."

She'd still done better than Viviane had. I thought about telling Jessa how I felt, but after the demon attack, it seemed too mean-spirited. Finally, we reached the Academy. I hoped we'd be safer within its walls. Maybe not. At the moment, I was having a hard time caring. Above everything else, I really just wanted to climb into bed and sleep for about ten years.

FOURTEEN

I DIDN'T GET TO SLEEP. Not right away. Professor Conrad, the man who'd rushed in to save us, told the faculty about the attack, and they wanted to question us. So I joined Jessa, Alexander, and Viviane in repeating the story to Du Lac and Celeste. By the time I returned to the dormitories, word had already spread throughout the school, and we were ambushed by half the girls in my dorm. Viviane had been there too, and I hoped she'd tell the story and spare me from having to. She had, but even then, I had to answer a dozen questions. And it was strange. I wasn't used to having so much attention. When I woke, it was late evening and the setting sun cast long, orange shadows across the floor. Viviane was gone. Jessa was still sleeping, but there were a couple of other girls in the dormitory—Kris, Tatiana, and...

I floundered on the last name. I thought it might be Marina.

Kris, dark-haired and petite, glanced my way. I could sense more questions coming, and I really just wanted to disappear for a while and clear my head. So I slipped from my bed and headed to the library. Hopefully, it would be quiet there.

I needed to think.

Guilt gnawed at my stomach. I wished I'd been more useful. Logically, I knew it would have been impossible to take down the demon myself, but I still felt like it was my fault somehow. At least the others had some training and magical ability. All I'd done was lift a sword I didn't know how to use. People were congratulating me like I'd done something amazing.

What if the demons were after me or something? That couldn't possibly be it, could it? I mean, even if I could hear them, it's not like I'd *asked* to talk to them. And I wasn't even a real mage.

I thought of Jessa, still fast asleep. She'd collapsed into bed and not moved in hours. Celeste had said Jessa would be fine, but what if something went wrong? What if she never woke up?

I didn't know where Viviane was, probably with Alexander. I hoped they were both all right. And then, there were the flames. I had no idea how those had happened. I had the sinking feeling that the voice in my enchanted sword had *made* them happen, and that...

That wasn't good. Was there a demon in my sword as well? But why would a demon fight another demon? All I knew was, I didn't belong here, and the longer I stayed, the more chances that somebody would get hurt. I just had to find Dorian's stupid journal so he'd let me leave. I'd had enough of the Floats.

There were too many people to try sneaking into the archives, so I wandered through the shelves and let my finger trace over the titles of the books. Growing up in the Scraps, I'd only seen a few dozen books in my whole life. And most of them were Gabriel's, which I hadn't been allowed to read. I wished I could just tumble into one of soft sofas lining the study areas and spend a year reading, but I knew that was never going to happen. Eventually, I pulled out a thick, heavy book which promised to be about different places and kingdoms. I carried the book over to an empty seating area and curled up in a chair with it. The opening pages featured a large map of Reverie. I picked out the places I knew. The Academy and the forum. Rosewood.

Down below I found Plumba. The Scraps.

I narrowed my eyes and ran my finger around the border of Reverie. An idea was beginning to form. Maybe I *could* share some of this wealth with Briar and Sterling. All I had to do was figure out where to drop things so they would find them.

We lived a mile from the Dregs. More or less. That was still a lot of territory. I needed to narrow it down some way.

The Gardens had been too far to walk to, as had Beryl—the realm on the *other* side of Plumba. But the Scraps were a large area. Gabriel had once said that the subway was transportation of some kind. That meant there had to be a logical reason for it being placed there. There had probably been something there once. A city or a town.

I flipped several more pages until I found one of the Scraps. There were only three towns. I pursed my lips together and tried to think. I didn't know of any towns in the Scraps. But I knew the Market. That would probably be considered a town, wouldn't it?

The Market had been within walking distance, but going there on foot was an all-day affair, which was why my uncle never went often. I flipped back to the other map and put my finger on the place between the beginning of the Dregs and where I thought the Market *might* be. Five miles between the two. Assuming they were in a straight line, if I dropped something off the edge of Reverie…

I would have to look. Carefully, I ripped the map from the book, folded it up, and placed it in my pocket. My best bet would be to walk Reverie's border and see if I could find any distinctive landmarks. And there might still be time. It was dark, but it wasn't late. I flipped back to the map of Plumba and surveyed it once more.

A throat cleared behind me.

When I looked up, Alexander was standing near me with a knowing smirk on his face. Had he seen me steal the page from the book?

"Hey—um, hello," I said, flustered.

"What are you doing?" he asked.

Alexander leaned over me, so close that I felt the warmth of his body with mine. My breath gave an awkward, embarrassing hitch.

"I—I'm trying to find my home," I said. "I've narrowed it down to—"

"Then, shouldn't you be looking at a map of Argent?" he asked. "And not Plumba?"

"I'm trying to familiarize myself with the nearby areas, too," I lied.

Alexander's eyes bore into mine. Such a soft, playful blue, and yet somehow so imposing. It wasn't fair for anyone to be so handsome. Especially so handsome and mean. And when he looked at me, it was such a strange feeling. It was like he could tell everything about me, see every lie and every deception.

"I don't see why you'd bother with *that* place. There's nothing worth seeing there," Alexander said. "Nothing good, anyway."

"Have you ever been there?" I asked.

"No," he said stiffly, "But everyone knows it."

Maybe he was right. Life had been terrible in the Scraps. But it was still my home, and there was something deeply comforting in the familiarity of the place. Or maybe the demon attacks and the quakes had made me think more highly of a place that had never really been that great.

"Can you go annoy someone else?" I said. "I'm reading."

"But I want to annoy you," he said.

"Why are you even here?" I asked.

"I was just walking around," Alexander said, "And I saw you through the windows. I thought I would exchange a few words."

A warm flush spread to my cheeks. He'd come here to talk to me. "That was nice of you," I said coldly. He was acting stiffly formal, but I wasn't going to fall for his fake charm.

Alexander shrugged. "Don't take it too seriously," he replied. "As a prince, it is necessary to ensure that the people of Reverie are well."

"Right," I replied. Was he bragging? I thought he didn't want to be treated like royalty.

"The fire you used was impressive. How did you accomplish such a thing?" he asked, his eyes narrowing. Ah, so this was an interrogation. I should have known I couldn't avoid it.

I swallowed. "Luck, I guess," I said, "Or I was scared. Remember what Celeste said? Sometimes, you perform more powerful magic when you're feeling something strong. Maybe it was that."

"Was it?" Alexander asked, his voice soft and dark. "Or was it something else entirely?"

"I don't know what you're implying."

"Then, maybe I need to be more explicit," Alexander said, leaning even closer.

His breath ghosted over my neck. Suddenly, I realized that he smelled nice, like something earthy. He put a knee on one arm of my chair, his hand on the other, as if worried I'd bolt if left an opening. For a wild moment, I thought of Sterling and how close he'd stood when he kissed me. Alexander kept finding me like this and trapping me places, and I didn't know how to react. My heart fluttered in my chest as he leaned closer.

"You can hear them, can't you?" he whispered.

"I don't know what you're talking about," I said.

"Don't tell anyone," he said. "Nobody hears them, except the darkest mages, and those always die tragically. Plus, it's forbidden. If you don't want to be executed as a traitor, keep your mouth shut."

Did he mean the hisses? If so, it meant maybe I wasn't just going crazy. I stood up quickly, pushing him away from me. He stumbled backward, kicking over a potted plant and knocking a few volumes off a shelf. I didn't get far before he grasped my wrist and pulled me back to him.

"Let go!" I snapped.

"I'm just trying to warn you," Alexander said, his voice soft. "Demons whisper evil temptations and destroy minds. You can't trust them. You must have an iron will to control such beasts, Wynter. If you don't, they'll possess you and make you do dreadful things."

It was the first time he'd said my name, and I realized how

close we were standing. His fingers were still clasped loosely around my wrist, sending warm tingles up my arm. His eyes were earnest, and there was something strangely protective in them.

But was it a warning, or a threat? Before I had a chance to decide, we were interrupted by Viviane's shrill voice.

***

"What are you *doing*?" her voice rose, as sharp as a knife. Alexander dropped my hand quickly, and I drew in a shaky breath and stepped away from him.

"We were discussing the demon today," Alexander said.

Viviane crossed her arms. "Great," Viviane said, "So now, you're finished?"

I didn't feel like getting between them or watching an argument.

"We are," I said, darting away. I shelved the book I was reading and hurried from the library, half-expecting Alexander to follow me. I left the Academy alone, and walked briskly across the grounds and through the front gates. It was cold out, and I rubbed my bare arms. I thought about returning to the dormitory and getting my coat, but instead, I kept going. I needed some time alone. The streets were lit with flames that danced and flickered in wrought iron lanterns, casting dark shadows over the path. Patches of ice clung to the edges of the sidewalk.

I thought of the demon attack and shivered. What if it came back? It probably wasn't wise to be walking around alone, but I couldn't have asked anyone to go with me. Not for this. I pulled out the map beneath the lights and set off towards the edge of

Reverie. It only took me ten minutes to find it. The entire kingdom was surrounded by a tall, silvery fence, composed of intricate swirls and floral patterns. It would be easy enough to slip objects through. I glanced around at the few people dotting the street.

I slowly walked along the edge of the fence, trying to match the map with the shape of the perimeter. When I peered from the edge of Reverie, I saw only darkness below. I wondered if anyone had ever fallen… or been pushed. A chill traveled down my spine. Maybe that's why the mage from Viviane's story cut the noblewoman into pieces first, so they'd slip through the fence more easily—if that story was even true.

Hisses whispered behind me. I froze, alarmed at first, but then I heard the laughter. It was soft and pleasant, like a bubbling spring.

I stepped away from the fence, melding into the shadows. My heartbeat quickened. I hadn't been doing anything wrong, but it was better if I didn't need to explain what I was doing out here by myself. A couple walked in front of me, their steps slow and easy. I recognized the man as Professor Gareth, but not the stunning woman whose arm was linked with his. The woman's snow-white hair was the longest I'd ever seen; it went all the way to her waist. Her knee-length coat was sky blue and trimmed in white fur and covered the top of her black, heeled boots.

"Well, *I* think it's fascinating. I'm sorry you don't agree, dear," Gareth said.

"I like seeing you passionate about it," she said, her voice light and teasing, "But maybe you should look more at *me* like you look at those sigils you love so much."

Hisses punctuated the conversation.

"I'll try to work on that," Gareth said.

What kept *hissing*? I looked around, searching for a demon, but none appeared.

"Thank you."

Still nothing. Once they'd passed, I slumped in relief against a building behind me. That was enough of a scare that I decided to head back to the Academy before I pushed my luck. With the day I'd had, I didn't feel much like talking to Professor Gareth, so I waited a few minutes before leaving my spot in the shadows.

I found him on the road, heading back to the Academy, but the woman was gone. I hadn't passed her going the opposite way. She must have gone into one of the nearby buildings, but which one? And how had she left so quickly? I sighed. Maybe I was reading too much into things, but in Reverie, it seemed like dangerous secrets lurked around every corner.

I sighed with relief when I entered the school grounds, and headed straight to my dorm. Tomorrow was going to be a long day. I'd have to actually go to class and pretend to be a mage. It would be obvious I couldn't perform real magic, and the longer I kept pretending, the sooner I'd be found out as a fraud. After everyone went to sleep, I'd try to access the forbidden archives. The sooner I got out of Reverie, the better.

FIFTEEN

BOOKS IN HAND, I HEADED down the hallway towards Introduction to Sigils. At least, I had some familiarity with what those were. Besides, they might be useful for figuring out how to open the locks on the third floor. From what I'd read on sigils, though, they weren't quite as easy as I'd imagined. Instead, they were made of a bunch of small symbols that had to be combined in certain ways, as specifically as possible, to receive the desired effect.

Apparently, there was something capricious about them, too, but it seemed that even the mages didn't understand what that *something* was. Two mages could draw the same sigil perfectly and receive different results, seemingly for no discernable reason. I could see why Viviane might have trouble with it, but there was definitely no way I could manage it. And this, unfortunately, didn't seem like something I could easily fake. Hopefully, everyone would assume I was one of those mages who just couldn't get it. Besides, it was only the first day, how bad could it be?

As I eased in the door, my eyes swept over the classroom.

It was massive, with rows of tables, each with a wooden box upon them, and seats before them. Was this what all classrooms looked like? An arm slammed into mine and I nearly dropped my book. Viviane smiled when I looked at her. "Sorry," Viviane said. "I didn't see you there. I thought you were the help!"

"Honestly, Viv," Alexander said. "Can you pick another day to score points? I don't feel like doing this today."

"My what a lovely dress," Viviane continued. "Didn't you wear that yesterday... and the day before?"

I frowned, suddenly self-conscious. In the Scraps, we wore clothes until they were dirty. All the mages, I realized, seemed to change outfits every day. What a waste. Still, if I was going to blend in, I'd have to pay more attention from now on.

When Alexander jerked his head towards the classroom, Viviane followed him in, muttering something in hushed tones. I took a seat a few rows behind them, shifting around to accommodate the sword. I'd seen other students wearing them, so I thought I might as well bring mine. I was enrolled in battle magic officially, after all, though it seemed strange to carry weapons into class. Viviane leaned her head towards Alexander and was whispering rapidly, casting glances in my direction. I ignored them and looked around the classroom, hoping for a familiar face. When I found none, I opened the box on my desk. It was filled with a few different bottles, goggles, a couple of plants and some copper cups.

Du Lac walked in. He gave me a sharp nod, but his smile had a predatory edge to it. It was strange because he hadn't actually *done* anything to me. I didn't really even know him, but there was something about him that just made my skin crawl. I wondered where he'd gone after his speech at the forum. It must've been embarrassing to have a demon attack right after he assured everyone it wouldn't happen again. I remembered what Dorian had said about someone releasing demons, and I wondered if that was true. What if someone was *trying* to make the Council look ineffective? But who would even do that, and why?

I couldn't afford to worry about the politics. All I had to do was keep my cover long enough to finish the job I was hired for. I opened my book and skimmed the first page. It seemed that magical objects were very important to mages, which I already knew a little about. I thought about how special and expensive mage tech was in the Scraps. How did that fit into all of this? The device was in my dormitory, tucked carefully beneath a pile of clothes and wrapped up in a pair of socks. For the first time I wondered how it worked. Was it the result of demons and sigils as well?

The door to the room slammed closed with such a sudden burst of noise that I jumped. Du Lac waved a hand, and I heard it lock, exactly on time.

"Welcome," he said, "To Introduction of Sigils. I'll be your instructor for this class. I am Dr. Markus Du Lac. I imagine most of you will know much of the material I'm going to cover today already, but for those of you who don't," he said, his eyes seemed to linger on me, "Pay attention. This is important."

I rolled my shoulders back and prepared to listen. I had seen what sigils could do, which was quite a bit, and even though replicating any of them was beyond my skills, it wouldn't hurt to learn a few things.

Laughter. Great. Now, the talking sword was mocking my efforts.

I'm not...

Then, what *was* he doing? Because it definitely wasn't encouraging. And why was the sword even talking right now, when it had been mostly silent yesterday?

Tired.

Du Lac passed out a polished wooden box engraved with complex, circular seal. I craned my neck to see what was being taken from it. Large, brightly faceted hunks of gemstone. I watched as the box slowly worked its way back, admiring the different colors.

When the box was passed back to me, I reached inside and pulled out a light blue one.

"These gemstones," Du Lac said as the box moved on, "Are enchanted to change color."

I frowned at the gemstone in my hand. Changing the color of an object sounded incredibly...wasteful. They were already beautiful. If a gemstone was going to be enchanted, shouldn't it do something useful?

"What I want everyone to do today is to practice making ink. Then, you'll use your ink to draw a sigil on your gemstone, hopefully changing the color. This activity requires very precise measurements and patience, so be careful."

I pulled a slip of paper from the box and furrowed my brow. This recipe had thirty different steps, and at the bottom, there was sigil along with a thirty-step process of drawing it, line by line, including which direction to draw the pen and how thick to make each mark. I began pulling objects out of my box; they were labeled, at least. Surely, this couldn't be too hard, right? Just mix a few things together in the right amounts.

More laughter, much louder that time.

The was probably a bad sign. I glanced hesitantly at my rapier, half-afraid that the demon might spontaneously appear and attack me.

You don't know anything about demons.

No, I didn't. But I'd seen them, and I'd feared the monsters in the Scraps. I didn't think the monsters in the Scraps were demons, but they looked kind of similar. They were dark and spindly creatures, but looked more like large animals than the demons, which were vaguely human. None of the mages seemed to believe the demons were good or even amicable. Alexander specifically told me I couldn't trust them. I still didn't know why this demon, the one in my sword, had even bothered to save me, though. Why fight his own kind?

But you're…student… You're supposed to be…

There was a bitter edge to the words. I frowned, unsure what the demon had been trying to say.

The first step. Three drops of quicksilver into a copper cup. I took the bottle of quicksilver and glanced around to see how everyone else was doing it. No one else seemed hesitant about this. Three drops. Was I just supposed to dump it?

I unscrewed the cap and slowly tipped the open bottle into the cup. Three drops. A small fourth drop fell before I tipped the bottle back. "How much does accuracy matter in this?" I whispered, hoping Viviane or Alexander might take pity on me and answer. Nobody responded.

The…whole bottle.

That sounded *really* helpful. It was just one extra drop. It couldn't make that much of a difference, could it? I moved to the next step, which involved sprinkling in quartz powder. I sprinkled it in, only to discover that I was supposed to roll the quartz powder in my hand first.

Maybe I'd only botched a couple of steps.

I worked to mix the rest of the potion. It was only a couple of mistakes, and when I was finished—long after most of my classmates—the copper cup was filled with a shimmering, silvery-lavender substance. Viviane's creation was silver, so my color wasn't *that* off.

I tilted my head, watching Viviane. She grabbed a paintbrush, dipped it in the substance, and drew a line directly across the gemstone. Nothing happened. I swallowed thickly and grabbed my own paintbrush. I drew the line across my gemstone and waited, but I had no more success than Viviane. I had managed to speak to the device, though, and it had worked for me. And then, my rapier.

But why? There was a demon in my sword, apparently. Was there a demon in the device as well? In this gemstone? Maybe the gemstone would do what I wanted if I talked to it. "I would really appreciate it," I murmured. "I know what you can do, and you're really powerful. And if you can change color, that would be great. Please."

Nothing happened. I swiped my thumb over the mark I'd left.

"No luck?" Du Lac asked, hovering over my shoulder.

"No," I replied.

"You're *supposed* to have a silver-colored substance," Markus said, "Like Viviane's."

But Viviane hadn't managed to make the stone change colors yet either.

"A pity," Du Lac said. "I'd expected to see something much better from you, especially after you put on *such* a show at your examination. What happened?"

Did I imagine that he was being…more obnoxious towards me than the other students?

"I guess I got lucky," I replied.

"For your sake, I hope not," Du Lac said. "Try again."

I emptied the copper cup in the sink, unleashing coils of green smoke. Then I tried again, doing my best to get the recipe exactly right this time. But even when I thought I'd gotten it perfectly, the gemstone still refused to change colors. Viviane's had changed. Alexander's had changed. The bells tolled, signaling the end of class. I frowned at my gemstone, as if I could force the color to change through the sheer force of will, but of course, it didn't.

"How terrible," Du Lac drawled, plucking the gemstone off the table before me.

"Maybe I'm only good with fire," I said. "I guess it's a good thing I went into battle magic instead of sigils."

"Oh, that's quite clear," Du Lac replied. "I think you need some extra work to help you catch up with everyone else."

"Extra work?"

Why was he singling me out like this? What had I done? It wasn't my fault I couldn't make the gemstone change colors, and when I looked around at other tables, I saw potions in all varying shades of color. But Du Lac hadn't made *them* do extra work.

"I want you to write a three-page essay about hegemonic discourse in sigil studies," Du Lac said.

"But I don't know anything about sigils," I replied.

I didn't even know what *hegemonic discourse* was supposed to be. It honestly sounded like Du Lac was just making words up.

"That's kind of the point," Du Lac said, smiling. A few

other students laughed.

Maybe this could work in my favor. If I had to write a paper, I would need to go to the library. Could I persuade someone to take pity on me and unlock the third floor? That would be my back-up plan if I couldn't get the door unlocked.

I clasped my hands in my lap. "I'll get to work, then," I said.

"You'd better," Du Lac replied.

He walked on, leaving before even most of the class did.

"It's a pity you couldn't figure it out," Viviane said, turning around in her seat. "Especially since you're trying *so* hard. Too bad there aren't any proper mages down in Argent. Perhaps they could have helped."

"It is too bad," I replied, "But I also didn't know I had magic for most of my life."

That was a good excuse, wasn't it?

"It shows," Viviane said, grabbing her books.

She seemed to have bought my excuse. I resisted the urge to sigh in relief.

"So when did you discover you had magic?" Alexander asked. Viviane rolled her eyes but waited at the door. "What happened?"

I scrambled to remember my cover story. "I worked for a merchant, and one day, I stopped a potential thief. I summoned fire."

"Without any ritual or training?" Viviane asked. "That's rare."

This was the second time she'd, essentially, said that my fire magic was too good to be true. But did she suspect I was a fraud, or was she just jealous because Alexander was talking to me?

That was such an obnoxious thing to worry about. Alexander didn't even *like* me.

"What's with the interrogation?" I joked, trying to divert her attention. "You were just telling me how terrible I am at sigils. Now, I'm a magical prodigy?"

Viviane narrowed her eyes. I realized that maybe I'd said the wrong thing. Maybe Viviane was suspicious because I was *inconsistent*. Too good with fire and too bad with sigils. But I didn't know how to fix that.

"Come on, Viv," Alexander said. "Don't we have dance next?"

"Right," Viviane replied. "Of course. I want to go to the dorms and drink a potion first, anyway."

I fumbled around and retrieved my schedule from my books. History of Reverie was next. The demon in my sword laughed.

That's an excellent…learning lies.

"I'll skip it, then," I muttered, yawning. It was only the first day of school, but I didn't see how a history lesson was going to help me find Nicholas Armenia's journal and escape Reverie unscathed. Besides, if every class was as bad as Du Lac's, I wouldn't make it through the day.

I'd feign a bad headache, take a nap, and when I woke— probably in the middle of the night considering the early hour— I'd head straight to the library. It was time to check out the restricted archives.

SIXTEEN

IT WAS DARK AND COLD. When I breathed out, my breath frosted the air. But it wasn't unpleasant. I looked around. There were trees, more trees than I'd ever seen in my life. In the Scraps, trees were short and scraggly. Most of them dead and broken. These, though, were something else entirely. They were massive and green. Beautiful. And they smelled strange. Sharp and young and new.

Hissing voices snaked through the branches.

"What is she?"

"Why is she here?"

"Can she hear us?"

I trembled, as I realized there were things moving between the trees. I caught glimpses of skin and limbs, wings and claws.

"You're far from home, aren't you?"

I recognized the voice.

I spun around, to see a boy laughing. He looked a few years older than me, and was every bit as handsome as Alexander. Maybe more so. But while Alexander was blond with blue eyes, this boy was dark-haired with eyes as dark as the night sky. His face was nice with high cheekbones and a thin, slightly upturned nose. When he approached me, he looked as if he came from the trees himself. He wore silver armor, which shined and gleamed from beneath his dark green cape.

"Lucian," he said, extending a hand. "Welcome."

"Where am I?" I asked.

"In a dream," he replied.

A dream? I didn't feel like I was dreaming. Lucian's hand was still held out.

I thought we were going to shake hands, but when I extended mine, he grasped it and gently pressed his lips against my knuckles. I felt the warmth of his breath against my skin. Fluttering spread from my chest all the way up to my face.

"Who are you?" I asked.

"You refer to me as the demon in your talking sword," Lucian replied.

My breath caught in my throat.

"It's all right," Lucian said. "I know the mages say such dreadful things about my kind."

There was a burst of soft light, pale blue. I blinked back spots from my vision, and once they were clear, I saw that I stood on a sanded place. Waves of water roared distantly. Was this the ocean? I'd heard of such things, but I'd never actually seen it. It was mesmerizing and beautiful—beyond anything I could have imagined. For several minutes, I couldn't look away.

"Lovely, isn't it?"

It was, but I pulled my gaze away to study him instead. Beneath the moonlight, there was something vaguely feline about his face. He didn't look like he came from the same world I did.

"I thought it was time we speak face to face. After all, we have a great deal in common," he said.

Now it was my turn to laugh.

"Like what, exactly?" I asked.

"We're both being exploited for someone else's benefit."

"I don't know about that," I said.

I shifted uncomfortably, and when I looked at my feet, I saw they were bare. I shifted my toes in the cold sand. It felt so real.

"Of course, you do. As nice as your nobleman may be to you, he's still making you do things you don't want to," Lucian said.

That was true. So why did hearing Lucian say it make me so uneasy?

"It's no big deal," I lied. "Not everyone has the luxury to do what they want."

"I would think after years of abuse, you'd be more receptive to any kindness," Lucian said. "Perhaps, I'll do you another. You need admittance into the library. I can show you how to do that. As a token of friendship. Perhaps, after I prove my value to you, we can speak again."

"Why would you help me? And why did you fight the other demon, who attacked me?"

"I wasn't doing anyone any good stuck in that storage closet. I yearned to be free; and now, my freedom depends on your survival. I couldn't let him kill you. Plus, I didn't know him. It's not like we're all friends."

He crouched on the sand, and I watched as he made a symbol—like the sun and moon intertwined—with a dark red substance. I bent close to it. "Try it," he said.

I crouched beside him, aware of the way he kept his eyes on me as I traced the symbol. "I can't actually do these," I said.

His finger slipped beneath my chin and brought my face to his. "I'll help you, of course," he said.

My throat went dry. Anything I might have said went spiraling out of my head. Why was I so terrible around handsome men?

"Um," I said.

Truly, I was the picture of wit.

"But isn't brevity the soul of wit?"

My face grew hot beneath his gaze. Reflexively, my hand twitched. I had a terrible wayward thought of putting my hand on his and pressing his fingers into my cheek.

"You are…" I trailed off. "Very nice."

"I would ask in what way you mean, but I fear that would only embarrass you."

With a mischievous smile, he turned his attention to my sigil. "It isn't bad," he said. "Try again. Make sure the ends all meet."

I copied his sigil again and again, tracing the lines and memorizing them. Finally, I managed to produce the sigil without correction.

"Where do I get the ink from?" I asked. "Will any ink do, or does it have to be a special kind?"

"Like that horrid ink you made for that professor of yours?" Lucian asked.

I nodded.

"It's not ink," Lucian replied. "It has to be your blood."

I gasped. My veins ran cold and I shivered.

"Blood magic? Professor Gareth specifically said it's

outlawed in Reverie."

"But I imagine," Lucian said, "Stealing is also outlawed in Reverie."

He knew far too much about me. Suddenly I was afraid he'd turn me in.

"Don't worry," he smiled, flashing his teeth. "Nobody else can hear me, and even if they could, nobody else would listen. There's only you."

Bells made me turn suddenly, and when I looked back Lucian's world was fading away quickly, until all I could see were his gleaming teeth in the darkness.

***

I came to awareness and lay in my bed, tangled in my blankets for several seconds. That dream had been far too real. And what did it mean? I drew in a sharp, shaky breath. I looked at my rapier, resting by my bed. Were demons behind every bit of magic in Reverie?

I wondered if Lucian's bloody sigil would even work for me. There was only one way to find out, but even then, I wasn't sure I wanted to try. Alexander had specifically mentioned that demons could be very cunning, and that I couldn't trust anything they said. What if this was a trick? What if that sigil did something awful?

The other girls were preparing for light's out. I watched a red-haired girl and a couple of her friends walk by. They looked tired. When I looked to my side at Viviane, she was drinking some sort of blue concoction that shimmered. It must be one of the potions she was fond of. Jessa was in her nightgown and roughly brushing her hair.

I hadn't had a chance to speak to her since yesterday. I smiled at her.

When Jessa saw I was awake, her brow furrowed in concern. "Wynter, how are you feeling?" she asked. "I heard you had a terrible headache."

"I did," I said. "I'm a little better now. How are you after…"

"I'm all right," Jessa said. "Exhausted. But I'll be fine. It's not uncommon to be tired when you've used a lot of magical power, which I did. It's expected, so it's a little different from a migraine."

Jessa was so open and concerned, I felt terrible for lying to her. I wasn't really used to people being concerned about me. Of course, Sterling and Briar had cared about me, but with them, I'd usually lied about *not* being in pain. Being able to complain and receive sympathy was a strange luxury, and I felt like I was taking advantage of it. Sure, Viviane was a jerk, and Alexander was hard to figure out. But Jessa seemed nice. Friendly, even.

Friendly. Hah!

Then, there were the demons. I sighed and turned over in my bed. Viviane walked by in a daze. She really did look awful. That second demon attack must've really upset her. As everyone prepared for bed, I flipped through my book for sigils, looking for a basic unlocking spell. I found something for unbinding metals, but that probably wouldn't work. Too bad I *didn't* have some actual magical power.

But then, Lucian seemed to think I could make his sigil work. Maybe mages and demons used magic in different ways. Or maybe Lucian's sigil wouldn't do anything for me, and he was just toying with me.

"I'm glad you're feeling better," Jessa said. "Pace yourself as best as you can. I know that's easier said than done, but once the semester really takes off, a lot of people get sick."

I nodded, but frowned. If I already couldn't handle myself on the first day, how was I supposed to survive when things became more difficult?

Viviane threw herself onto her bed and sighed. "While you were sleeping, Uncle came by," she said. "He said you should visit him."

I winced. Had Dorian expected me to have finished this already? He probably thought I was taking too long.

"I'll have to visit him, then," I said.

Viviane grimaced but nodded.

I remained in bed until the lights went out. Then I waited for everyone to fall asleep. I was so tired, but if Dorian expected me to visit, I needed to have *something* for him. When I was sure that everyone was sleeping, I slipped out of bed, grabbed the rapier and my device, and made my way quietly down the stairs to the front entrance.

In the darkness, the Academy was a very different place. It was vast and imposing with moonlight that seeped through the windows, silver on shadows. I kept close to the wall, but thus far, I'd seen no one. Soon, I reached the library, locked as expected. I pulled a pin from my hair and leveled it before the lock. The tumblers clicked, but nothing gave.

"Does that blood thing work on any door or just the third floor?" I whispered.

It opens most things, Lucian replied, *but these mages have all kinds of tricks I'm unfamiliar with.*

I could hear him much more clearly now. Was it because I'd seen him in a dream or something else entirely? I pursed my lips together, trying to decide whether I was desperate enough to try this. What if it was a trap of some kind? I had no way of knowing, but I also knew I should exhaust every other option before trusting a demon.

Footsteps. I bolted and ducked around the corner of the library, leaning into the darkness as best as I could. My heart pounded, and my head spun as I tried to think of a good excuse to be wandering the Academy grounds when everyone else was fast asleep. I probably couldn't get away with saying I was lost at this point; there would have to be something else.

The footsteps stopped nearby. I peeked around the corner at the cloaked figure standing at the library door. Silvery ink glowed on the lock—sigils, definitely. For several minutes, I waited, while the unknown person kept scrawling, writing and erasing over and over.

I dared creep a little closer, until I could see the outline of the person's profile beneath his dark hood and realized who it was. Alexander.

Why was he out this late at night?

If he gets the door open, you won't have to open it.

It was about time something worked in my favor. With a click, Alexander opened the door and slipped inside. I waited for just a second before approaching the entrance, and grabbed the door gently before it closed all the way.

But what is the little princeling doing in here this late at night? Lucian asked.

I slipped through the opening and silently closed the gilded doors of the library behind me. Alexander was headed towards the staircase in the center of the room. In the stillness, his footsteps echoed up the staircase; I wouldn't be able to follow too closely, or he'd hear me.

I darted between shadows, weaving my way through the shelves and books. I reached a small sitting area in one corner. Alexander's footsteps were still loud on the metal. I wondered if I would have any luck being quieter than he was. Alexander paused abruptly and leaned over the railing. I ducked into a dark corner, hoping he couldn't see me. I held my breath, until Alexander mercifully resumed climbing the stairs.

I sighed, and when I stood, a sudden burst of pain filled my skull. I hissed between my teeth and looked up to see what I'd hit my head on. It was a large portrait of a woman in a silver, floral frame. She was very beautiful. Her brown curls had been arranged over a dainty silver crown, lined with pearls and teardrop-shaped sapphires. Her eyes were a soft, gray-blue and set inside a soft, friendly sort of face. The woman's smile looked like she had a secret that she was just dying to share.

She looks a bit like you, Lucian said, sounding amused.

I tilted my head and squinted a bit, but I couldn't find whatever resemblance Lucian had seen. Besides, she couldn't look like me. My family was from the Scraps; they'd have never made it up here. "I guess we both have blue eyes," I said, "And dark hair."

Well, I have heard that everyone has a twin, Lucian said. *Maybe she is yours.*

"I've never heard that," I whispered.

And even if I did have a twin, I seriously doubted she would be a mage-lady.

I waited a few more minutes, then headed to the curved

staircase and began climbing. My footsteps seemed quieter than Alexander's, but I still jumped at every creak of the stairs. I would have to be careful; I didn't know where Alexander had gone, just that he'd gone up. *I think you should just set that princeling on fire. That would solve the problem.*

"I'm not going to set him on fire, Lucian," I murmured. "And stop making me talk to myself, I'm trying to be quiet. Besides, I couldn't even if I wanted to."

Are you sure? You never know until you try.

"Somehow, I don't think that would solve my problems."

Maybe. But it would be amusing.

I grimaced. "Sure," I replied, "until the Council or royalty or someone executed me. It would be great."

When I reached the second floor, I paused and waited to see if there was anything moving. There wasn't, so I continued to the next floor. Maybe Alexander had been on the second floor where I hadn't been able to see him. Or maybe he'd gone up to the fourth.

When I paused on the third floor, I saw the bookshelf had been pushed aside and there was a tell-tale gleam of silver around the lock.

My, the princeling certainly seems rather adept at getting into places he shouldn't be, doesn't he?

Lucian was right. Alexander *did* seem pretty skilled at getting through locked doors. And why would a prince need to be sneaking around at night, anyway? Surely he could gain access to the forbidden archives if he asked. But I wasn't about to complain about him opening doors for me. I hurried towards the door and turned the knob slowly, exhaling a breath as it clicked open. It was very dark inside, although I caught sight of a dim light in one corner. That was probably where Alexander was, so I moved away from it and darted behind a shelf. I waited to see if Alexander would come and inspect the door, but he didn't.

I held out a hand and traced the outline of the shelves, moving deeper into the archives. As my eyes adjusted I could see tall shelves of books fading into the darkness, illuminated only by the light of the moon falling through the high, gothic windows. Hopefully, Nicholas Armenia's journal wasn't right behind Alexander's head or something. I stepped behind a shelf and squinted at the books, but it was too dark to see. While I could make out shapes, I couldn't read individual names.

I was considering whether I could use my device without giving myself away, when a hand grasped my arm and shoved me backward. My eyes caught the flash of steel as a dagger rushed towards my face.

SEVENTEEN

I RAISED MY HAND, SQUINTING against the bright light Alexander was holding. He pressed close against me, pinning me against the bookshelf painfully. "Why are you here?" he hissed.

Very princely behavior. I clenched my jaw.

"I could ask you the same thing," I replied, trying to copy the haughtiness in his voice.

"Tell me," he said, shoving me again into the bookshelf, "or I'll shout for help."

He's bluffing, Lucian said.

"I'm just trying to find something," I stammered.

"Like what?" he raised an eyebrow.

Don't tell him, Lucian said.

"Something written by Nicholas Armenia," I stammered. It was a risk, telling Alexander the truth. But he shouldn't be sneaking around either. Maybe we could help each other.

Alexander released me and broke away abruptly. He studied me for a long moment, before heading towards the center of the room. "Follow me," he said, waving an arm.

Alexander walked to a place on the floor, covered with

books and a single lantern. He swept the lantern off the ground, lit it with a match, and continued down a narrow gap between the bookshelves. My heart beat quickly as we walked farther into the archives. This place was much bigger than I imagined.

"You've heard of him?" I asked, finally.

"Not exactly, but I know where to look."

Alexander finally stopped. His finger moved along the spines of books and bundles of papers, but there was no mention of Nicholas Armenia so far.

"Why are you interested in this man?" Alexander asked.

"I read his name somewhere," I replied.

"So you decided to break into the library, at night? I'm not a fool."

I frowned and pulled a stack of papers free as Alexander's finger passed over them. One bore the name *Nick* written in thin, slanted handwriting. This wasn't the journal, but it might be *something* related to this Nicholas guy. Something was better than nothing, wasn't it? Dorian had said the journal and anything else I could find.

Nick isn't exactly an uncommon name, Lucian said. *You probably want to check.*

That was a good point. I untied the ribbon binding the stack of papers together and unfolded the top one. Alexander held his lantern up and peered over my shoulder.

"Is this it?" he asked.

"Shh," I said, raising a finger. "Be quiet so I can read."

My Dearest Gwen,

I'm afraid I've not been in Argent until recently, so I've only just received your letter. Despite Amelia's assumption that I'm somehow responsible for Dorian's disappearance, I haven't the faintest idea where he is. I wasn't even aware he was gone until I received your letter. I can ask around to see if anyone in Argent recalls seeing him, and I'll certainly pass along anything I find. However, considering how much time has passed, I doubt I'll have much success. But I wouldn't worry too much. Dorian has magic and wits enough to look after himself.

As for me, my travels have taken me to northern Plumba. I've found a place that I simply must show you! I know you don't carry the same love for nature that I do, but I've found the most remarkable forest. It's just beyond the region's walls, about two day's journey from the ocean. It's the greenest place I've ever seen in my life, and completely isolated among the trees and ruins. A crystal clear lake hides statues beneath its surface, like a mirror into humanity's ancient past. I spend my days drinking tea by the shore, reveling in the expansive sense of liberty.

I expect to be returning to Reverie soon. Perhaps, I'll even arrive before this letter does. It's been far too long since I've seen your face or heard your voice, and despite my resolve to keep learning, I fear I can't bear to be away from you for much longer. Send my love along to your family, those of them who are willing to accept it.

Yours,

Nick

I wondered if those were the same forests Sterling sometimes went to, and if they were, why would a mage go to them?

Was this letter written by Nicholas Armenia? It seemed like a good bet. He definitely knew Dorian and his family, but this wasn't what I'd expected at all. Had Dorian sent me to get his family's letters or something related to them? Why were these personal letters even here in the forbidden archives? It's not like they were dangerous.

I frowned and flipped through a few more things as Alexander handed them to me. There were a few receipts for purchases and a couple sketches of people I didn't recognize. One was a woman with pale, wispy hair. The other was a dark-haired man; something about his face reminded me of Gabriel, but I couldn't figure out exactly why.

"Why are you looking through these?" Alexander asked. "The Rosewood family has enough secrets without you having to go *digging*. I mean, half of Reverie suspects Dorian killed his mother—"

"Killed his mother?" I said, looking up quickly.

Alexander rolled his eyes. "Do you really think a perfectly healthy woman just fell down the stairs and broke her neck? Really?"

It *did* sound a little hard to believe, and Dorian did really hate Amelia. But he didn't seem like a murderer. And hadn't he expressed his own doubts about her death?

I suppose that's one way to get your inheritance! Lucian declared, laughing.

It wasn't funny.

"No, I—I just saw the name in a book or something," I

said awkwardly. "I wanted to learn more about Nicholas. It's for that essay I'm writing on...the discursive of sigils."

Hegemonic discourse, Lucian corrected.

What did that even *mean?*

"I don't see why it's a big deal," I added. "I mean, after all, you're here."

Alexander pinched the bridge of his nose.

"Why don't you know *anything?*"

"Because I'm not from here," I said.

"The archives are forbidden to everyone except grand mages, and the most powerful members of the Council. It's not a place to come looking for—for frivolous things."

Only *grand mages?* Dorian had failed to mention that little detail. But if that was true, why were Dorian's family letters here? What could be so dangerous about those? Maybe they'd been taken with the journal and gotten separated somehow.

"It isn't frivolous," I said. Though I wasn't entirely sure what the word meant, it sounded like an insult. "But it seems like what I'm looking for isn't here anyway," I said.

Alexander shook his head. "You...you've clearly never...ugh. These are only the ones that have been cataloged."

"Catalogued?"

"The archives encompass the entire third floor," Alexander replied. "Just—follow me."

As he cut across the archives, I trailed after him, taking extra care not to drop any of the letters. We continued our pace across the floor until we reached another room full of wooden crates stacked in high piles. Hundreds and hundreds of them.

"Whatever you're looking for, it's probably in here somewhere," Alexander said. "Assuming that it hasn't already been moved or discarded."

Great. These would take forever to get through.

"If it was moved," I said slowly, "where would it be?"

Alexander shrugged. "Maybe somewhere on display. Maybe downstairs. Sold to someone. Borrowed by a visiting professor. I don't know."

I sighed, leaning back against the coolness of the wall, suddenly realizing the enormity of the task. It would take weeks for me to go through this much material, which meant I'd have to keep attending classes and pretending to be a pupil, despite sucking at everything.

"My turn for questions," Alexander said, his voice low in the dark. "Are you still hearing the voices?"

I bit my lip, as Lucian practically shouted at me to keep my mouth shut.

"Yes," I said quietly. Alexander was so close, the lamp sparkling in the intensity of his eyes. I had no reason to trust him, but something made me want to.

"*How?*"

"What do you mean?" I asked.

"How can you just *hear* them? I've had to work to understand them, and I can just barely make things out sometimes, if I really concentrate, and if it's quiet enough. I've had to work for it, but you…you've just arrived here. And you can already do it."

"What are you trying to say?" I asked, crossing my arms.

"It's suspicious," he replied. "I don't know who you are, but I think you're involved in something very dark and dangerous," Alexander said, his voice soft, "And what I—"

My heart pounded madly in my chest. "I'm not involved in

anything," I said.

"But we didn't have demons running around until you came here," Alexander said. "Three attacks in as many days. And then you keep showing up where you don't belong."

"You think I'm summoning them?" I asked, my eyes widening.

"I don't know what to think," he said, frowning. "But there's something about you. Something you're hiding."

"I'm nothing special; I can assure you of that," I said.

"I don't believe you," he growled. "Not for a second."

A faint, metallic thud echoed from the floor beneath us. Alexander gripped my arm and held his finger up against his lips. Someone was coming.

***

Who would even be awake this early in the morning? Alexander swore and shot across the room. I followed, stuffing the letters into the pocket of my cloak. Alexander cleaned up his area, roughly scooping all his books onto a shelf.

"What do we do?" I asked.

"I don't know," Alexander replied.

I glanced at the windows above our heads and wondered if it would be possible to open them or break them. Because we were on the third floor, there would be an overhang. If we dropped down, we could climb in on the second floor and run, which would put us ahead of whoever was climbing up.

"What happens if we're caught?" I asked.

"I'll likely be fine, but you'll be expelled for sure," Alexander said.

Panic rose inside me.

"Just for looking at some old books?" I whispered, feeling faint.

"Books meant for grand mages!" Alexander hissed.

My stomach lurched, and bile rose in my throat. If I was expelled, I'd have outlived my usefulness. Dorian would return me to the Scraps, and Gabriel would make me pay for it. He'd hurt Briar, and maybe Sterling, too. Briar had already taken a crossbow bolt to the knee because of me, and Sterling had lost a finger. I didn't want to think about what else they'd lose if I failed.

"I can't be caught," I whispered.

There had to be some way out of this.

There is one way, Lucian murmured.

The sigil he'd taught me? The one with my blood. I drew the sword and hesitated. This might not work. But the footsteps were getting closer and closer. I had to do something to escape, and if there was a chance Lucian's sigil could save me, I had to take it.

Alexander blanched when I drew my sword, but then leaned in curiously as I slashed my palm and dipped my fingers into the pooling blood. I took a deep breath and stood on a crate to reach the window. My hand shook as I traced the symbol over the glass.

"What is that?" Alexander asked sharply.

"Something I read in a book."

"With your *blood?*"

The symbol glowed bright red and then vanished. I frowned as a sort of heaviness entered my head. Nothing had changed. The footsteps became louder.

No, no, Lucian muttered. *Touch it.*

I reached for the glass, but where my fingers should have met a solid substance, they passed through as easily as they would have passed through air. Instead of unlocking the window, I'd made it intangible.

"*How?*" Alexander asked, his eyes widening.

"You really want to know, or should we get out of here?"

Gripping the metal frame around the window, I hauled myself up and onto the rough stone. Then, I held out my hand and helped Alexander pull himself up beside me. I was careful not to lose the letters as I crept along the edge, staying low to the roof.

Your princeling had best hurry, Lucian said.

I glanced behind me, where Alexander was still clutching the frame of the window, looking down at the rooftops of Reverie.

"Hurry!" I hissed. The roofing was wide and sloped, and for once, I was grateful for all the climbing over uneven surfaces that I'd done in the Scraps. But I'd never been this high up before. My heart seemed to lodge itself in my throat. If I fell, I'd likely break my neck. Or be in a lot of pain, at least.

Don't focus on the height, Lucian muttered.

That was easier said than done. I moved further up, more quickly than Alexander, who seemed uncomfortable with moving at all.

"How long will that sigil be there?" I muttered.

Not long, Lucian said, *And even if someone finds it, I doubt they'll recognize it.*

I rounded a tower and ducked behind it. I sucked in a deep gulp of air and fixed my gaze upward, trying to quell the panic rising inside me. Below me, the Academy grounds stretched out far and wide. The sky was dark but quickly approaching daybreak. A crescent moon hung low in the sky, surrounded by twinkling stars and partially obscured by dark clouds.

Alexander rounded the tower and stood beside me, so close that I could sense every rise and fall of his chest as he caught his breath.

"Now what?" I looked across the roof and found a tower with a window.

"What's that?" I asked, pointing.

Alexander leaned around me. "Probably an office," he said, "But I don't know which."

I kept low as I moved across the roof. Alexander followed. We stopped when we came to the edge of the room, and saw the tower was actually on another building, separated by a narrow gap. "Hold these," I said, pushing the letters to him. I didn't trust them not to fall out of the loose pockets of my cloak. He stuffed them into his satchel and tightened it around his chest. I nodded, then took a deep breath, before taking a running jump across the chasm and landing lightly on the opposite building. Then I moved out of the way so he could follow me.

Alexander's landing was much harder. He banged his knee and rolled towards the edge before I caught his coat and pulled him back to safety. He collapsed beside me, and we lay still for a second, arms entwined.

"Um, thanks," he said, clearing his throat and pulling away. I hurried to the window and drew the sigil once more. The glass vanished, and I stepped inside the tower. Spots danced in my vision as Alexander entered after me. The stone around us seemed to spin. I thought of Jessa and how tired she'd been after using her magic. But I couldn't use magic, could I? Lucian must be powering the sigil somehow.

My steps grew clumsier as Alexander and I descended through the narrow tower. I stumbled and he wrapped an arm around my waist, guiding me down the spiral staircase. There were more steps than I cared to think about, but finally, we emerged on a flat, narrow corridor. I didn't recognize anything, but Alexander seemed to know where he was going. He grabbed my hand and pulled me forward. There were no windows here, leaving us in near darkness. I thought of reaching for the device in my pocket, but fire would draw too much attention. If these were professors' offices, the last thing I wanted was to draw one of them out.

Laughter filled the air. Alexander darted close to the wall, and I followed his lead. The laughter continued, followed by a soft murmuring.

"I think it's coming from inside one of the offices," Alexander said, his voice low.

"Why is everyone awake this early?" I whispered.

In the darkness, I saw Alexander shrug.

"Stay here," he murmured.

Alexander swept away from the wall and crept forward. He paused by a door, leaned his head against it, and then, motioned for me to follow. When I passed the door, I heard Professor Gareth's voice.

"I'm telling you—" the professor began.

I wondered who he was speaking to so early in the morning. Perhaps, it was the same woman I'd seen him with, the one with the beautiful white hair, who had disappeared so quickly.

Alexander and I kept walking, keeping our heads low. Finally, the area opened and I recognized our surroundings. We were on the floor above the ballroom, and when I looked down, I could see the sunrise casting everything in a bright, orange hue.

"This is where we part," Alexander said. "My dormitories are on the opposite side of the castle."

"Be careful," I said. I realized we were still holding hands and pulled away suddenly.

Alexander waved a dismissive hand. "Thank you for…" he trailed off. "Thank you for getting us out." He pulled out the stack of papers and returned them to me. "I hope these were worth it."

"It was nothing," I said.

Nothing? Lucian asked, sounding vaguely offended.

"It—" Alexander cut off abruptly, and his face twisted into a scowl, as if he suddenly realized he was being too nice to me. "Well, good luck."

Without another word, he spun and walked the other way.

What a charmer, Lucian drawled.

No kidding. But still…

He was awfully handsome, and maybe that mattered a little more than it should.

I left the ballroom and turned down a corridor, back to the dormitories. Once I reached them, I slipped inside. For a few seconds, I waited, worried that the creaking door might have given me away. When none of the other girls stirred, I sighed softly and tip-toed back to my bed. I slipped the papers into the trunk at the foot of my bed and then climbed beneath the covers. Come the weekend, I'd take Dorian these letters to buy some more time. It had to be enough, for now. Maybe I'd even try to drop something for Briar and Sterling. Then, I'd have to work towards finding that journal, which meant revisiting the archives and hoping it was there somewhere. Unfortunately, if I was going to stick around longer, that meant I might actually have to start doing my homework.

EIGHTEEN

DELACROIX'S SWORDSMANSHIP CLASS TOOK PLACE outside. Past the sprawling gardens, there were fields of flat, grassy plains as far as I could see. It was a nice day, sunlit and breezy. I stood awkwardly around, rocking back on my heels and looking over my classmates, who were chatting together in small clusters. This *might* be the one class I could actually do well in. Swordsmanship wasn't a solely magical pursuit, and while I'd never learned proper fencing, I wasn't nervous around bladed weapons. I'd used knives and daggers before. I was even good with throwing them and hitting targets, something which had saved my skin a few times.

I like swordplay, Lucian said.

"It's too bad you didn't wait for Alexander or someone," I replied. "You might have—"

I, for one, am quite happy I wasn't chosen by Alexander, Lucian said. *Even as mages go, he's exceptionally intolerable.*

"He's not that bad," I muttered. "He explained the archives to me, and he sort of helped me find my way back to my room."

You saved him, if I recall, Lucian argued. *And he's only being nice because it's convenient for him. You can't trust him.*

"Funny, he said the same about you," I smiled.

I knew Lucian was right, I had no business hanging around a prince. Which was frustrating, because I couldn't get him out of my mind.

"Did you...how *did* you end up in this sword?" I asked awkwardly, changing the subject and hoping Lucian would drop Alexander entirely.

Lucian said nothing, but I felt him shifting and thinking. *The way most demons find themselves imprisoned, I suppose*, he said. *We fight a mage or two. Sometimes, it ends well for us. Sometimes, it doesn't.*

"Did you get to show off your swordplay, at least?"

Most definitely, Lucian said, but he didn't elaborate.

"So can you all make fire?" I whispered.

Or was Lucian even making fire? Maybe he was manipulating the device somehow.

No, Lucian said. *That device of yours doesn't make actual fire. It can only cast illusions and create light.*

I knew that. Sure, there had been the time at my testing when the drapes caught fire, but that had likely been Dorian's doing.

Lucian seemed to grow still in my mind.

Have you ever seen him use fire?

"No, but I'm sure he probably can. He's made ice, after all."

I think you should ask. But your device uses an entirely different branch of magic from elemental powers. And we all have different abilities. But I can only create fire because I'm recently captured. The longer demons exist in objects, the weaker we become.

"Weaker?" I asked.

We lose our magic and our wills, ourselves, Lucian said. *It's really a terrible fate, Wynter. Some of us, after we've been imprisoned for so long, can accomplish only weak, little magics. Imprisonment can take the strongest of us and reduce them to cleaning floors and windows. And eventually, you slowly lose things. Memories usually fade first, and after that, it's just...so terrible.*

"I'm sorry," I muttered.

I know you are.

"Is that why the demons are attacking?" I asked.

I don't know, Lucian replied, his voice careful. *I suspect those demons might not be attacking of their own volition.*

"Why would you assume that?"

Because if demons were trying to conquer Reverie or something, they wouldn't target schoolchildren. That wouldn't be advantageous.

"Maybe it's an assassination attempt. Alexander and Viviane are both important."

Maybe.

Alexander walked onto the field, Viviane with them.

Why is he even here? Lucian asked. *He already knows how to fight. She probably does, too, and they aren't even studying battle magic.*

"I'm in sigils class," I pointed out, "And I *am* studying battle magic. Maybe everyone has to take some of the same classes. Gareth did say we needed a variety."

I'd be delighted if you fought Alexander and absolutely obliterated him.

"Why?" I asked.

Because I don't like him, Lucian said bluntly.

"He's trying to understand you," I said softly.

And? He can't even understand girls his own age and of his own race. Do you honestly believe he'll ever understand my kind?

"Wouldn't you rather he try, though?"

Lucian made a disgruntled noise.

You're assuming his interest in demons is noble, and I really doubt that.

"And here you are telling me that *I* don't trust people," I whispered.

Still.

"But if you were going to guess," I said slowly, "Why would someone want to attack the Academy?"

Not the Academy. Children at the Academy, Lucian corrected, *and I don't know. Maybe this person is after something in the Academy. Maybe they're trying to ruin the Council's reputation.*

"How would a demon attack achieve that?" I asked.

Aren't they supposed to be the experts on magical matters?

"From what I can gather."

It doesn't look good if… Lucian trailed off, considering… *It doesn't look good if the Council can't find a cause for both the quakes and the demon attacks, and so far, aristocratic children have been attacked, right?*

"Aside from me," I said, "I think that's right."

Hm.

"So," I said quietly, "you think someone might be trying to make the Council and the aristocracy fight one another?"

It's a possibility, Lucian said. *Divide and conquer.*

My head spun, trying to figure it out. I didn't really understand politics at all. Professor Delacroix arrived, rapier in hand. She was a tall woman, the tallest I'd ever seen. Her hair was short and dark, and she had sharp brown eyes. My first thought was that she looked too young to be a professor. I was terrible at judging ages, but she looked to be in her early thirties.

She didn't introduce herself; she just jumped straight in and demonstrated stances, while we copied them.

You should bend your knees more, Lucian said, as I moved into a fighting stance.

I did, making adjustments. This actually wasn't so bad. I knew a bit about fighting without swords, and the stances weren't that different from those.

"Pair up!" Delacroix announced.

I quickly counted my classmates and realized we had an even number; this meant that someone would, inevitably, have to come over and be my opponent. I didn't know anyone in this class aside from Alexander and Viviane. It was too bad Jessa wasn't there.

Maybe you should try meeting new people, Lucian said.

"You hate literally everyone here," I murmured.

It's different degrees of hate.

"Where do I fall?"

Lucian laughed. *You have the dubious honor of being the one person here that I like*, he said.

I smiled slightly and rocked back on my heels. To my surprise, Alexander walked over to me, leaving Viviane to pair with someone else. I felt Viviane's eyes burning into me, even when I turned away. If looks were really able to kill, I'd have been struck by lightning.

"Did you come over here to beat me up?" I asked.

"No," he said. "I came to…thank you, I suppose. For this morning."

He sounds like he's choking on something, Lucian said.

"It was nothing," I said, "And you already thanked me."

"I just thought maybe I didn't thank you enough. That's

all." He paused, and brushed his hair away from his face. "The way you jumped across the roof like that… you're not like other girls, are you?"

"The other girls in Reverie you mean? Maybe you need to get out more."

"Maybe I do." He smiled, and my insides turned to butter.

"Where did you learn such powerful blood magic?" he murmured. "If it was really in a book, I would have found it by now."

Don't tell him.

"You'll never figure it out," I said. "Maybe there's more in Argent than you realized."

Alexander slowly nodded, as if considering the possibility.

"How often do you look in the archives?" I asked, keeping my voice low.

"Why?" Alexander narrowing his eyes. "Do you have plans on looking again?"

Does he know how to give a straight answer, or does mage royal etiquette include being as infuriatingly obtuse as possible? Lucian snapped.

"That isn't the first time I've almost been caught," he said. It was a warning, to make sure I understood the risk. I nodded quickly. I still wasn't sure if Lucian's sigil worked on the doors Alexander had opened, and if sliced myself open each night I wanted to visit the archives, I'd be too exhausted to attend classes and keep up the ruse of being an ordinary student.

"I might consider a partnership," he said, "With you. Assuming our goals align."

My heart fluttered a little at the thought of sneaking around with Alexander at night. But I'd have to be careful not to get too close. He was a prince after all, and I was pretty sure Dorian wouldn't want his schemes shared with the royal family. But before we could finish our conversation, class began.

"Let's start, everyone!" Delacroix exclaimed. "Remember your form!"

Alexander moved into a fighting stance.

"I have no idea what I'm doing," I said, "Just so you know."

He stifled a laugh. "That's quite apparent," he said. "Let me help."

I stood still as he adjusted my arms, lifting them slightly. It didn't feel like a comfortable position. If Delacroix hadn't walked by and given us a nod, I'd have assumed Alexander was trying to sabotage me. But warmth tingled through me with the slightest touch from his fingers. I caught myself staring at the way his lower lip rounded in concentration and the way his pale, blonde hair fell into his face, and a flush rose to my cheeks. Maybe he wouldn't notice, even though his gaze was focused right on me.

"You're very good at this," I said.

Alexander stepped back a few steps and tipped his head slightly forward. "Remember that the rapier is a thrusting weapon," Alexander said, "And give it a try."

I took a deep breath and thrust, trying to remember everything Delacroix had said about poise and posture. Alexander parried easily. "Was that good?" I asked.

"Terrible," he said, with a wry grin.

He's so encouraging, isn't he?

I frowned and thrust again. Another parry.

"You're not putting much force behind it," Alexander said.

"I don't want to hurt you," I lied.

Truthfully, I was just really bad at this.

"It's a *rapier*," Alexander said. "It isn't as if you're going to take my head off with it. At worst, I'll need a couple of sigils. That's assuming, of course, that you even *land* a blow."

I tried thrusting again, but Alexander was just too fast. Then, he went onto the offensive. I struggled to parry and tried backing away, but he kept following. Alexander probably could've chased me all around the field if he wanted. His blade swept past mine and tapped against the side of my neck, just as I tripped over a rock and tumbled into the grass.

"Looks like you're dead," he said.

"This isn't how I imagined dying, to be honest," I said.

Alexander raised an eyebrow, smirking. "How did you imagine it?"

So many different ways. People in the Scraps didn't live very long. If starvation or disease didn't kill us young, gangs or monsters did. My uncle snapping and killing me in a fit of rage was always an option, too. But I couldn't tell Alexander any of that.

"I don't know," I said, "Just not like this."

Alexander hummed and lowered his blade.

"Switch partners!" Delacroix announced.

Switch? We had to find someone else?

Alexander held out his hand and pulled me to my feet. He remained close to me, his arm on my elbow. The sunlight caught his eyes, catching the flecks of green and blue.

"Good match," he said.

He hadn't dropped my hand. Instead, he lingered. His finger gently swept over the delicate underside of my wrist, caressing the skin above the sleeve of my shirt.

"Consider my offer," he murmured, his breath hot against my neck. "I think we can probably help one another."

We don't need his help, Lucian said. *Tell him to throw himself off the edge of the kingdom.*

"I'll consider it," I said, speaking to Alexander rather than Lucian.

"Good," Alexander said. "I'd make a good ally, Wynter."

Potentially, Lucian muttered, sounding far from thrilled with the idea.

After he left, on to his next partner, I remained with my hand extended for just an instant. My skin tingled from where he'd touched me. I winced as Viviane stormed over, rapier in hand. But then, my eyes widened. This was the first time I'd seen her up close that day, and she looked awful. Her skin was very pale, noticeable even with her flushed face. Her breathing was hard; maybe her last opponent had given her a good fight.

"Let's go!" Viviane said, skipping any greeting.

I moved into a fighting stance. She struck first. I parried successfully, but her blows were fierce. Vibrations traveled down my arms. I thrust, but Viviane stepped aside easily. We exchanged blows, none of them landing. Clearly, this wasn't Viviane's first lesson in swordplay. She was fast and precise, and I only barely managed to keep parrying. It was too bad we weren't fighting with knives. I might have had the advantage, then. But swordsmanship was something else entirely.

And yet after a few minutes, Viviane seemed visibly strained. Her breaths came out alarmingly hard. I considered throwing the fight just so she'd stop.

I made a mistake, and Viviane swept in, bringing the blade

of her rapier against my neck. She smiled in triumph, baring her teeth.

"Nice win," I said, extending my hand.

Viviane scrunched up her face, and rather than shaking my hand, she raised hers and brushed a few strands of blonde hair from her eyes. For the first time, I noticed that she had a cut stretching across her bicep, just peeking out from beneath the sleeve of her dress. It was tiny, just an inch or so in length. I wondered how it had happened. It was an odd place to get a scratch.

"Of course, I won," Viviane huffed. "I've practiced swordplay since I was eight, and my father taught me everything he knows."

I hesitated. "You don't look so good," I said. "Is everything alright?"

"Oh, like you care!" Viviane snapped.

"I do care," I said carefully. "If you're sick or—"

Viviane grabbed my arm and pulled me closer. Her green eyes, cat-like and dark, looked me over with a sort of frantic, uneasy energy. "Stay away from Alexander," Viviane hissed. "I don't know what he sees in you, but you are not ruining my chances with him."

"I'm not trying to," I said.

"Sure, you aren't," Viviane snapped.

Delacroix whistled sharply, and all the fights stopped. Viviane slowly dropped my arm and stormed back to Alexander's side.

"Everyone did an excellent job today," Delacroix said, her eyes lingering on me, "More or less."

I winced.

"We'll continue practicing next week, although I do recommend practicing outside of classes. Swordplay isn't something that you magically succeed at. It's something that takes a good deal of time, effort, and dedication, and it's best that you practice at least every other day, preferably with a partner," Delacroix said. "You aren't going to be winning duels or mastering battle magic just by practicing once a week."

I sheathed the rapier. Hopefully, I'd never *have* to master battle magic, though I wouldn't turn down free fencing lessons before returning to the Scraps. I seriously doubted any of my classmates would offer to be my sparring partner. Maybe Alexander would consider making that part of our partnership.

Don't be ridiculous, Lucian said. *I'll teach you.*

"Really?" I asked, as I headed back to the Academy.

Of course. I'm a superior swordsman to Alexander anyway.

I arched an eyebrow, unsure if Lucian was serious or if this was some sort of masculine pride thing. But still, a sparring partner was a sparring partner. I had to maintain my cover until I found the journal, so I couldn't afford to get kicked out of the Academy, which meant I needed to get good at *something*. I'd picked swords because it was physical, something I could understand, and manage—but today I'd learned it was much harder than I'd imagined, all control, not wild swinging. And sure, I could practice, but a few weeks' worth of practice wouldn't put me anywhere close to people like Viviane and Alexander, who'd practiced all their lives.

***

That evening, I went down for dinner. The Academy had

a general dinner time and a dining hall, which I tried to avoid. Most often, I grabbed a few things to eat and went somewhere else, like the gardens or the dormitories. Whichever had less people. Francisca had drilled me in proper etiquette for weeks, slapping the back of my hands with a silver spoon whenever I did something wrong, but it would be too easy to make a casual mistake with so many people watching.

Today however, I wanted to try dropping something for Briar and Sterling, so I grabbed two plates and loaded them up. The problem with food was that it eventually went bad, but living in the Scraps, I'd learned not to be choosy. So had Briar and Sterling. Fruit seemed like a good choice, so I grabbed apples and oranges.

When one of the cooks looked strangely at me, I gave her a toothy smile. "It's for my study group," I lied, trying not to sound awkward about it.

But no one really seemed to care, so I grabbed a couple of muffins and a large handful of roasted cashews, along with a dozen raspberry-creme biscuits I knew my brother would love. Only when I could barely carry the plates without something falling off, did I decide it was enough. I returned to the dormitory, and noting with relief that it was empty, I placed the plates on my bed. Then I dug around through my trunk, searching for something to carry everything in. I couldn't just drop them one at a time, after all.

I pulled out the long, white dress. I could tear that up and wrap the food in it. No, that wouldn't do. It would be better to wrap the food in something warm, so Sterling or Briar would also have something they could wear or sell. During the winter months, wool and heavier fabrics fetched a good price in the

Scraps. Of course, this was assuming my uncle didn't get ahold of it. I pulled a scarlet red cape from my trunk and laid it across my bed. After wrapping the fruits in a wool scarf, the nuts in a pair of knotted up gloves, and the muffins in a thin linen shirt, I bundled them all into the cape and tied it up together. I tucked the letters into my coat pocket.

My arms full, I left the dormitories and the Academy grounds. It was nearing sunset, and the sky was awash with bright and vibrant colors. I walked at a quick pace, enjoying the wind in my hair. Rakes swept across the ground, brushing leaves into piles. There were people everywhere, milling through the streets. I walked past them and headed towards the place where I'd been the night I'd seen Professor Gareth and his friend. The place where Reverie overlooked the Scraps.

When I reached it, there were a few people scattered here and there. So I kept walking, edging down the fence until I saw no one. I didn't know if it was *illegal* to drop anything down from Reverie, but I couldn't risk unusual behavior. I was pretty sure this spot was the closest to my home. I bit my lip and glanced around me to make sure I was alone.

Then, I carefully wedged the cloak-wrapped fruits through the metal patterns of the fence. The fruits fell in a burst of red fabric, dipping beneath a layer of clouds. It was about the time Sterling and I usually headed to the Dregs, so I hoped he'd see them. If I did this every weekend, Sterling or Briar might be able to catch onto the pattern. I leaned out as the fruits vanished from view, pushing my head against the bars. I couldn't see where they landed. A gust of wind tilted the fence slightly, quickening my pulse.

I felt sick, imagining the fence breaking and sending me

toppling forward, down through the clouds from Reverie. Once, when I was very little, my uncle and I came across the body of a man in the Scraps. His bones had been shattered, and there was so much blood. My uncle said he'd fallen from the Floats. After that, I barely slept for a week, imagining bodies raining from the sky. Later I found out one of his own men had beaten the man to death.

I backed away from the fence, shivering and pulling my coat tighter. But before I left, I gazed back wistfully. Everything below was so gray and flat, with just a few tiny pinpricks of light from fires and lanterns. I said a silent prayer that Sterling and Briar were surviving without me.

I'm sorry they aren't with you, Lucian said. *I, too, know how it feels to be separated from your family.*

"It's not great," I muttered, staring down at the Scraps.

"But it's complicated," I said, trying to distract myself from how far up I was. "I don't miss my uncle. I don't miss *living* like that. It's nice being here. Sometimes. Even though the people don't like me very much."

I continued along the path, until I heard hisses. I tightened my hand on the letters in my pocket, and prepared to draw the rapier, but no demon appeared. I was alone, save for the two people walking ahead of me. It took me a few seconds to recognize Professor Gareth and the woman on his arm.

"—now, I think the problem," the woman said, "is that the aristocracy is so convinced that magic is *solely* the domain of the Council. Most of these aristocrats forget that they, too, are mages and responsible for the safety of this kingdom."

Gareth sighed. "Perhaps, that's part of it," he said, "But we've had these attacks happen before. You remember."

Have they? Lucian asked.

Yes. Someone had mentioned a rogue mage. The pathway was lined with large, red-berried shrubs. I remembered Dorian's warning about eavesdropping, but this seemed like a good chance to actually get some answers. I climbed behind the bushes, bending my knees to remain hidden. I hurried along until I walked beside Gareth and the woman. I caught flashes of them between the leaves and branches, but they didn't seem to see me. And it was growing darker.

"Yes," the woman said, "But we don't know that there's a connection."

The hissing continued, but it was a low rumble, like the sizzling noise of animal fat dripping on hot charcoal. Still no demon. I furrowed my brow.

Maybe there's a demon elsewhere? Lucian asked. *Or maybe you're hearing something else. That happened the last time you were here.*

"We don't," Gareth agreed, "But thus far, Viviane *has* been present during each of those attacks."

"But why would anyone wish to harm Viviane?" the woman asked.

"Perhaps, someone believes she's carrying Guinevere's charm and is trying to confirm their suspicions."

What charm?

"I have no idea," I whispered.

A pause. I suspected Gareth might be looking around to see if anyone was near. "We shouldn't speak of these matters aloud," he said.

But I wanted to know! Why would anyone want to hurt Viviane?

"But perhaps, I'm seeing connections where there are

none," he admitted, sounding resigned. "I'm so afraid, Elaine. Afraid for my students, afraid for Reverie—"

"You should be afraid for yourself," the woman, Elaine, replied. "If you speak too much…"

"I know the dangers," Gareth said.

"So did Guinevere," Elaine replied, "And look at her."

What did that mean? Did Elaine suspect Guinevere *hadn't* really killed herself?

Hisses. I barely noticed them now. Whatever I was hearing, it hadn't attacked me yet. Maybe it *was* just something about this place. Gareth and Elaine halted, and I crouched lower. When I peered through the bushes, I could see that they stood very close together.

"I don't know what I would do without you," Elaine said softly.

"I think you'd do fine," Gareth replied. "You've always been strong like that."

Elaine sighed. "Are you certain," she said, "That I can't convince you to go elsewhere? Somewhere far away. Beryl, perhaps. Maybe the outskirts of Argent."

"I've too much that needs done here, Dearest," Gareth replied.

"I know," Elaine said, "But sometimes, I wish you would think of yourself first."

"I'll be careful," he promised.

"I know. Is this where we part?"

"Yes," Gareth replied. "Good night, my love."

The bush beside me rustled. I jumped at the sound and felt a bit silly when I realized it was just a stray cat. Its yellow eyes glared from the darkness. When I looked up again, Elaine was gone. For a second, I wondered if she'd jumped. I raised my head just a little over the bushes and found Professor Gareth walking alone, as if nothing was wrong. Elaine was nowhere to be found.

NINETEEN

BY THE TIME I ARRIVED at Rosewood, it was already dark. I stepped around the fence and walked up the entryway, but hesitated before walking up the steps. This place looked especially foreboding at night. I remembered what Alexander said about half the kingdom thinking Dorian had killed his mother, and how Elaine implied Guinevere's death hadn't been a suicide. Could Dorian have killed her, too? What if he just had a penchant for slaughtering his female relatives? There had been a fairy tale about that, hadn't there?

"Miss Wilcox?"

I turned at the sound of my name. A woman stood several yards away. I squinted, trying to figure out if I knew her. Francisca, I realized. She walked towards me, swinging the basket looped over her arm. As she reached me, she dusted specks of dirt off her trousers. "Have you come to see my Lord?" she asked.

"Is he busy?" I asked. I was half hoping she would take the letters and let me leave.

"I'm sure he'll make an exception for you," Francisca said.

THE SOURCE OF MAGIC

"Follow me."

I'd assumed we'd go into the house, but instead, she led me around the side of the house, through the gardens. When I glimpsed into Francisca's basket, I saw it was filled with dark blue cherry-like fruits.

We found Dorian sitting on the ground before a large green bush, bearing the same fruit in Francisca's basket. Seeing us, he climbed to his feet. He pulled a lit cigar from between his teeth, and let out a long, smoke-filled breath.

"Wynter," he said, exhaling more smoke with my name. It floated into the air and arranged itself into small animal shapes before dissipating.

"Viviane said you'd come to see me," I said.

"Just checking in, making sure you're settled. I hope you've had time to visit the library?"

"I got into the restricted section," I said. "There's a lot of material, but most of it is unsorted."

"I see," he said, taking another long puff on his cigar. I pulled the letters from my coat pocket and held them out. Dorian took them and opened the top letter. For a few seconds, he silently skimmed its contents.

"Is that like what you wanted?" I asked.

"It's related to what I wanted," Dorian replied thoughtfully.

He didn't sound angry. I couldn't help but think of Amelia, but there wasn't really a tactful way to ask if Dorian had murdered his mother. And maybe all the rumors got it wrong. I shouldn't jump to conclusions before I had all the information.

"I'll keep looking through the rest of the archives. It's a lot of ground to cover," I said. "It might take a week, or more…"

"Good," he replied, without looking up from the letter. "Fran, I trust you have this handled? I'm going inside to read these more carefully."

For a second, I thought I saw a flicker of disappointment cross Francisca's face, but it was gone so quickly that I wondered if I'd imagined it. "Yes, Your Lordship," she said.

"I'll join you when I'm finished," Dorian added, "If there's still work to be done."

"I should get back to the Academy," I said, backing away.

"Nonsense," Dorian replied. "You'll stay the night. It's far too late for a young lady to be wandering alone at night, especially with the recent demon attacks. Do you remember where your rooms are?"

"Not exactly." Not from here anyway. The mansion was enormous and I'd never been into the backyard before. My face warmed as I followed Dorian inside, scrambling to think of an excuse not to stay with him.

Just don't close your eyes! Lucian exclaimed gleefully.

We entered through the back doors and emerged between the twin staircases that ran up to the second floor. Dorian snapped his fingers and lights flicked on, casting warm light down the stairs. I wondered if those were the same stairs Amelia had fallen down. We headed upstairs and down a corridor; most of the halls were a soft, brown-red color and decorated with tapestries and giant paintings, a lot of them featuring people who—I assumed—were related to Dorian in some way.

Quite suddenly, I realized that, aside from his servants, nobody except Dorian lived here. It seemed like too much space to go unused.

"Are you married?" I asked. Dorian was reading as he

walked, but he looked up long enough to answer.

"I haven't found a sufficiently advantageous match to make that worthwhile yet," he said.

He'd probably throw her down the stairs anyway.

I choked. Dorian opened a door and bowed; I couldn't decide whether he was mocking me or trying to tease me. "Your rooms," he said.

"Thank you," I replied. "Um…enjoy reading your letters and picking fruit. I guess."

"Fruit? That was deadly nightshade," Dorian said. "You'd only mistake it for fruit once."

"Why do you have…?" I trailed off.

"For poisoning my enemies, of course," Dorian replied with a wink. "Try not to let the ghosts of them keep you awake, little mage."

He was *definitely* playing some sort of trick on me.

I stepped inside the room and rocked back on my heels. "I don't believe in ghosts."

His face softened. "Ghosts exist, Wynter. Just not like you might expect."

***

Despite all the talk of ghosts, I slept soundlessly through the night. My room at Rosewood was spacious and quiet, unlike the dorms. This time I made full use of the soft mattress, and when I woke up, the early morning light streaming in the window chased away all my fears from the night before.

Dorian was already gone, but Francisca made me waffles with butter and syrup before I headed back to the Academy. I had a lot to think about, and I understood very little of it. If anything, listening in on Professor Gareth had made things more confusing. What was this charm he'd mentioned? Is that why Dorian wanted Viviane's necklace? Why would Elaine suspect Guinevere hadn't killed herself? I thought about asking Dorian if he knew, but I wasn't sure if *that* was a conversation I really wanted to have. Questioning a dead sister's suicide definitely seemed like a line that I shouldn't cross. And then, there was Elaine, who had seemingly vanished into thin air. I didn't know *what* to make of that, but I was sure that knowledge wasn't something I ought to just spread around. It was obvious Gareth and the woman were trying to keep their relationship a secret, maybe he was just having an illicit affair of some kind.

I crossed into the Academy grounds, my boots crunching on the early morning frost. The weather had warmed a bit, and more of the snow had melted, but it was still colder up here than it ever had been down in the Scraps. As I passed the ballroom, heading back to my dormitory, I saw Alexander in the nook that stretched across the second floor, extending into the balcony. He was leaning against the railing of the stairwell, reading a book, illuminated by the sunlight filtering through the glass. I bit the inside of my cheek as I watched him reading. He was wearing a charcoal gray suit that fit him perfectly, with a purple cape pinned at the shoulders. Despite having told him I'd consider his proposed alliance, I hadn't really thought much about it.

"Good morning," I said.

Alexander inclined his head in greeting.

"Are you going out tonight?" he asked, his voice low.

"I might," I replied.

Alexander nodded. "If you want to meet me at the

library…" he trailed off.

I think we'd do fine on our own, Lucian said. *Tell him to sit on his sword!*

I was *not* going to tell him that.

"Yes," I replied.

"Good," Alexander said. "I'll see you, then."

I nodded and leaned against the railing beside him, suddenly in no rush to leave. Alexander smiled at me, then went back to his book as I studied him. His haughty arrogance had been replaced by something much warmer; a relaxed confidence that was calming just to be around. He was the only person who knew I was hearing voices, and rather than condemning me for it, he was intrigued. By *me*. I dared to let myself wonder whether we were becoming friends, of a sort. A student with bright red hair walked past us. I saw her from the corner of my eye and scanned my mind, trying to recall her name. Tatiana. That was it.

"Crazy Tati," Alexander whispered under his breath. Just when I thought he wasn't so bad, he let out his inner asshole again. I glanced at Tatiana, but she didn't seem to have heard the remark.

"What do you—"

A hissing screech filled the room, so loud it shook the walls. I moved into a fighting stance. Alexander backed away from the balcony. Tatiana remained frozen in place. "What was that?" I asked.

"Let's not find out," Alexander said. He grabbed my arm and steered me towards the stairs, just as sound exploded behind us. Tatiana screamed and dove for the wall. The floor before me crystalized, ice forming and creeping up the wall. The windows across from me had busted in and lay in glittering shards on the floor below us. I brought my gaze upwards in time to see a massive, black dragon slip inside. Its clawed feet gripped the haggard remains of the window frame, as it snaked its head and fixed its large, blue eyes on us. When the dragon opened its wide mouth, ice spread across the walls. I'd always heard that dragons breathed fire; I wasn't sure one breathing ice was better.

Alexander still held my arm in a death-grip. We backed against the wall. I shook off Alexander's grip and unsheathed my blade; Lucian's flames burst immediately along the edge. Tatiana picked her way down the stairs; she was smart, keeping her back to the wall. I followed her. After only a few steps, I felt a sudden and strange tiredness, but I brushed it away. It was probably just a result of using Lucian's fire. Alexander came after me, his pen ready.

With a crash, the demon swept in. Its tail crashed into the stairs, spraying ice along the wood and carpet. There was a terrible sound, and I registered the stairs were crumbling before I realized we were falling. The impact with the floor below was sudden and sent throbbing, sharp pain up my left arm. Something pierced my leg. I felt the hotness of blood, and when I struggled to my feet, I stumbled. My mind raced, trying to find Alexander and Tatiana beneath the debris littered around me.

Tatiana's forehead was bleeding, but she was conscious. She screamed when the dragon stepped closer, spreading its massive wings. With a roar, the demon dipped its head and thrashed, as if it was being attacked by some invisible force. Then it swung its head back towards me and bared its teeth. Alexander crouched on the ground and drew a sigil I didn't recognize. Fire arched from the ground and lapped at the demon's legs. Its body began to melt like ice.

Tatiana gasped and clamped a hand over her nose, blood dripping from between her fingers. She must have used too much magic. The dragon burst from Alexander's flames and lunged towards us. I tightened my grip on my rapier, with a very badly conceived, half-formed thought of attacking.

Do it, Lucian said.

When the dragon came close again, I thrust the rapier forward. The fiery blade slipped between the demon's scales and sank in past the skin. I felt something tougher give way, maybe muscle, until the blade was lodged all the way to the hilt. The demon screamed inside my mind, and I felt a piercing agony in my chest, as if I could feel the creature's pain. Blue fire burst around me when I pulled the blade free.

My arm hurt so badly I was dizzy with pain, my leg throbbed, and there was this new, deep ache inside me. I just wanted everything to stop, and the second that I hesitated felt like a century stretched before me.

I remembered the gala where Dorian had slain a demon without any hesitation. He'd encased it in ice and shattered it apart. But I didn't want to kill this demon. What if it was like the ones Lucian had told me about? Imprisoned so long he'd lost all reason. Now, finally freed, maybe he was just trying to escape. But then, why was it attacking us?

The demon's head snapped forward, its teeth shining in the dim light. Tatiana screamed as it dove towards her. I stabbed upwards, through the roof of the dragon's mouth. Fire burst from the sword. My knees shook and threatened to buckle beneath me. The world spun, and all the colors around me rushed together. The dragon grew slack as I pulled the sword free. Blue blood dripped along the blade's silvery surface and pooled between my fingers. Slowly, I sank to the ground and gasped for air. I pulled my injured arm close to me and curled around it, as the dragon thrashed on the ground below me.

"Wynter!"

It was Delacroix, with Celeste at her heels.

"Alexander! Tatiana!" Delacroix exclaimed. "Is everyone all right?"

Celeste didn't say a word. She swept to the ground and began drawing the sigils, presumably to seal the demon away. Delacroix was talking to Alexander, but all her words seemed to come from far away, and I couldn't make out their meaning.

I felt frozen, watching as the demon became encased in bright light. Was that how my sword had been created? Was this what happened to Lucian? The dragon sank its talons into the walls, ripping off shreds of wallpaper, desperate to escape.

Celeste drew a shimmering, amethyst crystal, about the size of her palm, and tossed it forward. The demon's wings were spread, and I stared at the membrane of them. They were beautiful. Like darkness and starlight, a deep purple cut by spots of brilliant blue. And below that, there were sigils that gleamed faintly.

But if there were sigils…

Then, it's a mage controlling them, Lucian murmured. *And it must be a very powerful mage to control a demon like that.*

I gasped for breath, and my blood seemed to freeze in my veins. I trembled as the dragon screamed and thrashed. It shrank smaller and smaller, before it was finally pulled into the gemstone and trapped.

"Wynter," Delacroix said. "Are you all right? Are you

injured anywhere?"

I snapped my head towards her.

"There were sigils on it," I said, "Doesn't that mean someone was—"

"You're mistaken," Delacroix said simply. "I think you may have hit your head."

I hadn't, though. I knew I hadn't. I felt a little fuzzy, but I wasn't imagining things. I shook my head. "I saw sigils," I repeated, more slowly this time so they'd understand. "On the dragon. Maybe I could draw them out—"

"There weren't any sigils on it," Celeste interrupted. "Wynter, I was right beside it, and I didn't see them."

"But I…" I trailed off. How had they missed them?

I *had* seen them, hadn't I?

You did, Lucian replied. *They're lying to you.*

But why?

"Here," Delacroix said, helping me to my feet.

I stumbled against her. My leg had gone numb, but my arm still ached. And I felt like I just wanted to…to…

"Alexander, Tatiana," Celeste said. "Don't worry. We'll get you fixed up."

Tatiana looked as pale as death. For the first time, I noticed the blood on Alexander's shirt, just over his collarbone. "Did you see them?" I asked dizzily.

"No," Alexander said curtly.

Something flashed in Tatiana's wide, green eyes. Maybe some sort of deep-seated sympathy, so profound that I couldn't really understand it.

I had to lean on Delacroix just to walk. Dimly, I heard the clatter of metal and realized I'd dropped the rapier. Dropped

Lucian. Why were my professors all lying to me?

They're mages, Lucian said. They always lie.

TWENTY

WHEN I WOKE, I WASN'T sure where I was. Everything was sparse and white. I moved my arm and noticed it felt heavy and sluggish. There was a sort of dull pain all over and a persistent fuzziness at the edge of my vision. Or was it my vision? Maybe it was just my head in general. I saw beds to my right. A girl lay in one, her red hair pulled back. It was like…I couldn't hold the thought. It was like something.

"Am I dead?" I asked.

"Hardly."

I turned my head to the left. A dark-haired man sat nearby, wiping a cloth over my rapier, and my breath hitched at the sight of him. "I—I'm getting up, Uncle. This isn't—"

"I'm not Gabriel, Wynter."

I blinked a few times, trying to figure out if that was right. It sounded right. I couldn't remember my uncle's eyes being that pale blue color. I couldn't remember him ever wearing *lilac* either; that dye cost too much.

"Take your time. You've been unconscious for a few days now."

It wasn't Gabriel. I knew this man, though. What was his name? All at once, my vision cleared and my memories came rushing back.

"I'm sorry, Dorian," I said, unsure of what I was even apologizing for.

"Don't be. Considering the amount of magic you used, some disorientation is to be expected."

I hadn't been apologizing for that, though. I didn't think.

He doesn't seem surprised that you used magic, does he?

Lucian. That was Lucian. I furrowed my brow and tried to figure out if Dorian *should* be surprised or not.

"The state you left this blade in, however…" Dorian trailed off. He finished wiping the blade and turned it into the light. It was as brilliant as ever. No evidence remained of it having run through a demon. *I* ran it through a demon.

"Thank you," I said.

Dorian nodded. "It's a nice sword," he said. "I could give Lillian an earful for leaving it in such a horrific state."

"Lillian?"

"Delacroix," Dorian replied. "As an accomplished swordsman, I'd expect she'd know something about sword upkeep."

I frowned, unsure if he was trying to be funny.

"Are…are Tatiana and Alexander all right?"

"About the same as you," Dorian replied. "Alexander has already returned to his room. Last I saw, Viv was with him."

I forced myself up onto my forearms; everything felt sore and numb. Dorian tensed, like he wanted to help but wasn't sure how. "What happened to me?" I asked.

"You defeated a demon. You fell unconscious, and you

woke up here with a broken arm and a gash on your leg," Dorian said, "With some expected magical fatigue."

Yes, I realized suddenly. Dorian ought to be surprised I'd used magic, but he didn't seem to be. Maybe it was best not to ask about that, though. Because *I* wasn't using magic. Not on my own.

"And you're here?" I asked.

"Of course, I am. You were injured."

"You're weird," I said.

"That isn't a very lady-like thing to say," he chided.

It was getting a little easier to think clearly. "I'm not used to people caring I'm hurt," I said awkwardly. "Your…kindness is weird."

"It's nothing as noble as kindness," Dorian said, "But I've always heard we give the gifts we'd most want ourselves. I suppose there's truth in that, at least."

"Then, what is it?" I asked.

"We've talked before about men and mystery," Dorian replied.

"When do I get to have mystery?" I asked.

"When you've grown and experienced more," Dorian said. "Mystery ages like wine."

I felt like he was toying with me, but I couldn't quite figure out why. Slowly, I settled back onto the sheets and pillow. What if I told *him* about the sigils? Would he believe me? I bit the inside of my cheek.

But I saw Celeste heading towards us. I knew I couldn't tell him, then. Not in front of her. I knew she'd just ignore me again. "I didn't know you were here, Your Lordship," Celeste said. "As you can see, Wynter is doing well."

"This is what you call well?" he asked.

"As well as can be expected, given the circumstances," she amended smoothly.

Dorian sheathed the rapier and placed it on my bed. "I'd still prefer that my little mage not be fighting demons," Dorian replied.

"As would we all," Celeste said. "But these are difficult times."

Dorian patted my shoulder. "Until next time," he said.

I nodded. The moment he was gone, I turned my attention to the girl in the bed beside mine, Tatiana. I remembered the blood flowing from her nose, so much of it. I wanted to cry because it had all been too much, and I hadn't even *wanted* to hurt a demon. I'd hesitated, and she got hurt. And I didn't know if that made me something better or worse. I wanted to ask Lucian, but he'd gone unusually silent.

***

Falling from the stairs onto the ground floor and summoning Lucian's fire had taken a lot out of me. And even though my broken arm and the gash on my leg had been healed with magic, they still throbbed. I'd remained in bed for a day afterward, finally dragging myself out of it when I realized that I was already doing terribly in my classes, so I didn't need to miss them, too. If I got kicked out of the Academy before Dorian was finished with me, my uncle wouldn't be happy. And if my uncle wasn't happy, that meant Briar and Sterling would pay for it. Plus, I really needed a shower.

Professor Gareth's History of Reverie class was small.

Alexander and Viviane were in it, along with a handful of other people I recognized. I tried to get Alexander's attention, but he didn't see me come in. Others, however, twisted their heads in my direction.

"Wynter," Kris turned around in her seat and whispered excitedly. "Did you really slay a demon?"

Alexander and Viviane looked at me, then—along with most of the class.

"No," I said. "I only weakened it, so Celeste could seal it away."

"But she did strike it in the heart," Alexander said quietly. I wanted to think he was standing up for me, but something about the bitterness in his tone gave me pause.

Viviane curled her hand around Alexander's arm, like she was marking her territory. I was too tired to even care. Kris nodded and turned back around to a couple of her friends.

"See, I *told* you so," she said.

Then, Tatiana walked in. We exchanged nods, and she shyly held out her hand. "I don't think we've ever even spoken to one another," she said, "What a way to meet."

She smiled, but there were dark circles under her eyes. She must have been exhausted after our ordeal. I saw a faint red crease at her hairline where she'd been injured. I shook her hand and smiled back. "Maybe it'll give us a sense of mystery when we're older."

Viviane sounded like she was choking on something. Tatiana laughed. "Maybe," she said, dropping my hand. "We'll definitely have to talk more."

She went to her seat. I sank down a bit in mine. I really just wanted to sleep, but if I had to sit through a professor's class, I was happy it was Gareth's. He'd always been nice to me. He entered and immediately began a passionate lecture about the government in Reverie. I fell asleep at one point and only realized it when I jerked my head up from the table. Gareth had the grace not to say anything.

"Now, it was at this time," Gareth continued, "that the people of Reverie began to suspect that the old system of choosing a monarch based solely on his or her magical talent might not be the best approach. Instead, it was agreed that two parties would govern Reverie—the monarchy and the Council."

I vaguely recalled hearing about this, but I couldn't remember who'd told me about it.

"Of course, this did not magically fix all of Reverie's problems," Gareth continued. "The Council was composed of the kingdom's most powerful mages, people who would have been competitors for the throne, had the governing system not changed. Many of these mages were unhappy of suddenly having to share their places with the newly formed aristocracy. And thus, a rivalry between the two has persisted."

"So why don't we go back to the old system?" Tatiana asked.

"That's an excellent question, Tatiana," Gareth replied, "But—despite our differences—the Council and the aristocracy continue to solve issues together. The more minds we have together, the more effective solutions we can find. We might argue sometimes, but ultimately, I think it behooves us to spread out the power amongst many people. This gives us different perspectives on the many issues Reverie faces on a daily basis."

All those people and barely an ounce of sense between them, Lucian lamented. It was the first he'd spoken since the attack, and he

THE SOURCE OF MAGIC

sounded as tired as I felt.

Considering the poor job they've done of figuring out what's causing both the quakes and the demons, I think it's a fair assertion. Especially considering that—apparently—it's one of their own causing this.

"Be nice," I hissed.

The girl beside me edged away. I winced, and my face reddened. I needed to be more careful when I talked to Lucian.

Oh, I'll bet these mages did just wonderful things to people they think are mad, Lucian said. *Do you think they'd lock you up somewhere or just send you off the edge?*

He was being unusually cruel today, but I kept my mouth shut this time.

"Professor," another student said, "What about the demons? I've heard some people say that they're being released *because* we abandoned that old system. We no longer have a powerful sorcerer-king to rally around, so the old magic is fading and they're getting loose from their bonds."

Our classmate, a short dark-haired boy, raised his palms. "I don't mean any offense. I'm just saying that we didn't have these problems *before*—"

Alexander muttered under his breath and kicked the chair in front of him.

"These problems," Gareth said lightly, "Have existed before the formation of the Council and the aristocracy. We have a few historical records indicating—"

"A few!" our classmate argued. "Now, there are demon attacks all the time!"

Some of my classmates looked towards me. I shifted awkwardly. Their attention wasn't unfriendly, but I wasn't used to being noticed.

"I mean, did you *see* the ballroom?" another student asked. "I just looked in, and—"

"The ballroom is closed for a reason. Stay away from it," Gareth cut in. "There have been three demon attacks thus far, and I promise the Council is looking into it. However, if *turning away from magic* was the primary issue, wouldn't these problems have occurred directly after we changed our course?"

"What if both the demons and earthquakes are the result of Reverie falling out of the sky?" Tatiana asked.

Laughter burst around her.

"Sure, Tati," a classmate said, "And I'll bet you think the Kingdom of Aubade is secretly governed by a race of cat people."

"Only crazy people believe that!"

"How hard *did* you hit your head? You're joking, right?"

"It's not a joke!" Tatiana insisted. "My father has been doing serious research into this phenomenon, and—"

"Where? In the gossip columns?"

"Class!" Gareth cut in. "You are *not* going to tear down your classmates."

I sank deeper into my seat. The arguments brought forth all the deep-seated anxieties within me. Arguments weren't good where I came from. They always led to real violence.

"Tatiana, tell us about your research," Gareth said.

"Oh. Well," Tatiana said, sounding surprised. "My father realized that the Lower Realms have a history of quakes which split apart the ground, and these quakes happen along things called fault lines. Basically, the Lower Realms rest on a series of plate-like structures, and sometimes, these structures brush against one another. So quakes happen."

Gareth gave an approving nod.

"But," Tatiana continued, "Reverie has no fault lines or plates. This means that we shouldn't have quakes. So my father—"

"Who is clearly crazy," the girl beside me muttered.

"—has done calculations to look at where the force of these quakes is coming from, and he's determined that mathematically the quakes are occurring because we're slowly slipping downwards," Tatiana said. "It isn't a conspiracy theory. It's physics."

"I disagree with your father," Gareth said, "As does the rest of the Council. However, we *don't* presently have an explanation for the quakes. Therefore, we should encourage theories—no matter how outlandish they may seem. If we begin dismissing theories, we're narrowing our potential avenues both for research and for solutions. That being said, Tatiana, Reverie always floats up or down every few centuries. When I was a child, the Council said we were rising too close to the sun."

Sure. But my professors also said that I hadn't seen sigils on a demon, and I *knew* I had. What else were they covering up? If a mage was controlling the demon attacks, could they be behind the earthquakes as well? It was so hard to piece things together.

"Right," Tatiana said, clearly disagreeing.

"Students," Gareth said, smiling gently. "I realize that you're all worried about the demon attacks. I am, also. However, this lecture isn't about demons, and I'm afraid I can't offer much information. I'm not an expert on demons."

"Are there experts on demons?" I asked suddenly. "I mean, people who can understand them?"

Another smattering of laughter. I flinched.

Not in Reverie. Demons are experts on demons, Lucian said, chuckling to himself.

"Didn't one almost kill you?" Kris asked. "What more do you need to know?"

"Class," Gareth said, more sternly. "Let's keep in mind that not everyone comes from Reverie. Yes, Wynter, there are experts in demonology, although I'll admit it's a field beyond my expertise. I'm very much a sigil man."

"Thank you," I said.

Gareth smiled, then returned to his lecture on Reverie's history.

"Following this separation, some early aristocrats weren't happy with the Council consolidating magic in the Academy, so an agreement was reached between the Council and the aristocracy. The king designated five noble houses to safeguard stores of magical objects, so magical depositories would be spread throughout the kingdom."

I leaned my hand against my cheek as Professor Gareth kept talking. I still didn't entirely understand why Reverie needed an aristocracy *and* a Council. While members of the aristocracy inherited their positions, members of the Council were only accepted after passing rigorous tests involving magic. It seemed like it would have been easier just to have members of the Council learn politics alongside magic, but maybe I just didn't understand how things worked.

After class, Alexander turned around and met my eyes. I thought he was waiting for me, so I joined him at the door.

"Library tonight?" I asked quietly.

"With you?" he asked with a sneer. "I think not."

What was his problem?

I crossed my arms and stormed out of the class. Whatever. I didn't need prince charming. If he didn't want to help, I'd just have to go by myself.

TWENTY~ONE

THAT NIGHT, I WAITED UNTIL everyone was asleep before trying the archives again. I rolled up my sleeve and looked at the scars I'd received from Gabriel, searching for a place where I could draw enough blood to use Lucian's sigil. Had I really been brought to this? It felt like I was punishing myself now. And I was still so sore and tired from the demon attack. I stared at the library and considered whether or not I had the energy to go through with this venture. I thought Reverie was a paradise, but it was darker and more dangerous than the Scraps had ever been, and the people were far meaner. I just needed to find the journal, then I could go back where I belonged.

I made a small cut near my elbow to draw blood, and carefully sketched the sigil across the main door. It burned with blue light before fading, and I stepped through the thick wooden door. I took a deep breath when I'd reached the other side, before heading upstairs to the restricted archives. Once inside, I flicked on the device, so I could sort through the large trunks in the light of the blue flame.

"I don't suppose," I said, pulling out a thick stack of

documents and folders, "there's some magical way for you to find what I'm looking for?"

Even if I was tired, using a magical solution sounded more manageable than spending hours sorting through books, papers, and heavy boxes to find the journal Dorian wanted.

Not really, Lucian replied. *At least, not with the information you've been given. Maybe if you had some of Armenia's blood, you could do it.*

"I somehow doubt Dorian has a man's blood just…laying around his house," I said.

You never know. I wouldn't put it past him.

"What is the deal with blood magic, anyway?" I asked. "I'm not a mage, so why does the sigil need my blood?"

Magic requires a sacrifice, Lucian said, as if that explained anything.

"So what makes blood magic so much worse than the others?" I asked.

Lucian seemed to consider the question for a moment. *I don't know. When demons use blood magic, it doesn't hurt us as badly as it does you. There's something about mages or the way they're using our magic that isn't working.*

The answer felt only half-true. I wondered what Lucian was leaving out.

"So you're having me use a type of magic that's hurting me more than it should, a type of magic that *you* don't even understand," I said slowly.

You haven't died yet, Lucian pointed out.

I flipped through the materials, sorting them into different piles, and then carefully stacked them back into the leather trunk before moving on to the next.

"I just wish there was a way I could help," I sighed. "The school is under attack and I'm sneaking around. We got lucky this time, but people could have died."

It's not your fight. You're only here to steal for a haughty nobleman, Lucian said.

"I know that," I replied, "But…if it was Briar or Sterling, I would do all I could. If it was their lives at risk, I'd do whatever it took. That's why I'm still here. Because if I fail, my uncle will take it out on them, and I—I couldn't live like that."

But it isn't Briar or Sterling.

"That doesn't make it fine for me to do nothing," I said, "And Viviane, Alexander, and Tatiana have people who care about them. I wouldn't want them to get hurt, either."

Why do you care? Viviane has been nothing but awful to you, and Alexander isn't much better. And they're mages! They're all disloyal and treacherous, self-serving monsters. Let them die. You can't save everyone.

I shook my head. "If I can save them, I should. It's the right thing to do, and that's got to be enough."

It won't be, Lucian said. *That will never be enough for someone like you.*

"Is that a bad thing?"

Yes.

I sighed, digging through the materials in the second box and finding nothing. I'd barely made a dent in the uncategorized section of files, but my eyes were already glazing over. I couldn't do this tonight. Maybe Dorian would understand. He'd seemed sympathetic when I was injured. At least, more than Gabriel always was.

Congratulations, Lucian said dryly. *The nobleman doesn't maim you. Truly, a high standard.*

I tried to be as quiet as possible as I headed down the steps and out the front entrance. I remembered what Alexander said about professors patrolling the floors at night. Those patrols were likely on a schedule; I wondered how hard it would be to find it. If I could, it would be much easier to time these trips out.

As I continued down the corridors heading back to my room, I kept to the shadows. Already, the sun was rising; its light drifted in through the windows and cast slats of light upon the walls. I heard someone approaching and darted down another hallway, fleeing the footsteps as quickly as I could. This route took me further from my dormitories, but the longer route was worth not being caught. I rounded a corner, and there was Professor Du Lac. I was so startled that I gasped.

"You're out early," Du Lac said.

I silently swore. "I—I wasn't—"

"Follow me," he said, setting a brisk pace.

I considered running, but it wasn't as if Du Lac wouldn't find me. And I didn't know if I actually *could* run. Instead, I followed him, struggling to keep up with his fast pace. My muscles were ridiculously sore, and I began to feel light-headed. "Where are we going?" I asked.

"To my office."

As we made our way down the corridor, I looked around, half-hoping that someone would swoop in and somehow help me from having to face Du Lac alone. But it was just after sunrise. There wasn't anyone to see us, except the marble busts and oil portraits of long-dead mages. We halted by a door, which Du Lac opened with far more force than necessary. "Inside," he said.

I stepped tentatively into his office. It was small and dark, appropriate for him, really. Books were crammed everywhere—into shelves, on floors, spilling over onto his desk. He sat and waved me into the chair opposite him. Rather than remaining behind his desk, he pulled his chair over and set it directly before mine. His eyes were intense, so sharp that I felt like he could look right into me and see every terrible thing I'd ever done.

"I can explain," I said.

"You don't need to," Du Lac said. "Quite frankly, I don't care what you were doing. Maybe surviving the demon attacks has made you think you're invincible, but I assure you that isn't the case. It isn't safe to be wandering around the school at night."

"I'm sorry," I said.

Du Lac smiled thinly. "Really, I'm surprised you've survived this long. It isn't easy learning to be a mage. I've seen students pulled through magical portals never to be seen again. I've seen students burned alive because they lost control of their powers. I've even seen students possessed by demons, and that is always messy business. It's very difficult to force a demon from someone."

He's just trying to scare you, Lucian muttered.

I swallowed. "I—"

"I had a student once," Du Lac continued. "She was a very gifted young lady. I'd never seen anyone so naturally gifted in sigils. She was from one of the noble families, but I was certain she deserved a spot on the Council."

"Why would she want one?" I asked. "She was already a noblewoman."

Du Lac looked at me like I'd just said the stupidest thing he'd heard in his life. "And do you think that's something to be proud of? Getting power because you're just born into it? The nobility knows *politics,* but that's all they know. It's the Council that truly holds the power and the knowledge, which made this student all the more remarkable. If she'd have earned her spot in the Council, she would have been far more of an asset to Reverie than those petty nobles. Something like that very rarely happens, but anything less would have been a waste of her exceptional talents. But she chose her friends poorly. She was head over heels in love with some student from the Lower Realms."

The Lower Realms?

"And he was a piece of work," Du Lac said, "Always sneaking around, getting into trouble."

"What happened to her?"

"Why, together they began exploring all manner of forbidden magic. Eventually, it drove her mad, and she leaped to her death," Du Lac said. "I've heard she didn't die immediately. Instead, she lay there on the ground and slowly bled out."

This story sounded like another version of the one I'd heard from Viviane, but which one was true? Did she kill herself, or was it murder? In the Scraps, we'd had little rhymes about a mage-lady going mad with magic and falling to her death. She'd been as pale as death with eyes as black as night. Broken bones bleached in the morning light. Some said she killed girls who looked like her, to spare them from a similar fate.

My pulse raced, as I suddenly realized I *knew* a noblewoman who'd killed herself. Potentially. Was Du Lac talking about Dorian's sister? In the forum, he said the last time demons were loosed was seventeen years ago, by a rogue mage... was this rogue mage the same as the student from the lower realms?

"So if you *were* involved in any dark magic or knew anyone involved with it, you would tell me, wouldn't you?" Du Lac asked.

I thought about Alexander in the archives and about the potions Viviane kept drinking. But I didn't want Alexander to get in trouble, and I wasn't even sure if Viviane was doing anything wrong. I was the one talking with demons, but I couldn't tell him that.

"I—I was just out of my room past light's out," I said. "That—that has nothing to do with dark magic."

Du Lac rummaged on his desk and grabbed a stack of papers, covered in sigils. I didn't recognize them. "I found these among your things," Du Lac said. He smiled triumphantly, as if catching me in a lie.

"These aren't mine," I said, flipping through the stack. "I—I don't know how they ended up in my things. I would never—I can't even manage regular magic."

Why was he looking through my stuff?

They might just check periodically, Lucian said.

"You seem to have mastered fire fairly well."

Only because I'd cheated with the device and had Lucian helping me.

"But I'm terrible at sigils. You know that," I said. "I—I can't even change the color of a gemstone. What good would these sigils even do me?"

Du Lac frowned and placed the papers aside. "But if they aren't yours, what were they doing in your dorm?"

"I don't know. Maybe someone put them there as a joke," I said. "I—not many people here like me. Maybe someone is trying to get me expelled from the Academy. Do—do you think I was out tonight because I was trying to find information about dark magic? The only thing I was doing was, um…"

"Was?"

I fumbled for an excuse. "I wanted to practice my swordplay," I said, "Since I couldn't sleep anyway. After the demon attacks, I—"

Oh, that's good, Lucian said. *Do you think you can make yourself cry?*

Probably not. But I could try.

"I've just been so afraid!" I exclaimed. "I—I can't defend myself well enough, and I'm worried that something terrible will happen! So I thought I would practice."

I forced a couple of sniffles. I almost felt guilty about manipulating Professor Du Lac, even if he was a huge jerk. "Because I *really* want to master battle magic," I said. But I'm so awful at everything! I was lucky with the demon. It's just unbelievable—"

My eyes burned. I'd managed a couple of tears.

"And I'm under so much pressure not being from here—"

"Enough!" Du Lac snapped.

I sniffled. "Sorry, Professor," I said, trying to sound deeply upset.

"So," Du Lac said, "What am I going to do about your late-night escapades? I could have you expelled for this. If I can prove these are yours, I can ensure you're sent right back to whatever hole you crawled out of in the Lower Realms. But I doubt you want that, do you?"

Could he really do that? That punishment sounded

excessive to me, but I didn't know if it really was or not. What I did know was that I absolutely could not be expelled. Not yet.

"I don't want that," I said.

"Then you're going to have to buy my silence with a favor," Du Lac said, smiling wickedly. That didn't sound good.

"What do you want?" I asked.

Du Lac stood and went behind his desk, sorting through papers. Finally, he retrieved a small, ink-drawn picture. It was a woman with dark hair, pulled back and tucked into a crown. She looked vaguely familiar, but I couldn't place where I'd seen her before.

"Do you see the tiara she's wearing?" Du Lac asked.

I remembered that tiara. This was the woman from the library.

"Yes," I said.

"I need you to retrieve it for me." I frowned. This woman was clearly an aristocrat, and stealing from an aristocrat sounded like a good way to get killed.

"But how am I supposed to do that?" I asked. "I can't just go to the palace and steal—"

"You don't have to go to the palace," Du Lac replied. "This tiara has been in the Rosewood family for centuries, so—"

"So Dorian has it," I said.

Would the punishment for being in the corridors at night really be worse than the punishment for stealing from Dorian?

Not if you don't get caught, Lucian said.

No, but what were the odds I could steal an expensive, probably priceless family heirloom from his estate without anyone noticing?

"I saw sigils on the demon," I said quickly, hoping to gauge

Du Lac's reaction. Maybe I could use it as leverage somehow. He considered me for a long moment, before leaning back and crossing his fingers over his stomach.

"You didn't see anything," he said.

"All my professors keep saying that," I said, "But what will Dorian say?"

"Going against the word of the Academy's faculty would be political suicide," Du Lac said. "He'd either tell you you'd imagined it—which you did—or he'd ruin himself trying to prove you were right."

I say you steal this tiara, give it to Du Lac, and let that be the end of it, Lucian said. *I seriously doubt Dorian is going to galivant around wearing a ladies' tiara. He probably won't even notice it's missing.*

But it was still his, and I was working for him.

Not because you wanted to!

No, but maybe I sometimes thought a little…fondly of him. Job or no, he was nice to me.

Because it benefits him, Lucian said. *Why can't you see that?*

Maybe because I didn't want to. Or maybe because I believed there really might be *something* more to Dorian. But it didn't matter. If Du Lac really had the power to expel me, it meant I'd never complete my mission, and I couldn't risk that. I'd have to steal *from* Dorian so I could steal *for* him. I sighed, fixing Du Lac with a resigned gaze.

"I'll do it," I said.

***

The next few days at the Academy were strange. My classmates met me with respectful nods and smiles. Everyone knew I'd defeated a demon, and it seemed like that had made me one of them. A mage like them. A celebrity even, or a hero. That was, of course, except for Viviane. She continued glaring at me in Du Lac's class, challenging me in Delacroix's class, and bumping into me in our dormitory. I dealt with it. Now that Du Lac was blackmailing me, I knew it was even more important that I behave myself and disappear as much as possible, but that was hard to do with people watching me all the time.

I sat in Du Lac's sigils class, trying to copy the patterns he'd made in the air. It was supposed be a fire spell, which I felt Du Lac had chosen just to mock me. He kept smirking at me because I couldn't create it. I was tempted to use the device in my pocket to create the illusion of fire, but I knew that was a bad idea. I didn't need to show off, especially not to spite him.

A few of my classmates had already managed it. I grimaced at my paper, black with ink. "What am I doing wrong?" I whispered. "It looks just like his."

I tried tracing the lines again, making them thicker and darker. "Please, make fire," I whispered.

Viviane turned around and scowled at me. "Are you talking to yourself?" she asked.

"Yes," I replied.

"Well, stop it. *Some* of us are trying to concentrate," she said, flipping her hair.

"Sorry," I replied.

I sighed and turned my attention back to my paper.

"I think it's in the way you've drawn the lower half," Alexander said.

I looked up at him, surprised he'd offered to help. He'd barely spoken to me since the accident. He cleared his throat and ran his finger down the lower half of my sigil. "The way you've curved the bottom looks a little shaky for me. That's why you aren't getting the fire you want."

I frowned and tried adjusting the bottom curve, making it more obvious. Still, nothing happened. "Please, work," I murmured.

The air around me crackled. A distant roaring filled my ears. A small plume of smoke appeared, rising upwards. I jumped. How had *that* happened?

And the smoke kept rising, its tendrils white and curling in the air. Suddenly, Du Lac was there. "The goal was to summon fire," he said, his arms crossed.

Where there's smoke, there's fire, Lucian said. *Tell him that.*

"I tried," I replied.

"And are you expecting praise for a poorly drawn sigil just because it did *something*?" Du Lac asked. "Clearly, you lack the temperament for this, if you consider *anything* to be a success."

The tendrils of smoke were growing higher and higher. Still, no fire appeared. But the smoke was becoming *thick*. Alexander and Viviane both shifted away. I clambered out of my seat. The smoke wasn't stopping, and I had no idea why. I didn't even know how I'd done this!

"What did you *do*?" Du Lac snapped, breaking into a fit of coughs.

Why didn't he know? He was the sigils professor!

"I don't know!" I yelled. What if the smoke just didn't stop? What if it just kept going and going until it filled the whole room?

Du Lac stormed across the room and swiped the pen of his desk. My heartbeat raced. The black smoke was rising to the ceiling and spreading like a cloud.

"Nice job, Summer!" Viviane snapped.

But if it was coming from my sigil, maybe I could stop this by messing with the sigil. Smearing the ink or something. I grabbed my pen and drew a line through the sigil, hoping it would stop the smoke. Du Lac grabbed my arm and pulled me back. "Don't do that!" he snapped. "What if you—"

With a roar, lightning erupted from my sigil and shot towards the ceiling. My jaw dropped. As the smoke cleared, I saw a black, charred mark spread across the stone ceiling.

TWENTY~TWO

I SPENT THE NEXT FEW nights digging through the archives, but found nothing. Not only was I returning to Rosewood empty-handed, but this time I was supposed to steal a priceless tiara from Dorian's dead mother. On Friday, I loaded up on food to drop for Briar and Sterling, in case this was my last chance. The way things were going, I'd either get caught stealing for Du Lac, or for Dorian, or expelled for blowing up half the school.

How had I created lightning? That hadn't been the device, or Dorian, or Lucian… that was *me*, but that was impossible, wasn't it? I'd always thought there was a concrete difference between humans and sky dwellers. You were either a mage, or you weren't. But if *I* could make magic happen, that meant it wasn't true, and anyone could learn magic if they knew the steps and rituals that went with it. I thought about my entrance exam and the burned curtains. I'd *assumed* that had been a trick of Dorian's, but what if it hadn't been? What if that fire had actually been *me*? It didn't make any sense. Maybe Alexander had done it somehow. Of course, he had no reason to be so helpful, but maybe he'd decided that we were something like friends. Despite how he'd been treating me recently.

After school I headed to the edge of Reverie to drop the bundle of food through the grate, along with a letter about how everything was going up here. I didn't want them to worry, so I only told them the good things. I hoped they were eating most of the food themselves, at least some of it, before they took it back to the Scraps. Or was Sterling's mom keeping it hidden? Maybe they'd ferreted some away to trade. I was bolder this time, and included some cured meat, sausages and half a raw cabbage I'd stolen from the kitchen. It was almost satisfying to rip up one of the fancy dresses Francisca had folded neatly into my trunk, wrap it around my illicit contraband, and drop it off the Floats. A small act of rebellion against an untenable situation. Once the food was dropped, I headed to Dorian's estate.

The intricate, wrought iron fence that ran around the length of Dorian's estate was only five minutes away. I arrived shortly before sunset, pushed open the gate and walked down the stone pathway to the entrance of his house, although calling it a *house* seemed absurd. This place was practically a castle. The door opened before I reached it.

"Miss Wilcox!" Francisca greeted, waving me in. "Welcome."

"Thank you," I said. "I—um—like your dress."

It was a pretty dress, pale blue with sleeves that fell off her shoulders. "So does my Lord," Francisca said, her brown eyes bright with mischief. "Lady Eleanor says it's far too extravagant for a lady of my station."

"Oh, is she here today?"

"Speaking to my Lord, in fact," Francisca said. "Shall I inform them of your presence?"

"No," I said, shaking my head. "That's not necessary. I'll just wait until Dorian is finished."

"Certainly," Francisca replied. "Do you require anything else? Refreshments, perhaps?"

I shook my head. This was so weird.

Not really, Lucian said. *She's treating you like the guest of a nobleman.*

"Very well," Francisca said. "Do let me know if there's anything further you require."

"Thank you," I said, excusing myself as quickly as I could. I was in no rush to speak with Lady Eleanor, and the distraction gave me an opening to look for the tiara. But could I really do this? As I walked across the wide, marble floor towards the stairs, I considered just waiting for Dorian and telling him everything. He might be angry that I'd been caught, but he wasn't unreasonable. I bit the inside of my cheek, trying to weigh the odds. In my experience, adults usually couldn't be depended on. Even if they let your mistakes go, they collected them up for later and threw them back in your face. "What do you think I should do?" I asked.

Personally, I loathe mages, Lucian said. *Steal a few more things while you're at it.*

Dorian wasn't a *bad* person, though. I had never stolen from someone who was nice to me before.

He's protecting an investment, Lucian said. *You just haven't seen his teeth yet.*

Maybe not. But I'd worked for Gabriel, and he'd never

cared anything about me.

So one of them is a better businessman, Lucian replied, an edge to his voice. *The nobleman realizes that you must nurture an investment until it bears fruit.*

Hearing that shouldn't have hurt as much as it did. And anyway, I didn't have to decide until I actually found the tiara. Maybe if I couldn't find it quickly, I could abandon the endeavor then and just ask Dorian for it. But for now, I'd see if I could find it myself while he was distracted. I tried to remember the brief tour I'd gotten on my first night at Rosewood. My rooms were on the second floor. But I had no idea where anything else was.

I walked down a long, carpeted hallway and frowned as I looked at room after room. "Lucian, if you had to hide a tiara, where would you hide it?" I muttered.

I don't know, Lucian said. *I'm not exactly the tiara type, in case you haven't noticed.*

I tried a door to my left; it opened without difficulty and revealed a massive ballroom, decorated in green and gold. Probably not in there. I frowned and closed that door. One down, a hundred or so to go.

I kept going, checking door after door. Some of them opened easily; others were locked. I made a mental note of those and kept going. If I didn't find the tiara in one of the unlocked rooms, I would have to go back and look through the locked ones at night. A few servants walked past me, but they never tried to stop me from looking around.

I climbed the stairs to the next floor and looked through the rooms once more. There was no way I could search every room before Dorian came looking for me. It would've taken a week just to look everywhere. For now, I was just doing reconnaissance. Dorian had never said that I *couldn't* look around his estate. But if I couldn't find that tiara, what was I going to do about Du Lac?

I don't suppose setting him on fire is an option?

"I'm not setting him on fire!"

I walked into another room. This one appeared to be a bedroom, one of *many* bedrooms that Dorian appeared to have in his estate. The room was rose and gold, clearly a lady's room. Across the doorway, there was a massive window and a balcony that overlooked the vast gardens. I could see the gleaming silver fence around Reverie and the line where the land ended and met the sky, and if I'd been on the balcony, I was sure I could've looked straight down to the Lower Realms. I shivered. I'd never realized how close we were to the edge before.

I drifted in, walking past a large cherrywood piano, a table, and chairs. There wasn't any tiara that I could see. I entered a parlor, pausing by a massive portrait of Amelia. That seemed promising, at least.

This was the largest bedroom I'd ever seen, featuring a giant bed and a good deal of furniture. At the foot of the bed, there was a trunk like the kind we had at the Academy. I crouched before opening it. There were clothes cluttered together with musty-smelling books and papers. I shuffled through it, searching for anything that looked remotely like a tiara.

I moved to the dresser. It was mostly empty, save for a few scattered buttons and bits of jewelry. I'd expected something more. I slammed the drawer shut and opened the next one. It was just as sparse. Another drawer and no tiara. I shut the last drawer a little harder than necessary. Why was all this furniture empty? "It's not here," I muttered. "Where is it?"

"Ahem," a polite cough made me jump. Lady Eleanor stood in the doorway, her eyes fixed on my hands, which were still in the open drawer of her mother's bedroom.

***

"Wynter, was it?"

She wore a bright scarlet dress; her mother's mourning period must've ended. "I don't think we've been properly introduced yet," she said. "I am Eleanor, Baroness of Sherringford."

I curtsied. "It's a pleasure to meet you, my Lady."

Eleanor turned her gaze to the dresser and pulled open a couple of the drawers, before slamming them closed again. Her movements had a wild, sharp sort of energy. Finally, her attention landed on me. I half expected her to scream for help or zap me with magic. Instead she crossed her arms and strode into the room.

"I wish I could say the same," she said, lowering her voice. "You haven't listened to Viviane, so perhaps, you'll listen to me. I don't know *why* Dorian has brought you to Reverie, but if you sabotage Viviane's courtship with Alexander, I *will* see to it that you're never heard from again. I have worked far too hard to have my plans undermined." Her eyes were manic, almost hysterical.

Maybe if she can't win the princeling, she doesn't deserve him, Lucian said.

"I'm not trying to sabotage anything," I replied.

"I'd like to believe that, Wynter," Eleanor said, "But I just don't." She thought *Dorian brought me here simply to ruin Viviane? Would he really be so cruel?*

This family is exhausting, Lucian said. *Can you imagine being related to any of them? I think I'd flee the kingdom.*

A throat cleared. Dorian stood leaning against the doorway. Eleanor's attention snapped to him. "Where is our mother's jewelry?"

"You mean *my* jewelry," Dorian replied.

Eleanor's eyes narrowed. "You haven't sold it all for money, have you?"

"No, I merely prefer to keep my wealth where it can't be stolen. I'd be more concerned about *your* finances. At the rate you're going, poor Viviane might have to marry a merchant's son to free you from debt."

"Then, perhaps, you ought to employ for help. I'm appalled by how few servants you have. It's no wonder the place is crawling with thieves." She let her gaze drop to me pointedly.

"And I'm appalled by how obvious your husband is with his affairs. That reflects so poorly on you, Eleanor."

"Be careful, Wynter. If you anger him, he might hurl you down a flight of stairs."

"If I hurled everyone who angered me down the stairs, you wouldn't be here," Dorian replied.

Eleanor smiled sharply and strode from the room with a sort of affected regality. Dorian beckoned for me, so I trailed along and fidgeted with my hands. I looked away as Eleanor and Dorian exchanged their farewells, and all too soon, the doors were closed. I wondered how they could kiss cheeks after all the hateful things they'd said about each other.

Did Eleanor really suspect Dorian of murdering their mother? Was he really so terrible, and I just couldn't see it? Maybe Lucian was right. Francisca appeared out of nowhere and handed Dorian a glass of red wine. He looked utterly bewildered by its appearance.

"What's this for?"

"You're always in a dark mood after speaking with Lady Eleanor," Francisca said, "With all due respect, my Lord."

Great.

"You always make *with all due respect* sound profoundly like an insult," Dorian replied.

"It's difficult to respect a man who is so terrible at cards," Francisca said. "I'm afraid that has given me a terrible impression of your whole character."

She's rather friendly with him, isn't she? Lucian asked mischievously.

Was she?

"How *ever* shall I redeem myself?" Dorian asked, adding a theatrical sigh.

"I'll be quite happy to help you find your road to redemption, Your Lordship."

I'd rather not watch this woman's dismal attempts to charm her master, Lucian said.

Maybe Francisca was just being nice.

"Thank you, Fran," Dorian said, in a dismissive tone.

Francisca bowed and walked away. Despite Lucian's complaints, I really hadn't wanted her to leave. Dorian took a few sips of wine before finally looking at me; his face was hard to read.

"Do you want to explain what you were doing, rifling

through my mother's drawers?" he asked. I exhaled sharply. The only chance now was to tell the truth and hope he'd forgive me.

"I was caught," I admitted, wringing my hands together.

"Quite clearly," he said.

"No, not by Eleanor. Outside of my room when I wasn't supposed to be," I replied. "Professor Du Lac said I could be expelled."

"*Where* outside your room?" he asked.

"Just the corridors," I said.

"And you believed him? I was caught outside my room all the time. The worst I ever had to do was clean the ballroom floors."

My face flushed in embarrassment. "He said he found evidence of dark magic in my things, but I haven't been…I don't know where those came from."

"I see. Please continue."

"So he wanted me to steal a tiara from you."

Dorian looked taken aback. "*Markus* wants you to steal from me," he repeated.

"I know your mother wore it," I said. "It's sapphires and pearls."

"But why would Markus want that?" Dorian asked, seemingly more to himself than me. "There's nothing special about it."

"Maybe he's looking for the charm?" I suggested.

"What charm?"

"I overheard Professor Gareth mention a charm that Guinevere might have," I replied. "I'd assumed you were looking for that."

"I'm not. I've never even heard of it. I'm…trying to

recover stolen property," Dorian said carefully.

But what could be so valuable that it would be worth so much trouble?

My guess is that it's either sentimental or magical, Lucian mused. *Maybe both.*

"This certainly complicates our relationship," Dorian said. "You realize, of course, that you could've *asked* me for it."

"I—I thought about telling you," I said, "But I just couldn't."

"Why not?"

I swallowed the lump in my throat. "Because I can't afford to fail this," I said. "You've made it clear you're only interested in the journal. I thought, if I bought a little more time, I could find it."

"That's all the more reason to be honest with me," he said dryly. "You *aren't* the only one with stakes in this."

"You can't send me back," I said. "Not yet. And you can't tell my uncle."

"Can't I?"

"He'll hurt the people I care about," I said. "To punish me. If you really are a gentleman, you'd be honorable, right? I don't think an honorable man would be fine with innocent people getting hurt. Not when it can be avoided."

For a long moment, Dorian watched me and said nothing. I didn't like that about him, the way he silently thought everything through before he reacted. I'd have preferred he scream at me, so I'd know where we stood. I didn't realize the tears welling up until I wiped them away. They might have worked on Du Lac, but Dorian was too smart for that.

"I'll gladly let you cut off one of my fingers if you just—"

"Finally, an opportunity to maim an adolescent girl. Truly, something all gentlemen dream of doing," Dorian said, his voice dripping with sarcasm.

"I didn't want to get in trouble," I said. "I mean…I didn't know."

I sounded so pathetically childish.

Dorian was quiet for a long time. "Did you tell Markus anything about who you really are?" he finally asked.

"I haven't told anyone," I replied. "Why?"

"It seems like quite a wager to assume that you would *steal* from me rather than telling me about his plan," Dorian replied, "And I don't believe Markus would have told you to unless he *expected* you would actually do it."

"I don't know," I replied. "Have you told anyone?"

Dorian offered his arm. "A few people. Maybe there's a spy in my house. That's something Fran and I will need to investigate," he said. "Let's take a walk."

He offered his arm, and I took it almost out of habit.

"But isn't it bad if Markus knows I'm stealing for you?"

"We don't know if that *is* something he knows," Dorian said. "It's a guess. If he has an informant, he may think I'm having you steal to cover my gambling debts. The only person who knows I'm after something else is Fran, and she wouldn't tell anyone. Either way, he'll probably be watching you very closely now."

"What about the tiara?" I asked. "Are you going to give it to him?"

"*You* are going to give it to him," Dorian said, "And for now, we're going to pretend I know nothing about this. I know there's nothing special about that tiara. But if Markus wants to waste his time looking, I see no benefit in dissuading him. It might even work to my advantage."

"So that's…it?" I asked, still worried that he might have some punishment in mind.

"Far from it," Dorian replied.

He steered me out into the gardens, and I realized the fence here was much shorter, only waist high. I trembled as we drew up next to it. All it would take was one good push to send me tumbling over the edge of Reverie.

"I'll confess to being frustrated with the way my investment in you is playing out," Dorian said, gazing out over the horizon with his hands folded behind his back. "This deception should have run its course by now. The longer we continue, the more likely we are to be caught."

I winced. "I'm sorry."

Down below, I could see the glint of domed rooftops in the Gardens, an assortment of marble salons, lavish fountains, and carefully cultivated gardens, red in the setting sun, like the whole city was on fire.

"In two weeks, the Academy will hold its winter examinations. If you fail those, you'll be dismissed, and I'll lose the access I require. So I need you to find that journal very quickly. I'm aware you've managed a little magic, but I can't count on you passing examinations meant primarily for people who have spent their whole lives in Reverie. We managed to cheat and gain you entrance to the Academy, but we won't be able to cheat at these."

This was it, then. I was almost out of time, and I wasn't even entirely sure how I'd managed the little magic I had. The fire was Lucian. But what about the sigils? I'd made lightning somehow, but it was an accident. I had no hope of passing official examinations when I couldn't even keep up in my classes.

"So maybe you're in need of some additional motivation," Dorian said. That sounded a lot like a threat. I looked up at him quickly, my pulse jumping.

"You aren't going to…hurt anyone, are you?"

Dorian shook his head. "There's something your uncle Gabriel has failed to grasp, and that's this: if you abuse the people around you too much, eventually, one of them is bound to slip oleander in your tea," Dorian said. "If you want people to perform well, you need to be willing to give them a little, and I think you'd like a new life with Briar and Sterling, far away from your terrible uncle. In the Gardens, perhaps."

My throat tightened. It felt like a trap somehow. Like an agreement with too many unspoken rules. He was offering me a way out, the one thing I'd always wanted. But why would he promise so much, for one stupid journal?

"Really?" I asked.

He nodded. "You have my word. You're a smart, resourceful girl. It's up to you, now."

It sounded too good to be true, and it all hinged on Dorian's word, which meant after I'd done everything he wanted, he *could* just rid himself of me. But maybe this was the best chance I'd get. He certainly had the means. For a luxurious moment, I looked down over the sweeping landscape and dared allow myself to dream of a life of freedom.

He's just trying to win your loyalty, so you take more risks, Lucian said.

Maybe. But if that was what it took for Briar and Sterling

to escape my uncle Gabriel, it didn't really matter all that much. I'd have sold my soul to make them happy.

TWENTY-THREE

THE TIARA WASN'T PEARLS AND sapphires, actually, it was pearls and blue diamonds. I knew it was probably the most expensive thing I'd ever held, and although it was in a completely nondescript box, as I returned to the Academy I was terrified that someone would figure it out and try stealing it from me. There were so many people in Reverie, and most of them were far more powerful than I was.

You realize, Lucian said, *that this nobleman's word is probably only good when it benefits him. There's no reason for him not to drop you right back where he left you when this is all over.*

"But so far he's been honorable."

He hired a teenage girl from a terrible person he met in the Lower Realms, and despite his talk of honor, he's seemed fine until this point letting your uncle's threats control you. Your nobleman is fine with dishonorable behavior, as long as he isn't doing his own dirty work.

"So what do you think I should do?" I asked.

Pawn the crown and buy a new life. That's more guarantee than a nobleman's word.

He was right. That idea made more sense. And what if I

couldn't find the journal in the two weeks? My only option, then, would be to pass the final exams. Without cheating, which seemed impossible.

And you're assuming that he'd be content to let you keep trying, Lucian said. *Eventually, he's going to want to cut his losses.*

"You also said we should steal this from Dorian," I pointed out.

So I was wrong once, Lucian replied. *Besides, it wouldn't have been a problem if you hadn't gotten caught.*

"I'm going to find that journal. It has to be…" I trailed off, thinking.

Dorian and Du Lac weren't looking for the *same* thing, but maybe there was some overlap. Dorian had only denied looking for Guinevere's charm; he hadn't denied looking for *something* tied to her. If it wasn't in the archives, maybe Du Lac had the journal. I knew where his office was, and I even had a reason to be there. I could at least look.

So you're casting your lot with the nobleman, huh? Lucian asked bitterly.

"I have to hope he'll be true to his word," I said, "And besides, if I steal it, we'll be on the run forever."

Lucian sighed. *Fine, if that's really what you want to do. I think this is a terrible idea.*

Of course, it was. But it was a terrible idea that might make life better for Briar and Sterling, without having to worry that some mage was going to hunt me down trying to retrieve a stolen tiara. And it was a much better deal than I'd been offered so far, which was to risk my life for nothing more than the chance to return to the drudgery and hardship of the Scraps.

I sighed in relief as I walked into the Academy. Almost

there. I headed upstairs, tracing the path back to Du Lac's office. I half-hoped he wouldn't be in, so I could search through his private library. That would make my life easier. But I was also eager to get rid of the priceless tiara so it wouldn't be my responsibility any longer. After rounding the corner, I found the door to Du Lac's office open. And there he was, at his desk and bent over a massive volume.

For a few seconds, I stood awkwardly in the doorway and waited for him to notice me. When he didn't, I cleared my throat. Du Lac's eyes snapped up. "Close the door."

I stepped inside and did as he asked. Then, I placed the box on his desk. He opened it and pulled out the tiara. It glittered like a cluster of stars, all the gemstones and metal brightened by the flickering candles and lamps in his office. I had an irrational fear that if I so much as breathed on the tiara too hard, it would shatter to dust.

"Hm," Du Lac said. "So you *are* good at something. Thievery is to be expected, considering where you're from."

Did he think I was a lady from Argent, or an orphan from the Scraps? Either way, I bristled. I was a lot more than a thief, and I'd have loved to prove it to him. But I had to focus. "What do you want that for?" I asked.

I didn't expect him to tell me. I was stalling for time, so I could look over his bookshelves. He had so many books, though. I was surprised that the room wasn't falling apart simply from the weight of them all.

"That's no business of yours," Du Lac replied. "Your time would be better spent worrying about your exam. At the end of the semester, all students participate in a tournament showcasing their skills, and if your performance in my class is any indication of your *other* talents…"

"It isn't," I replied.

He smirked and waved me out. I let out a breath of air and headed to the dormitories. I'd have loved to show Du Lac that I really *could* use magic like the mages. It wasn't as if my sigils didn't do *anything*. They just didn't do what I wanted. I wished I could prove to him that just because I was human didn't mean I was worthless. But the ability to control magic was everything up here. Without it, it was obvious I didn't belong.

I collapsed on my bed, vaguely aware of Viviane. I expected her to immediately begin interrogating me, but when I looked over at her, she was busy looking at a jar of berries and trying to compare them to something in a book. No, not berries, I realized. Deadly nightshade.

"Are you going to poison someone?" I asked.

"No," Viviane replied. "If you pick deadly nightshade by moonlight and freeze it, you can use it for potions."

So maybe Dorian wasn't poisoning his enemies.

"It's for class." She added quickly. I wasn't sure if she meant, she was taking a potions class, or if she was taking potions *for* class.

"You like potions a lot," I said, remembering the blue concoction she liked to drink.

"They're useful," she replied, sounding thoughtful.

"I'm sure," I said.

After that, she said nothing. I furrowed my brow and watched her for a few minutes. This was the nicest she'd ever been to me, and that worried me. Something was definitely wrong.

***

I was in a clearing surrounded by trees. The full moon shined overhead, luminous and orange, accompanied by a dotting of stars. A faint breeze drifted through the clearing, causing the grass and the treetops to sway and bend. And there was Lucian, his dark eyes watching me.

"Do you make this place?" I asked. "In my dreams?"

"Yes," he replied. "I can't do it to everyone. It's pretty, isn't it?"

"I've never seen anything like it," I said.

"I think there's a good deal you haven't seen," Lucian replied.

"So why am I here?" I asked.

"I thought you might want to practice—just in case you do have to take the final examination," Lucian said. "I think I did promise to teach you some swordplay. Don't worry, you'll wake up as rested as always, maybe more so."

"You aren't going to set me on fire, are you?" I asked, drawing my rapier.

Lucian laughed and unsheathed his blade. It gleamed in the moonlight, with a delicate, engraved handle and a slight curve. It was larger than my rapier, but Lucian spun it over the back of his hand like it was as light as a feather.

"I'll try to refrain," he said.

I moved into a fighting stance and waited. When he struck, he was fast and elegant. The green gemstones on his silver armor caught the light as he moved. I parried and shifted my weight, hoping to turn the movement into a strike of my own. But Lucian was too quick for me. I struck again and again. As I struggled to keep up, I began to get careless, forgetting everything I'd ever learned about swordplay and just trying to hack through his defenses. Each time I thought I saw an opening, it was just a trap to pull me off balance before flicking the tip of his blade to scratch across my skin. He was right, he was better than Alexander. Smooth but unpredictable.

Our blades crossed, and he shoved me backward until I struck a tree, sending a jolt of dull pain up my spine. Lucian pushed, until my own blade lay across my throat. "Never let yourself get pinned by a stronger opponent. What you *should* have done, is either stepped aside or pulled out a knife," Lucian said, voice light with mischief. "You should always keep one with you during swordfights. You could've stabbed me in the thigh or my stomach and used the distraction to move away."

"That doesn't sound very honorable," I replied.

"I've never thought much of honor," Lucian said. "It's a completely unsustainable system, built on the assumption that everyone in the world is equally honorable. And sometimes, you *must* do dishonorable things for your own survival, and there's no shame in that. But you know that already, don't you?"

Lucian lowered his sword and offered me his hand. I pushed it away and felt for the mark I was sure he'd left on my neck, but there was nothing there. Apparently, I couldn't get hurt in our shared dream, and I also didn't seem to be running out of energy. I lunged at him again, taking him by surprise, and landed my third strike against the plated armor across his ribcage.

"I know that sometimes you have to do bad things to survive," I said, brushing back my dark hair. "But that doesn't mean it's right."

"And I'm sure after some scoundrel kills you," Lucian replied as we traded blows. "He'll really enjoy listening to your ghost recount to him the many benefits of being honorable."

"But what if you're like Gabriel?" I asked. "He survives by doing awful things. I'd rather die than be like that."

"Then, think of it as evening the field," Lucian said. "Most of your opponents are going to be more skilled than you, so you need every advantage you can get. It's hardly fair for someone who's only learned proper swordplay for a season to be expected to compete with people who have learned for a decade."

Somehow he managed to stab through the hilt of my sword and yank it away. He flung it to the side where it embedded into a tree with a twang. He pointed his sword at me, but I spun around the tip of the blade and wrapped my arm around his neck, pulling him down to the ground with me on top. It was a move I'd practiced for weeks with Sterling.

I smiled in triumph, until I felt the warmth between our bodies. I knew this was just a dream, but this felt *too* real. Lucian was handsome, at least in this form. But is that what he really looked like, or was this just a form he thought I'd find pleasing—an illusion like the rest of our surroundings? For the first time, I wondered what monstrous shape he'd take in the real world.

"What about magic?" I asked, walking over to pull my sword free from the tree.

"Hm?" he asked, standing up. Was it just me, or were his cheeks flushed?

"How can I use it? I'm only a human."

"What's the difference between a mage and a human? Intention and confidence. They are bred to know magic is possible; you are raised with the understanding that it isn't. It is our beliefs, not our abilities, that position us in life."

"So what, just believe in myself and I can move mountains?" I scoffed.

"Something like that," Lucian shrugged. "I wish I had the answers. But I don't know mage magic much better than you do. Perhaps, all humans can learn magic, and the mages haven't told them. It wouldn't be the first time they've called a race inferior based on falsehoods."

"I'm sorry, Lucian," I said. I still didn't know exactly what I was apologizing for, but I could tell he'd been hurt by the mages.

He nodded distantly. "Keep a knife close at hand," he said, giving me a brittle smile. "You never know when you'll need to stab someone."

"Right. In the thigh or the belly."

"Or anywhere," Lucian said. "I wouldn't be above stabbing a man in the back. Gabriel deserves nothing less. A cowardly end to a cowardly man."

"I'm not going to murder Gabriel," I said, "Even if this doesn't happen like I want."

Lucian sheathed his sword and approached me. He lightly grasped my arm, pushed up my sleeve, and traced his fingers over the scars he found. I trembled at his touch but tried not to show it.

"Why not?" he asked. "He hurts you and the people you care about. He's utterly irredeemable."

"He's my uncle," I said, as if that explained everything. "And I don't think I could just kill someone. No matter how bad they were."

Lucian sighed. "It's admirable that you want to solve your problems without resorting to violence," Lucian said, with a note of chilling finality, "But someday, your eschewal of bloodshed is going to get you killed."

TWENTY~FOUR

I COULDN'T SEARCH FOR THE journal during the day, so I decided to study. If I didn't find it in the next two weeks, I'd be out of options—unless I was somehow able to pass the exams and buy myself more time. The library was packed with students preparing, so I checked out a few books and settled in the shared area of the dormitory. It was an oval-shaped room filled with comfortable chairs and long study tables. There was even a small kitchen with hot water for tea and a never-ending supply of cookies and sliced fruit. I sat on the rug before a massive fireplace, surrounded by piles of books. The flames popped and crackled cheerfully as I read over regulations for what was and was not allowed in a magical duel.

Jessa frantically poured over her notes at a nearby table.

"You passed last year," I pointed out, flipping through pages of what looked like dancing positions.

"I know," Jessa said, "But they expected less of me last year! This year, they'll expect me to be so much better, and if I'm not, they'll cut me."

"They would be fools to cut you," I said. I thought about

her attempts to fight the demon, but wasn't sure if I should bring that up. "You're so enthusiastic about learning. Look at all the notes you have on dancing and…plants."

I waved a hand at her papers, full of nearly incomprehensible writing. Jessa's smile was forced. "I take a lot of notes in the hopes I'll do better, but…"

"I saw you grow flowers," I pointed out, "And make those vines come up."

"Yes, but you're already summoning fire!" Jessa exclaimed with a longing sigh.

I felt a sharp jolt of guilt for not really summoning fire. The other students were envious of my abilities, but they didn't know I'd cheated on the entrance exam and that most of the magic I'd been able to produce had come from the demon I wasn't supposed to be speaking with.

"Hey!" Kris shouted at us from the doorway. "The whole dorm is going downtown to celebrate before final examinations have us all wanting to jump off Reverie. Are you two coming?"

A few more girls were clustered around her. I recognized Tatiana and Viviane right away. Marina was there. And Jeannette, who I'd never spoken to but knew from Delacroix's class. There were two other girls—second-year students like Jessa. I thought their names were Bridget and Lily.

"Well…" Jessa trailed off. "It would be nice to get out. What do you think, Wynter?"

"I don't really—"

Jessa and Tatiana were smiling at me, and I liked both of them. I'd already studied so much that the words were starting to blur together on the pages, and it was still too early to look around Du Lac's office. Besides, Jessa looked like she really needed a break.

"All right," I said, closing my book.

Jessa and I joined the group, and we headed out from the Academy. It was late evening, and the streets were bustling. We headed downtown towards the forum. I hadn't seen what lay past that in this direction.

"So is studying for the exams killing anyone else?" Kris asked.

"Exams?" I asked. "I thought there was only one."

Kris laughed. "Oh, I wish! No, you have one for every class. It's just that *those* aren't going to have you dismissed from the Academy. You're allowed to fail your exams and retake classes until you get better, as long as you pass the final examination. But if you fail that one, you're out."

"Only having one exam would be great!" Lily said, twisting a strand of blonde hair around her finger. "I'd rather get it all over with at once. I'm seriously questioning my decision to focus in battle magic. I can barely manage water, and Delacroix already expects me to form ice."

"Ugh. I hate Delacroix," Marina said. "I can never tell where I stand with her."

"She's very…dedicated to her job," Tatiana said.

"I'd take Delacroix over Celeste," Viviane said.

"Really?" Lily asked.

"You aren't serious," Kris added.

"Celeste is nice, though," I said.

Viviane rolled her eyes. "Oh, sure, she's nice, but there's just something about her that bothers me. It's like she's *too* nice."

"You only say that because your mother makes you take extra classes with her, Viv," Kris replied.

We stopped before a building made of cobbled together stone. The doors were wide open, unleashing a torrent of music and conversation onto the streets. My eyes widened as I gazed over the stone floors, the wooden counters and tables, and the crowd of people. "Is…is this a tavern?" I asked.

Kris laughed. "You don't have clubs in the Lower Realms?" she asked. "Life must be so boring for you. Come on!"

They all went in, so I did, too. Still, I remained close to Jessa and Tatiana. Kris didn't hesitate in going to the bar and asking for her drink. I waited back and listened to what they were ordering. I really didn't have any familiarity with specific types of alcohol. There were only a few taverns in the Scraps, and they sold ale and brandy.

When the barman turned his attention to me, I asked for red wine. I didn't know anything about wine, but I'd seen Dorian drink it. I was fairly sure I could mimic the way he did it, and if I couldn't, I could take my cues from Viviane, who'd also picked a wine.

Kris commandeered a table in the corner, and we all shuffled in around her. I sat on the edge of my chair, listening and swirling my wine around in its glass.

"How was lunch your mother?" she asked.

"The usual," Jessa said, sounding deflated. "Honestly, I feel like a brood-mare sometimes."

"I understand that," Marina replied, "But at least, you *have* marriage prospects. My engagement to the viscount fell through *again*."

Viviane laughed bitterly. "I think I'd best hope my dear uncle dies young and childless. Maybe I'll begin slipping arsenic in his tea."

"Ah, it is unfortunate about Lady Eleanor's estate," Bridget said. "Are her finances truly as bad as the rumors suggest?"

"They must be if Eleanor is hoping you eventually marry *Alexander*," Kris said. "I mean…"

These girls were all far too young to be worrying about marriage. I wondered if it was a nobility thing. I didn't understand it, so I took a tentative sip of my wine and immediately grimaced. It was the most awful thing I'd ever tasted. Like moldy woodchips. Lucian laughed.

"You don't like it?" Kris asked.

"Not really," I replied. "I thought it would be sweeter."

"You should try something else," Jessa said.

"Do you want a sip of beer?" Lily asked, pushing her tankard towards me. "Truly, a drink worthy of demon slayers."

I felt sick at the comment. I hadn't even slain a demon— just fought it.

Without warning, Viviane reached across the table and took a large gulp of my wine. She swirled the glass around and considered it. "It tastes fine to me," she said. "You're likely just sensitive to the tannins."

"The…what?" I asked.

"Viv, you know wines," Bridget said. "Why don't you get Wynter something sweeter?"

Viviane rolled her eyes but left without any complaint.

"I don't like wine either," Kris said.

"What about you," Marina asked. "Any boys in Argent?"

I thought of Sterling. I felt a rush of emotion, but it was the same kind of love I had for my brother. Loyalty, protection. Nothing like the mess of emotions I felt when I was around Alexander, or the heat I'd felt with Lucian the night before.

"There's a boy, but I'm not sure how I feel about him," I said. The others leaned in, but I didn't know what else to tell them. "He's kind, handsome, and loyal. And he loves me. But his family isn't wealthy." Understatement of the century.

"How romantic!" Jessa exclaimed. "It's just like a fairy tale. Star-crossed lovers." I practically spit out my wine at that. They were all assuming I was some rich heiress from the Gardens, instead of a street rat from the Scraps. The truth was, Sterling and I were the same. We belonged together. But then, why didn't I feel anything for him?

"Speaking of fairy tales," I changed the subject. "I heard there was a mage from the Lower Realms who was in love with a noblewoman, but it ended tragically." It was an awkward transition, but everything seemed to lead back to Guinevere. Maybe if I found out more about what really happened to her, it would help me understand what Dorian was really searching for, and why.

"Oh, *that* story!" Kris said. "He started hearing voices, so he cut her into pieces and drank her blood. My father used to tell it to me all the time. I think it was his way of keeping me away from boys. Or have a proper respect for the dangers of magic."

"Kris!" Jessa exclaimed. "You don't have to be so grotesque with it!"

"That never happened," Tatiana said. "If a noblewoman was really dismembered, why don't we know her name?"

"Tati, you believe the sky is falling," Lily said, drawing peals of laughter. "How is this any less likely?"

Poor Tatiana seemed to wilt in her seat. I smiled at her, hoping to offer some measure of reassurance.

Lily leaned forward and looked sharply around.

"And we do know her name. She was one of the Rosewood siblings. Gwendolyn?"

"Guinevere," Bridget said, looking uncomfortable.

"I thought she killed herself," I said.

"Oh, that's what everyone *says*," Lily replied, "But we all know Viviane's uncle went a little strange after that. He was *convinced* someone murdered Guinevere."

"Or he had a difficult time understanding why his sister killed herself," Jessa said. "I'm sure most people would."

"But that's interesting! I heard after the man chopped her up, he threw her body off the edge of Reverie and down to the Lower Realms. Then, he jumped himself," Kris cut in. "Isn't the Rosewood estate near the edge?"

"It wasn't just some random mage though," Lily said. "He was a student in the academy, from the Lower Realms."

My heart pounded at this news. Du Lac had mentioned a student from the Lower Realms as well. Was it the same man in all the stories? The one dating Guinevere before she died? The pieces were all starting to fit together. If so, the man I'd been searching for, Nicholas Armenia, was from the Lower Realms before being accepted into the academy, just like me.

Maybe he's also the rogue mage blamed for loosing demons last time, Lucian said, adding to the puzzle.

"If any of us disappear and end up dismembered," Lily said, smirking at me, "We know who to blame."

Kris gasped. "We've given her ideas now! What if this was all part of Wynter's evil plan?" The others laughed, but quieted quickly with nervous eyes when Viviane returned and planted a new glass of wine before me. For a few seconds, no one said anything. Marina broke the silence by whistling between her teeth.

"Viviane, you and Wynter kind of look alike," she said.

Viviane scowled. "Hilarious," she said sarcastically. "Honestly—"

"But they *do*!" Kris said, leaning forward.

Viviane stormed back to her seat, clearly irritated. I took a few sips of the wine, and surprisingly, this time it wasn't that bad. It looked exactly like the first one, maybe more purple than red, but much sweeter.

"You could pass for cousins," Tatiana said. "I don't think sisters, though."

"Can we talk about something else?" Viviane said. "We were supposed to be out to enjoy ourselves. I'm going to watch some drunken fools attempt to dance."

I looked around and didn't see anyone dancing.

"More like join in," Kris said, standing and swaying her hips. "Let's go!"

Everyone filed out of the nook, and I followed. We walked upstairs to another room, filled with so many people that it was nearly suffocating. Pink, neon lights flashed from the ceiling, and a few people were playing instruments in the corner, although the crowd was too thick for me to see them. Kris and Marina joined in with the people dancing without any hesitation. The other girls formed a circle around them, until I was left with my glass of wine and Tatiana.

"I'm not much of a dancer," I told her.

After a while I headed back downstairs. I returned to the bar and lingered there, trying to pick up pieces of the conversations. "—did you hear about that 'sky is falling' man?"

That had potential, and it came from a table behind me.

"—I heard the Council found him dead this morning! They're saying a demon might've killed him!"

It seems like the demons aren't only attacking students, then, Lucian mused.

But why hadn't we all heard about that at the Academy? I thought about the sigils on the dragons and how my professors had lied about those. Maybe lying was just the way things were done in Reverie. I wondered if the 'sky is falling' man knew Tatiana or her father. I hoped it *wasn't* her father.

If I had to guess, I'd say the Academy doesn't want people to panic, Lucian said.

It didn't matter, anyway. I couldn't let myself get distracted with mage politics and demon attacks. All that mattered was the journal I was supposed to find. With a burst of inspiration, I walked over to the table and smiled at the two men I'd been eavesdropping on. "I'm looking for Nicholas Armenia. Have you seen him?"

Blank looks. It had seemed like a good idea at the time, but unfortunately, no one had any idea who I meant. I was surprised it hadn't worked. I began to feel groggy, and the room was spinning.

It's probably the wine, Lucian said.

I hadn't even noticed I'd finished the whole glass. With a sigh, I dragged myself back upstairs. I spotted the other girls quickly. Kris, Jessa, and Marina were still dancing, all together in a group. I didn't see Tatiana, Lily, or Bridget.

Viviane remained against the wall, sipping her wine. She met my gaze and waved me over. I joined her, and she smiled wryly. "Do you want to go back?" she asked. "The two of us should be fine."

She was being... uncharacteristically nice. There was a strange fuzziness echoing in my ears. I frowned and wondered if this was what being drunk felt like.

"I wouldn't mind going back... but not with you!" I blurted.

I clapped a hand over my mouth, unsure what had just happened. It didn't feel like I said it. Instead, it felt as if someone else had said it *for* me.

Viviane smiled. "You shouldn't have drunk that wine," she said.

"Did you poison me?" I asked.

"No," Viviane replied. "I just slipped you a truth potion. You aren't really a lady from Argent, are you?"

I choked in my attempt not to answer. "No," I replied, through gritted teeth. "Viviane, you can't—"

"Why?" Viviane asked. "Are you afraid you'll say something I can use against you?"

I turned to run, but Viviane tightly seized my arm and dug her nails into my skin. "Of course, I am!" I replied.

"I've thought there was something odd about you since the beginning. Why are you here?"

I pulled my arm free and tried to run, but I couldn't force myself to do it. I felt like I was choking, and there didn't seem to be enough air in the world.

"I'm stealing for your uncle," I said.

Surprise flickered across Viviane's face, but it disappeared, quickly replaced by something angry and cold. "Consider this a warning," she said slowly. "Stay away from Alexander, or I will ruin you." I laughed at her threat. I was being blackmailed for so many different reasons now, it was hard to keep them straight. And the idea that she was going through all this trouble over a boy seemed ridiculous to me.

"If you ruin me, you'll ruin Dorian, too," I said simply. It was the truth.

Viviane seemed to waver for just a second. "So be it," she said. "My mother has been trying to ruin Dorian for years, so she can be Countess of Rosewood. Betraying my uncle would make Mother prouder of me than she ever has been."

A jolt of fear shot through me as she stormed away. Viviane was the *last* person I'd have wanted to realize I was a fraud. And now that she knew the truth, it was only a matter of time before she told Alexander everything.

TWENTY~FIVE

I WALKED HOME ALONE, PULLING my cloak against the cold air. I was so flustered, I got turned around twice and had to backtrack through unfamiliar streets. At one point, I crossed a narrow bridge over nothingness. The stars above were obscured by a thin mist, like the distant lights of campfires and torches in the Lower Realms down below. My head was spinning, and for a second, I couldn't tell which way was up or down. It was like I was standing in the center of the universe. Only the hissing lamplights guided me towards the right path. I wondered if there was a demon in each one, burning every night just so drunk mages could find their way home? What a waste of magic.

I'd been lucky Viviane was so focused on Alexander. She should have asked *how* I was a fraud, or doing the magic, or what we were trying to steal. As it was, her accusations would be weaker without any specific details, and despite her threats, I didn't think she'd really be so keen to destroy Dorian's reputation. He was still her uncle, after all. I hated the idea of Alexander discovering the truth, but there were more important things to worry about than how some rich prick felt about me.

With any luck, I'd find the journal and be long gone before he learned who I really was. If Dorian kept his promise, Sterling and Briar would be safe, and that's all that mattered.

Despite the awful experience at the bar, I still forced myself to go to Du Lac's office. It was too early to go home, and I didn't want to risk running into anyone else until the truth serum wore off. I hadn't brought my tools, but I used Lucian's sigil to pass through the door as easily as through the glass in the archives. I felt even more light-headed than usual, but it was probably just the alcohol. For the first time, I realized how valuable I'd be if I returned to the Scraps now.

If Gabriel knew what I was truly capable of, there's no way he would ever let me go. I searched carefully through Du Lac's bookshelves, but couldn't find anything that looked like a journal, and there was no mention of Nicholas Armenia. I clenched my jaw and pinched the bridge of my nose. Where else might it be? I'd only searched through a third of the archives, so I'd just have to keep looking. I'd already spent too much time in Du Lac's office, and it was well past midnight, so I headed back to the dormitories. The crisp air cleared my head, but I was exhausted from lack of sleep.

I walked in slowly and saw the full moon through the window across from me. Its silvery light fell over the three beds near me. The two closest to the wall belonged to Dahlia and Ariana. Dahlia was nice, if a bit quiet. Ariana was eccentric and in Gareth's History of Reverie class, although she rarely attended. And of course, Viviane. She must have gotten home before me. I climbed into bed and stared at her for a long time. Viviane knew I was a fraud who'd—at least—lied about my past and was stealing for Dorian. The question was, would she tell

THE SOURCE OF MAGIC

anyone? Or had she already? I drew in a shaky breath.

Viviane seemed to be having a fitful sleep, tossing and turning every few minutes. I wondered if she was caught in some terrible nightmare and unable to escape. Briar sometimes thrashed like that. Maybe I did, too, and just didn't realize it.

Viviane mumbled softly and rolled onto her back. I noticed blood smeared across her sheets and my eyes widened. I quietly slipped from my bed to look closer. Viviane's skin was pale, nearly clammy. The blood was coming from a cut in her upper arm, and although Viviane remained sleeping, she wiped a finger through the dripping blood and drew sigils down her arm. I took a step back, expecting some burst of magic, but nothing seemed to happen.

"Is that normal?" I whispered, stroking the scabbard of my rapier absently.

No, Lucian replied. *I've never seen anything like this before.*

I climbed back into my own bed and continued watching.

"Should I tell someone?" I whispered.

Lucian hesitated. *It might be unwise to wake her*, he said. *If you startle her, it's possible she'll unleash a spell of some kind, and I've no idea what it might be.*

I nodded and stayed awake, watching Viviane. I knew I should be furious at her, for betraying me in the bar and forcing a confession. I'd always considered her a spoiled aristocrat, but it seemed like she was wrapped up in something dangerous.

I slept for a few hours, but opened my eyes just before dawn. The sigils had faded from Viviane's arm by morning. When she woke, she saw the blood and swore softly.

"Viviane," I said.

Viviane glared at me with enough venom to kill a horse.

"Quit watching me, Summer. It's creepy."

I wondered if Viviane had planted her sigils in my trunk and if she'd even realized she'd done it. If so, what kind of dark magic was she wrapped up in?

After a few seconds, I climbed out of bed and dressed, pulling on my uniform. They weren't strictly required, but they were comfortable, and I didn't feel like picking out a dress. Plus, I'd already tossed several of them out already, and wasn't sure how many clean ones I had left. I smoothed over the knee-length skirt and after thinking it over, pulled on my sweater and left my coat.

It was getting warmer, so there was no need for both. I skipped breakfast and went straight to the library. Because it was early, it was mostly empty. The journal wasn't in Du Lac's office, and it hadn't been in the archives, at least not in any of the boxes I'd checked. Was it possible it had been moved somewhere in the school? I scoured the spines of books, but there was no sign of Armenia. Frustrated, I scowled at the books as if I could make what I wanted magically appear.

When it didn't, I sank into a nearby seat, beneath the same portrait of Countess Amelia that I'd once bumped my head on. I tried to study, but I was too anxious to focus. The exam was still two weeks away, but I didn't trust Viviane to wait that long. She'd been trying to get rid of me since I first got here. Even if I passed the exams, that still left Viviane and Du Lac as direct threats, not to mention the occasional demon attack. I promised Briar I'd return to the Scraps, but what good would that do if we remained slaves to Gabriel our whole lives? I had to find that journal.

"Wynter?"

I'd been so distracted I hadn't seen Alexander approach. I tipped my head back against the seat and looked at him. Alexander leaned close to me and put his hands on the arms of my chair. I sighed. I was getting so tired of people trapping me in places.

"Alexander," I said.

"You look tired," he said. "Worried about exams? I think it's my princely duty to tell you that it'll be fine."

"You've never seemed all that concerned with being princely."

"Apologies," he said. The smug look disappeared from his face, replaced with an expression of deep sadness I'd never seen before. "I'm sorry I've been distant lately."

"Why were you?" I asked. "What did I do wrong?"

"Nothing," he said. Then he scowled and sat down next to me. "It wasn't you. I was just... angry at myself. Angry at you. You stopped that demon, when I couldn't. And I'm a prince, and you're just a—"

"A nobody from Argent," I said.

"I was jealous, you've been given this power and you don't even want it."

"That's stupid," I said.

"Yes, I suppose it is," Alexander sighed. "I guess it's just that I have so many expectations on me. My older siblings have all done great things. How do I stand out when I'm the youngest of six children?"

"I don't know," I replied. "I don't care much about standing out. If anything, I'd want to disappear."

"You don't understand," Alexander said.

"No," I replied. "I guess I don't."

287

Alexander leaned closer. Even in the half-light of the library, I was taken aback by the intensity of his blue eyes. Just staring at him made my face warm. Viviane's warning rung in my ears, and I glanced furtively around the library to make sure we were alone. Alexander was the one thing that could burn everything down. I knew I had to stay away from him, but I was glad he was speaking to me again.

"What about the demon attack?" I asked. "Did you see what I saw?"

Alexander was quiet for a long time. Slowly, he sank into the chair beside me.

"Yes," he admitted quietly, "but telling won't do any good."

"Why not?" I turned and curled up in my chair, so I could face him. The fabric backing of the chair was soft against my cheek. "Because the Council cares too much about Reverie looking strong," Alexander said, "And the aristocracy is too busy fighting over trade agreements and worrying about Reverie's many enemies."

"Reverie has enemies?" I asked.

"Of course, we do."

"Do you think that—assuming a mage is controlling these demons—they're trying to assassinate specific people?"

Alexander shook his head, looking as if he pitied my lack of political insight.

"If someone wanted to plan an assassination to weaken Reverie, they'd likely target either my parents, Celeste, or Du Lac. If I was assassinated, it'd be sad, but I have six older brothers. It's not like I'm the heir apparent. I might work as a hostage, and I wouldn't be a good hostage if I was dead. And

Viviane? Sure, her family would be furious. But it wouldn't be a kingdom-destroying blow or anything."

I wondered again about the charm Gareth mentioned. Nicholas heard voices, did that mean he could talk to demons, like I could? Alexander was jealous, because he wanted to be able to communicate with them as well. Was that different from a mage using demons to do their dirty work, binding them to their will with sigils? What was the connection?

"You're forgetting, too," Alexander said, "that you and Tatiana were also present. I don't imagine anyone is going to try and kill either of you."

"You should be careful anyway," I said, "So should Viviane. She doesn't look good. You've noticed, right?"

Alexander's jaw clenched. "Of course, I've noticed," he said.

"I know it's not my business," I said, "But I just…I think maybe she's involved in something she shouldn't be. Maybe you are, too."

"You're worried about me," he smirked. Alexander tilted his head back. His hands curved over the armrests of his chair.

"You wouldn't understand what I'm trying to do," he said. "If we can improve our mastery over demons, we can save Reverie."

"Save it from *what*?"

"From the quakes, from the demons," Alexander said. "From *everything*."

"I think whatever you're involved in is too much for Viviane. Remember what you told me?" I asked. "Not everyone can master magic."

"Can we talk about something besides Viviane?"

"Like what?"

Alexander vaguely waved his hand. "I don't know. Anything. Tell me—tell me about you."

"There's nothing to say," I replied.

"Sure, there is. What was your life like before you came here? Did you have friends?"

Why did he want to know about me?

"One," I said. "Sterling. And my brother."

"Older brother?"

"Younger."

"They must be very proud," Alexander said, "Having a mage in the family."

"I don't know about that."

"What do you mean?"

I felt awkward lying to him, but I wasn't sure how much to tell him. "Um…I live with my uncle, and he just doesn't like me much. I could be the most powerful mage ever born, and I don't think he'd care."

"How unfortunate," Alexander replied.

"It is what it is."

"So…" Alexander trailed off. "How do you intend to occupy yourself after this semester?"

"I suppose it depends on whether I pass the exams or not."

Alexander looked at me askance.

"If you do and decide to stay in Reverie over spring break," he said, "I could give you a tour. If you wanted. Obviously."

Alexander was acting really weird. Really nice, suddenly. And the way he was looking at me was making me feel warm and fuzzy inside. I liked the thought of spending time with him.

You need to be careful, Lucian interrupted.

Lucian's warning snapped me back to reality. Did Viviane already tell him I was a fraud? Was he trying to use his charms to get more information out of me? Even if it wasn't, I knew I couldn't afford to spend time with Alexander. Besides, if he found out who I really was, he wouldn't be so eager to spend time with me.

"I've got to go—" I said, reaching for my things.

Alexander reached forward and cupped his hand around my cheek. I froze, as all my protests fell away. His hand was soft and warm, and he leaned forward, my heart raced a million miles a minute. He was so handsome that it wasn't even fair. I thought of kissing Sterling, and I wondered what it would be like to kiss Alexander. "Think about it," Alexander said. "Won't you?"

I nodded mutely.

Alexander leaned in and pressed his lips against mine. It was nice, and I felt a soft tingling spread through me. My hands fluttered. I wasn't sure what to do with them, but I had a sudden thought of curling them in his hair. I wondered if he'd done this before. Of course he had, he'd probably kissed dozens of girls.

I saw blue light from the corner of my eye and abruptly broke our kiss as flames burst around the edge of my sword. Alexander backed away quickly, looking almost comical in his confusion.

Then he burst out laughing.

"I guess it really is instinct with you," he said

Heat flushed to my face. "I'm so sorry," I said.

"Don't be," Alexander said. "I think it's…well, it shan't be a kiss I soon forget."

"I…I thought you and Viviane were…" I trailed off.

"Wynter," Alexander said, "Don't keep bringing Viviane

into this. Despite what she may have led you to believe, the two of us aren't having some elaborate romance."

My breath hitched.

"I think I'd very much like to know more about you," Alexander said, his voice low. "We could be great together; you know. You have a real gift for understanding demons, and I'm working to understand them. I'd bet we can discover some exciting things, you and I."

Alexander abandoned his chair and left me alone again. I stared after him for a long time, confused and unsure. My heart beat madly in my chest. I took a deep breath and tried to ignore all the girlish fantasies I'd suddenly concocted about Alexander sweeping me off my feet. Maybe I could even tell him the truth about this all. Maybe he could help me.

You're being an idiot. Viviane warned you to stay away, and now you're letting him kiss you. What do you think she'll do when she finds out?

"You almost set him on fire!" I hissed. "And for what? He didn't do anything!"

What? You only want my fire when it's useful to you, hm?

"I don't want you to hurt people!"

But it's fine when it's hurting demons. You are just like the rest of them!

"I didn't choose to be here or fight demons, Lucian."

No, but when this is done, you—at least—get to do something! You have a royal heir interested in you! The nobleman has agreed to help your family—

"Only if I can find what he wants me to," I said, "And they have *names*, Lucian."

Why should I care? They've never been invested in knowing the names of the demons they enslaved. Do you think your nobleman knows the name

THE SOURCE OF MAGIC

of the demon in his blade, the same demon whose ice magic has protected him all these years? Do you think this prince or Viviane know the names of the demons in their pens? Look. I said her name. Are you happy now?

"This has nothing to do with me," I said. I didn't understand why he was getting so angry. I knew he didn't like the prince, but this seemed deeper. It was just a kiss.

Nothing? Wynter, do you think you're the only person to ever hear my kind? Because you aren't. And like all the others, you'll keep using my powers when you want to. Then, you'll marry the handsome prince and continue subjugating my race! Maybe you'll even learn to stop listening, so you can sleep at night.

"That isn't going to happen," I said, "And if I married Alexander, I would do as much as I could to help!"

Then, you have no problem with freeing me, do you, demon slayer?

I took a deep breath and froze, my head spinning. I walked quickly out through the front gates of the school, past the sculpted gardens, and sat on a bench near a large fountain. White doves were pecking seeds from between the cobblestones of the pavement.

"What are you talking about?" I whispered, after making sure we were alone. Lucian's reply came low and dejected, like the anger had left him.

I thought, if I could help you, protect you, prove myself a worthy ally, eventually you'd let me go.

"Let you go?" I repeated.

Do you think I want to be trapped in a sword, doing the bidding of a first-year mage student; when the mages have enslaved my race? Do you think I don't also have family and loved ones I miss and hope to return to?

Guilt ate into my stomach. I never even considered that Lucian would want to be freed, or that I would have the ability to grant him such liberty.

"So everything you've done," I said slowly, "it's all been to warm me up, just so I would free you?"

Alexander was right. You could never trust a demon. Yes, Lucian had been helpful. I couldn't deny that. But I couldn't ignore the demons that had attacked us. I couldn't deny all the dire warnings I'd heard about the dangers of demons.

"I…I can't," I said finally. "I can never trust you. Not really."

I know.

***

The first day of exams finally arrived, and Lucian hadn't said a word since our argument. Viviane had been avoiding me as well, but her silence was a relief. I was anxiously expecting a confrontation when she somehow learned I'd kissed Alexander. Why hadn't she told anyone about me yet? What was she waiting for?

The dormitories were loud with panicked girls, worrying over exams and trying to study last-minute. And because I still hadn't found the journal, I was one of them. I had to at least try to pass winter examinations. Somehow.

After grabbing an apple from the dining hall, I headed out to the grounds. They were green and radiant in the spring sunlight. The sky was a cheerful blue all around me, spotted with soft and fluffy clouds. I took a bite of the apple, relishing the sweetness of it. We'd never had apples that fresh in the Scraps. They'd always been bruised and half-rotten, and even then they were a rare treat. I wondered if Briar and Sterling had gotten the food I kept leaving for them, or if it was rotting away in the Dregs.

The bells rang, announcing that it was time for us to gather. I finished my apple, letting the seeds drop onto the ground, and headed back inside. The ballroom, once destroyed, was now fixed and packed with a hundred or so first-year students. The older students, like Jessa, would be having their exams later in the week.

I spotted Viviane and Alexander. They weren't standing as close together as they normally did. I wondered if Viviane had told Alexander anything. Alexander caught my eye and smiled, but he didn't invite me to join them. So I remained where I was, against the wall and out of everyone's way.

Professor Gareth stood beside me and leaned against the wall. I still hadn't figured out how Elaine had vanished in thin air. Maybe it was a spell of some kind. I kind of wanted to ask, but it wasn't really my business. And I certainly didn't need to be involved in another mystery.

"Excited?" he asked.

"A little nervous," I admitted.

"I think you'll be fantastic," he said. "I've never actually *seen* you use magic, but I've heard you're wonderful with fire. It'll be enjoyable to watch you compete in the dueling tests."

"Thank you," I said, "But I'm really not that great."

"I think you're too modest," Gareth said.

"I wish that was it," I replied, "but I haven't learned as much as I'd hoped."

"Perhaps, that means only that you're a smart, young lady," Gareth offered. "I would be more concerned if you *did* think you'd learned all you should have learned. But you are doing better on my tests, for what it's worth."

I offered him a small smile.

A whistle split the air. Celeste and Du Lac stood on the balcony above us. I felt like Du Lac was looking straight at me, even though I stood behind a large crowd of people. The feeling sent shivers down my spine.

"Good morning, students," Celeste said. "Today is the day you've long waited for. These examinations will determine the students who pass from this year to the next. Written tests will take place this morning. Testing in sigils, rituals, and potions will take place during the evening. Tomorrow, testing in swordsmanship and dancing will take place in the morning, followed by the final testing which will occur in a series of duels. Your opponents have been selected, and each winning student will move to the next round. Please, note that losing one of these duels does not automatically indicate a failing grade."

The only one that really mattered happened tomorrow evening, then. I could fail the others. But not that one. I still had nearly two days to find the journal, but just in case I didn't, I needed to pass these exams so I could keep looking. I knew it was possible, in theory. I hadn't thought that humans could even *do* magic, but if Lucian was right, I just had to pretend I was really a mage, and believe in myself. I didn't have to do better than everyone; I just had to pass.

From the ballroom, we went to the halls outside. Schedules of tests had been posted along the wall. I stayed at the back of the crowd, waiting while everyone else rushed in to see who they would be facing. Finally, I edged my way to the front, my eyes skimming down the list until I found my name and time.

Tatiana was my opponent. I didn't know much about her

magic.

"What do you think, Lucian?" I asked, "Can we beat her?"

He didn't answer. I bit the inside of my cheek. By myself, I'd only managed to—what? Draw lightning by accident. Possibly set some curtains on fire. I'd drawn Lucian's sigil, but I had no idea whether that was his magic or mine, and I doubted it would be a useful skill during the duel. Lucian's powers had been dependable and strong, and I needed them. Maybe I was more like the mages than I wanted to admit.

Without Lucian's help, I seriously doubted my cobbled together assortment of magic was going to be enough to keep me in the Academy, which meant going back to the Scraps empty-handed. It should have been a relief. At least I'd be back with Sterling and Briar, unless my uncle followed through on his threat and sold Briar off to someone else.

Viviane knew my secret and the prince had kissed me. Everything was falling apart, and I had less than two days to find what I couldn't find all semester.

TWENTY~SIX

THE SECOND I LAID EYES on the first test, my confidence plummeted. I twirled the pen between my fingers, staring at the sheet of paper before me. I'd managed to get about half the questions right, which was more than I usually managed. But the others? I had no idea. I filled in all the questions about foreign kingdoms with *Aubade* because it was a kingdom I remembered. When I got to the questions asking about different royal families and parts of the Council, I just scrawled in whatever first came to mind. I didn't know if King Gregory, Alexander's five-times great-grandfather was *really* responsible for writing some legislation involving forcing the people in Argent to mine coal, but it sounded as reasonable as anything else.

I let my cheek rest in the palm of my hand and stared at my exam. Several of my classmates had already left. Which mage was responsible for the creation of potions as a discipline? I scribbled down a name pulled from my memory; I had no idea if it was correct.

"Students," Gareth said. "Your time is up."

I looked around. To my relief, I wasn't the only student still left. Dahlia hadn't finished either.

"I have another obligation," Gareth said, "But if you want to finish, you may take your exams to my office. I will assume that you're being honest and not taking advantage of my kindness."

"Thank you, Professor," Dahlia replied.

Gareth smiled and nodded. After he left, Dahlia sighed. "I don't suppose you know why I'm supposed to care about Geoffrey, the thirty-ninth Baron of Eastbriar?"

I frowned, unsure if this was or wasn't cheating.

"It's my last question," Dahlia said. "Please."

"Didn't Geoffrey first propose enlisting people from the Lower Realms to help Reverie in the war against Aubade?"

Dahlia snapped her fingers and wrote down the answer. "I think that's it! Thank you. Did you have any you were stuck on?"

I bit my lip. Maybe one question wouldn't hurt. I'd answered one for her. I scanned the test and found one that I was really stuck on. "During the formation of the Council, members of the aristocracy were uneasy about leaving magical affairs *solely* at the discretion of the Council and by extension, the Academy," I said. "As a compromise, five noble houses were charged with safeguarding large stores of enchanted objects, a practice which continues today. Name those five noble houses. I have Eastland, Willowbrook, Northhaven, and Mauverine."

Dahlia's lips moved as she repeated the names. "Rosewood," she finally said.

My skin prickled. How had I missed that? So Dorian had a vast store of magical items hoarded beneath his estate?

"Thank you," I replied, filling in the answer.

Dahlia gathered up her test. "Don't mention it!" she

replied.

I looked at my test and slowly went through the answers, filling in a few blank spaces with random guesses. Any answer was better than none at all. After I was finished, I headed for Gareth's office. Although I'd never been inside, I'd heard him talking in it before. When I arrived in his office, I knocked on the door before opening it.

Gareth's office was brighter and more spacious than Du Lac's, but it was still overflowing with books and papers. I found Dahlia's test easily, sitting atop his desk. I placed mine with hers and glanced around Gareth's office. He must've just stepped away for a few minutes. I paused, considering. Gareth knew about Guinevere. If this did all involve her, maybe *he* had the journal. And I was here, alone, in his office. I felt bad stealing from the one professor who'd been kind to me, but I couldn't afford to think about that now.

I pushed away my guilt and began sifting through the papers on his desk, before combing through the bookshelf. The volumes were in no discernable order, but I didn't see anything relevant. Then I turned to the drawers on his desk. They all opened, except for one. I bit my lip and pulled out my sword, slicing a thin cut through my forearm to draw blood. As I drew the sigil, my hand shook. I felt my energy wane as usual. Slowly, I reached my fingertips towards the locked drawer; my hand passed through without difficulty. I groped around, feeling papers and something leathery. My fingers closed around it, and I pulled out a couple books and a few scattered papers.

I heard footsteps approaching, so I stood quickly and wiped the smeared blood off the desk. My heart raced and my palms were slick with sweat. There wouldn't be time to look through everything, so I pulled off my sweater and tucked the books and papers behind it, hoping to pass off the things as my own.

I smiled as Professor Gareth walked in. "I finished my test!" I declared.

"Oh, good," Gareth said. "Thank you."

His kindness was like a dagger in my stomach. I wanted to thank him for being so kind. That was more than I expected or deserved. And odds were, I wouldn't see him again after all this. Worse, I was carrying an armful of his things. So many questions ran through my head, but this wasn't the time or place.

"It's been a great semester, Professor," I said, backing up towards the door.

Gareth's eyes crinkled at their corners. "It has," he said.

I gave him one last smile before heading out. The corridors were bustling with students making their way to class. I spotted Kris among them, but she didn't seem to notice me. I darted into the dormitories. They were crowded, but as long as I didn't let on that something was wrong, everyone would just assume I was studying. I unfolded the sweater and dumped the contents onto my bed. There were two books. I pulled one open and flipped through the pages. There were rows and rows of sigils, tiny drawings of flowers and stars, and snippets of texts. Had I found someone's class notes? The other book did appear to be a journal of some kind. The leather was stiff and the pages yellowed from age. I flipped through it quickly, searching for any names I might recognize.

I miss Guinevere so much these days. I knew it would be hard being apart from her, but I hadn't anticipated it being so lonely. I wish she'd agreed to come with me. She'd have loved it here; it's a bit like Reverie.

Whoever's journal this was, it belonged, at least, to someone who knew Guinevere, which seemed promising. This might be right, but there was only one way to know for sure. I gathered up everything but the journal and shoved them in my trunk. I was supposed to go to Du Lac's exam, but at this point, what difference did it make? He'd probably fail me anyway. If this really was Nicholas Armenia's journal, there was no point in showing up now, pretending to be a mage.

I headed downstairs and left the Academy through the front gates. It was a pleasant day with a faint breeze that played in my hair. My heart fluttered in my chest. Everything was so beautiful up here, I felt a painful longing in my chest. Was this really the end of everything? Could I really go home after this? Dorian hadn't said he needed anything else. Would he honor his word and help me get away from my cruel uncle?

I made my way quickly to Rosewood and pounded up the entryway steps. A sudden thrill filled me now that I was on safe ground. Briar and Sterling could have a new life, and I could leave Reverie. I didn't belong here, I never had. So why wasn't I happier about leaving?

When I raised my hand to knock, the door opened. Dorian stood in the doorway, Francisca close behind him. I slowly lowered my hand. "How is it that you always know when I'm on my way?" I asked.

Francisca rolled up the sleeve of her blouse, revealing a dark blue sigil over her forearm. "It gives me a sense of where people are. No one ever sneaks up on me," she replied.

That was certainly useful.

I held out the journal. "Is this it?" I asked.

My heart was in my throat as Dorian took the journal and flipped through it, his brow furrowed. "I'm not sure," he said at last.

For a long moment, I just stared at him, unsure if I'd heard him right.

"What do you mean?" I asked.

"I mean, it could be a forgery," Dorian said, "Or the wrong book entirely. I'll need to have someone verify it is what I'm looking for."

"How long will that take?" I asked.

"Probably a week," Dorian replied.

I froze, my heart plummeting.

"But the final examination is in two days," I said slowly.

"So it is," Dorian replied. "Given that we don't yet know if this is Nick's journal, I suppose you'll just have to pass the exam, won't you?"

I had a sinking suspicion he'd planned this somehow. Maybe he already knew whether it was Nick's journal, and he was just playing with me. Or maybe he was trying to weasel out of our agreement.

"But I'm not a mage," I said, panic rising in me.

"Didn't you summon fire to fight a demon?" Dorian asked.

No, *Lucian* had, and Lucian hadn't spoken to me since our fight. I should have told Dorian the truth. I was more of a fraud than even *he* knew. Or did he suspect it already? Maybe he knew I'd fail the exam, or be discovered as a fraud, and then he wouldn't have to honor the promise he'd made me. Maybe he and Viviane were working together to ruin me. Maybe even

Alexander was in on it. Maybe Lucian was right about everything.

"But if that *is* Nick's journal, you'll do what you promised, right?" I asked. "And if it's not and I pass, you'll...you'll let me keep looking?"

"As long as I get what I want, little mage," Dorian replied.

I drew a shuddering breath. At the moment, I'd have given about anything to actually *be* a mage. But I wasn't going to give up when Sterling and Briar might have a chance for a better life. No, I was going to take that exam, and if I wanted to pass, I'd have to practice.

***

Battle magic was my best bet, with or without Lucian. I wasn't the best in the class by a long-shot, but I was pretty sure I could overcome Tatiana with brute force and a few of the tricks Lucian had taught me in practice. I was sure I'd already failed Du Lac's class by not showing up, but maybe I could make it up in the final duel, which carried the most weight.

Once I returned to the Academy, I headed through the grounds and to the fields where Delacroix's class had always taken place. There were a few other students practicing. The ones I knew gave me nods and smiles. I unsheathed my rapier and moved into a fighting stance, but it was hard to practice without a partner. I hesitated.

"You really aren't going to help me, are you, Lucian?" I whispered.

No answer. Maybe I didn't deserve one. It was going to be difficult to perform in a magical duel without his fire. Despite

Dorian's insistence that I couldn't cheat my way out of this, I thought about the device tucked away and hidden in my things. I could use it as a distraction at least, and the fake flames might even pull some extra marks from the judges.

"Wynter!"

I turned around at the sound of my name. Alexander waved and jogged to me. "Do you want a partner?" he asked.

I thought of Viviane, who knew I was a fraud. At least, she knew I'd lied about where I was from, and I doubted everyone would believe me over her.

"No, I'm fine," I said. My eyes flicked to his lips, remembering our kiss in the library, but it was too dangerous to be near him now that Viviane knew my secret.

Alexander unsheathed his blade and moved into a fighting stance.

"Come on," he said, smirking. "I'll go easy on you, I promise."

I rocked back on my heels and resumed a fighting stance. I *did* need to practice. I thrust the rapier forward; Alexander parried as expected. I tried feinting, seeing if he would fall for a trick. He didn't. Instead, he broke past my guard and tapped the side of my neck.

"I'm beginning to think," I said, blowing a strand of hair out of my face, "you really just want to kill me."

Alexander laughed. "How absurd," he said. "I just want you to pass your swordplay exam. I've already made plans for your summer, remember?"

My heart raced. It was a nice dream, but one way or another, Alexander was going to find out the truth, and then he'd never look at me the same way again. I remembered what he said once about the Scraps, that *nothing* good could come from it. Including me.

At best, I'd return to a better life with Briar and Sterling; at worst, everything would go back to how it was before. Maybe I didn't want that, not exactly, but I knew these summer plans were never going to happen. I thought of telling Alexander that we would never work, but that would mean admitting everything. I couldn't do that, not yet. No matter how this ended, I was never coming back.

I thrust again. He parried.

"Your form is good," Alexander said. "Delacroix will like that."

Yes. But her exam wasn't the one I was worried about. Her exam wasn't the one that would have me dismissed from the Academy. The final duel was the one that really mattered.

Alexander lunged forward. I parried his blade and tried to turn the move into a thrust, but he stepped aside. When he thrust, I parried with the edge of my blade. I pushed against him, trying to knock him off balance, but Alexander dropped his blade and swept aside. I stumbled, overbalanced with the sudden loss of resistance. Alexander's blade tapped against my shoulder.

I took a fighting stance once more and thrust. My form *was* good, and that was more than I'd had when I came to the Academy. Alexander parried and went to swipe his blade beneath mine. I parried and feinted. I saw an opening and thrust my blade towards his neck in desperation. The edge of my rapier grazed just beneath his jaw, drawing blood.

I gasped and nearly dropped the rapier. "I'm sorry! I didn't mean—"

Alexander laughed and put a hand to the side of his neck.

When he pulled his hand away, a tiny spot of blood stained his palm. "It's just a scratch," he said. "I think I'll survive."

"But you didn't cut me," I replied, wincing.

"It happens," he said, sheathing his blade. "Let's take a break. I'll show you how to do the healing sigils."

He pressed his hand once more to his neck and then offered me his arm. I hesitated before sheathing my rapier and linking my arm with his. "I really am sorry," I said.

"If I'd known a little cut was going to get this much attention from you, I wouldn't have fought so hard against you," Alexander teased. "I'd have let you nick me and feigned as if I was dying."

My face warmed. "You—you aren't being serious," I said.

Alexander smiled. "I'm being completely serious," he said, his voice low and husky.

I had no idea what to say. Alexander tucked a wayward strand of hair behind my ear, sending little sparks of warm through me. What was I supposed to do with this…this nicer Alexander who was suddenly paying attention to me? I felt all flustered and warm, even though—rationally—I knew these feelings were dangerous. I couldn't afford to piss Viviane off before the tests. Too much was riding on this.

"For what it's worth, I really do think you'll pass," Alexander said. "Maybe you don't see it, but you have improved since coming here."

Of course, I had improved. I just had no way of knowing if it would be enough. For all I knew, I'd given Dorian a useless journal and was poised to fail the final examination. And now, Lucian wasn't helping me anymore. I hadn't realized just how much I needed him. And more than that, I missed him. Having him around all the time had been annoying, but his sudden absence felt like a black hole in my heart. I couldn't blame him for wanting his freedom, but what if I let him out, and he was just a monster like the others? What if he hurt someone, and I was responsible for it? I couldn't take the risk, at least not now.

TWENTY~SEVEN

THE NEXT MORNING, EVERYTHING SEEMED even louder. The corridors were full of a sort of frantic, anxious energy that I understood all too well. It was a relief to leave the bustle of the buildings and go to the fields outside. Delacroix and a handful of my classmates had already gathered. I stood by Alexander, who gave me a small smile.

"Wynter," he said.

"Alexander," I nodded. "Are you ready for this?"

"I don't think it'll be a problem for me," Alexander replied.

"Of course, it won't," Viviane said, grasping his arm. "It's a pity, Summer, that no one taught you swordplay in *Argent*."

Alexander shot her an irritated look and awkwardly pulled his arm free. Viviane glared. But not at him. No, it seemed her ire was reserved only for me. I wondered if she would reveal me right then and there. I edged away from Alexander, giving Viviane her way.

"Wynter! Viviane!" Lily waved and ran over to us.

"Why are you here?" I asked.

"I'm making notes on form and such for Delacroix," Lily

said.

I looked at Delacroix, who seemed to be counting us all. She clapped her hands together and drew her blade. "Circle up!" she exclaimed.

We formed a ring around her. She was one of the few teachers who wore pants instead of a dress or robe, which only made her seem taller. During class, she wore a leather vest embossed with floral patterns and metal plates that protected her knees and shoulders. Today her dark green tunic brought out the flecks of emerald in her eyes. She was pretty, in a severe looking way.

"So who's going first?" she asked.

"We're going to fight you?" Alexander asked.

Delacroix shrugged. "I am the best swordsman here," she replied with a smirk. "That makes sense to me."

But wouldn't she get tired? I looked around at my classmates. Surely, Delacroix couldn't fight *all* of us, could she? Not that it mattered. This wasn't the exam that really counted, but brushing up on my swordplay wouldn't hurt.

"Who is going first?" Delacroix asked again.

"I will," Alexander replied, unsheathing his sword.

She and Alexander took fighting stances. I held my breath, waiting to see who would make the first move. Without any warning, Alexander lunged, thrusting his blade. Delacroix parried easily and slashed the air before her. Alexander parried, Delacroix's blade sliding off his. Once more, Alexander attacked. Delacroix parried and slipped her blade beneath his. She was holding back. I gulped.

Once Delacroix began attacking, Alexander immediately went on the defensive, trying desperately to parry her blows. He clearly struggled, his movements becoming more and more haphazard with every one of Delacroix's strikes. Then, Alexander parried, and Delacroix lunged. Her blade slid beneath Alexander's guard and tapped against his clavicle. "Done," she said. Alexander stood still a second more, catching his breath, then his shoulders slumped. If she handled Alexander this easily, Delacroix was going to cut me to pieces.

Delacroix went back to Lily, making notes in a large, leather-bound book. The two of them whispered together for a few minutes before Delacroix returned to us.

"Next."

I waited, letting my classmates go one after the other. I'd hoped that Delacroix would eventually tire, but she seemed to have boundless energy. I bit my lip.

"Who's next?" Delacroix asked.

I took a step forward and unsheathed my rapier.

Delacroix smiled and moved into a fighting stance. I mirrored her pose and waited. I wasn't going to strike first, not against her. But Delacroix seemed fine with waiting. She stood across from me, patient and silent. Without warning, she lunged. I parried her blade, vibrations darting down my arms. She was powerful and fast.

She struck again and again. I parried each blow, but Delacroix didn't give an inch. She feinted, and I saw an opening. I went for it, my blade aimed for her neck. She parried and swept my blade aside. Another strike. I parried, stumbling from the force of Delacroix's blow. Another blow. I tried to parry but was too late. Delacroix's blade tapped my ear.

"Dead," she said. "You need to work on protecting your left side, Wynter. You have a tendency to leave that side open when you fight."

Although I nodded, my heart sank. Had I passed? Had I failed? I'd lost, but thus far, no one had won against Delacroix. That was a good sign, right? Delacroix walked back to Lily and spoke with her, while I rejoined my classmates.

"You did well," Alexander said. "I said you would."

Beside him, Viviane's grip tightened on her rapier. She narrowed her eyes and leaned close to me. "I'd expected something more," Viviane whispered, "Considering who you work for."

"Be nice, Viv," Alexander said.

"It's just a little gossip between girls," Viviane replied, smiling sweetly. "Nothing that you need to worry about, right, Summer?"

I nodded. "Right," I replied. "Nothing at all."

***

Staff and students were allowed to watch their classmates duel, so I joined my classmates on the lower floor of the ballroom and watched the first few bouts. The faculty sat at a table before us, ready to judge the duels. I kept thinking about the demon, too. The demon I'd weakened and allowed to be imprisoned in this very room. Alexander came and stood beside me. I felt an instinctive uneasiness that Viviane might join him, and I sighed in relief when Tatiana came over to us. She smiled brightly and extended her hand to me. "May the best mage win," she said. "Please, don't burn me too badly with your fire."

I felt a sharp pang of guilt. "I promise I won't," I replied.

"Who are you facing, Alexander?" Tatiana asked.

"Brian. I don't know if you've met him," Alexander said, nodding at a wiry boy with dark hair and lean muscle.

"We have dance together," Alexander said, shrugging. "He's in sigils, too. And I think Viviane is facing Kris."

Tatiana hummed. "I haven't seen Viviane all morning."

I hadn't either, but I wasn't going to complain about that.

Celeste stood and turned around to face us. "Students, the final examination will soon commence. The exam will be completed once one of you surrenders or can no longer continue to fight. The other judges and I may also call an end to the duel at our discretion, if we believe it too dangerous for either of you to continue. You should duel one another, but your primary goal is to demonstrate what you've learned. The first competitors will be Sean Abernathy and Haley Chevalier. Please step forward.

Sean and Haley took their positions and began. From there, the duels commenced mostly how I'd anticipated them going. It soon became clear that there were differences in skill levels, but everyone had managed *some* magic. Each bout was a surprising combination of tricks, dancing, magic sparks, and distraction. It was like fencing, but on a whole different level. My heart sank, worried about what Tatiana would do to me.

I bit my lip. Without Lucian, what did I have? A sigil that would let me pass through objects and one that could make lightning, if I could remember it. Rudimentary swordplay skills that weren't very impressive without Lucian's fire. Would any of that be enough? I felt like I might be sick. I really hoped I'd found Nicholas Armenia's journal, and not just someone who happened to know Guinevere and Dorian.

After a while, Celeste called a break. Some of my classmates went outside for pretzels and hot chocolate, but I remained where I was. Celeste smiled as she walked past me. I smiled back and fidgeted with my hands. This was too much. I silently cursed myself again for not just fleeing with Dorian's tiara and pawning it. The faculty took their seats again. Viviane entered and stood stiffly beside me. "Good luck," I said awkwardly.

Viviane looked at me. I expected a snide comment, but she said nothing. Instead, hand shaking, she pulled out her pen. Alexander walked past her and stood beside me, but Viviane didn't react to him either. Something was wrong. Her pupils were wide and dark, and I could see the sheen of sweat across her pale skin.

"Vivi—"

"Viviane, Lady of Sherringford, and Kristiana, Lady of Northwell!" Celeste announced.

Viviane and Kris took their places.

"And begin!" Celeste exclaimed.

Kris crouched to the ground and began drawing her sigils; Viviane drew them directly on the palm of her hand. I tensed and waited. The ground rumbled, and crystals burst through the ground, shimmering like jagged bits of glass. Kris yelled, seemingly in surprise, as the crystal spikes shot from the ground, coming closer and closer. Before Viviane's crystals could reach their target, Kris unleashed a flurry of thick roots that wrapped around them.

"Since when is Viviane that good?" Alexander muttered.

I had no idea. From what I'd seen of Viviane's sigils, they rarely worked.

"I guess she's been practicing," I said.

More crystals emerged from the ground, roaring and

forming around Kris. They smothered Kris's roots, choking them out. Kris rolled up her sleeve and pushed her pen against her forearm, but before Kris could launch any spell, Viviane vanished.

"Is that invisibility?" Tatiana asked.

There was a chorus of murmuring and a few scattered cheers from the audience. We hadn't covered invisibility in our textbook. I looked towards the faculty. Celeste's brow was furrowed and she was muttering to herself; it seemed like she thought there was something strange about this, too. Beside her, Delacroix was whispering to Gareth. Du Lac looked fascinated.

Kris slowly turned around, putting her back to Viviane's crystals. I didn't see Viviane, but I saw blood form along Kris's side. Kris screamed and struck out with her arm. Sigils glowed bright green, and thorned vines sprang from the ground, crowned with red roses. They rose upward toward the ceiling, before diving like a flock of birds.

Viviane yelped and reappeared, wrapped in the vines. She dropped to the ground surrounded by leaves and bright red petals, while Kris, gasping for air, stood over her. After a few seconds of thrashing, it didn't look like Viviane could free herself. The thorns tore at her skin, drawing blood.

"That's enough!" Du Lac shouted.

I frowned and looked towards the professors. I hadn't expected *him* to interfere. Maybe Celeste or Gareth.

"No, it isn't," Viviane said, her voice so quiet I barely heard it.

"Viviane, it's over," Kris said. "It was a great match!"

Viviane screamed in frustration, hastily drawing new sigils on her arm before swiping her fingers towards Kris.

The ground before her crumbled as jagged crystals emerged around her like shards of glass, slicing through the vines and leaving deep cuts on her arms and legs. Without pausing, Viviane swiped her fingers through the blood dripping down her trembling limbs and sketching more symbols in a wide arc in front of her. They crackled with power, radiating golden light. The ground shook, knocking over the ceremonial urns in the corner of the room.

Viviane floated above the wreckage, her hair fanning out like she was underwater, and then cast out her hands quickly. More crystals stabbed like knives towards the edge of the ballroom, splitting open the floor. I leaped back, trying to avoid being cut. Some of my classmates screamed.

"Viviane!" Du Lac shouted.

She whipped around and glared at him, but her eyes were unrecognizable, glowing with white energy. Kris's vines fell away, as Viviane stepped lightly toward Du Lac. The arm of Viviane's dress had been torn during the struggle, and a row of angry, red sigils had been revealed. They looked like the same sigils as I'd seen on the demon. I drew in a sharp breath as I realized what that meant. *Viviane was being controlled by someone else.* But who would do such a thing?

Kris tried to run, but Viviane unleashed a row of tall crystals, blocking her path. Viviane's eyes burned with inner fire, sending up sparks of magic like a shimmering crown. She was out of control. Someone was going to get hurt. I looked around me, but the professors were too busy protecting the other students. Everything was so loud and panicked. I drew my rapier and ran to the edge of the crystals. I sliced my arm and drew Lucian's sigil quickly. My head spun, but I leaped through the crystals and stood before Kris. "Come on!" I shouted.

Kris ran to me and passed through the crystal barrier, right where I'd come through. Suddenly, the ground beneath me rumbled, knocking me off my feet. My heart pounded so loudly I heard it in my head. Cracks of skylight snaked through the broken floor beneath me. Viviane wasn't just creating crystals. She was splitting Reverie clean apart.

"Viviane, stop!" I shouted.

A hand grabbed my shirt and pulled me to safety. It was Alexander, pen in hand. "Stay behind me!" he yelled.

"She's being controlled!" I exclaimed. "By—I can tell by the sigils!"

Blood dripped from Viviane's nose, but she still drew another row of sigils along the palm of her hand. I turned to the crystal, ready to draw another sigil so we could pass through it. Before I could, it exploded in my face like shrapnel. I fell backward, hitting the ground hard. There was blood and ringing in my ears. I held onto my sword like a lifeline.

Delacroix scrambled over the shattered crystals came to a halt before us, rapier drawn. "Viviane," she said, "Stand down."

Viviane scowled. Her face was covered with blood.

"Viviane, this isn't you," Delacroix said. "You've fallen prey to a terrible enchantment, but I can help you."

Du Lac and Gareth joined Delacroix and flanked her as she approached Viviane. For a second, Viviane seemed to hesitate. Something flashed in her green eyes. "M—my mother is going to kill me," she said.

"No, she isn't," Delacroix said soothingly. "You haven't done anything—"

Viviane vanished, and Delacroix screamed. I didn't see

what happened, but she fell to her knees. Blood poured from her chest, thick and viscous. Du Lac grabbed my arm and pulled me back. "Run!" he snapped.

I darted away, Alexander close behind, but Viviane blocked our path. Her skin was nearly gray. There was a pop and a flash of light, someone's spell, and Viviane collapsed, her breaths tearing from her throat. She writhed on the ground, her arms snaking like live wires. Her hands flopped like fish out of water, drawing another row of sigils.

Crystals burst from the ground, rushing towards me. They were coming too fast. I thrust my rapier forward, but there wasn't even a hint of flame. Alexander pushed me out of the way, and Viviane's attack struck him hard, knocking him off his feet. I scraped my arm on the shattered crystal and winced, then looked up as Viviane stood over me.

"You," she said. "This is all *your* fault."

"Lucian, please," I rasped. "Help me stop her."

The ground beneath me rumbled. I staggered to my feet as more crystals formed beneath me. Some of them tore large chunks through the ground, revealing the empty sky beneath us. I watched them fall, as if in slow motion. We were so high up. There was no way to survive a fall like that.

Gareth slowly approached Viviane from behind. Before he could surprise her, she screamed and whipped around. She punched him squarely in the jaw. Gareth grabbed her right wrist, and with his free hand, he tried to swipe his pen across her arm. But she threw him to the ground with superhuman strength.

If you can burn the sigils, you can likely disrupt the spell, Lucian said. His voice was quiet, as if far away.

I breathed a sigh of relief as my rapier burst into flames.

"Thank you!"

I thrust the blade into the ground, and the crystals melted like candle wax. When Viviane turned back to me, I was ready. I thrust the blade into her forearm, right through one of the sigils.

When I drew the blade out, Viviane dropped a hand to the wound and swayed on her feet. Delacroix, blood staining her blouse, placed her sword at Viviane's neck.

"Wh—where am I?" Viviane asked. "Did I pass?"

Her knees buckled. Du Lac caught Viviane as she fell, and lowered her gently to the ground. She looked close to death.

"Wynter?" Viviane asked distantly. "I wasn't—did I—"

Alexander crouched Viviane. "It's all right," he said, squeezing her hand. Gareth tore apart Viviane's sleeve and traced his finger over the sigils.

"They were on the demon, too," I said. "What are they?"

"A type of magic that should have remained buried long ago," Du Lac replied hesitantly. "I've never…I've never seen magic like this used on mages before."

Delacroix flopped to the ground nearby and tipped her head back. Blood was quickly seeping through her blue blouse. Celeste stepped delicately through us and began drawing healing sigils along Delacroix's collarbone. Either I'd missed Celeste in all the confusion, or she'd been evacuating students. I realized, quite suddenly, how quiet the ballroom was. It was mostly empty now, except for a handful of students and teachers.

"You can control demons through their blood," Gareth said slowly.

"And you think someone did this to Viviane?" I asked.

Who would do something like this to her? And for what?

"No one can know about this," Celeste said. "There will be panic if word gets out that there's a rogue mage controlling people."

"No," Viviane mumbled. "No, I—I won't keep—"

"Let's get you to the infirmary, Viviane," Delacroix said, "So you can recover."

"You, too, Wynter," Gareth said.

Gareth crouched at my feet and drew careful sigils around the crystals until they all sank and melted away.

I slowly sheathed my rapier. Immediately, Alexander was at my side. He said nothing, only looked solemnly at me. We slowly made our way across the destroyed ballroom. Whatever Viviane had done, it was terrifying. In some places, the floor was cracked so badly that I could see slivers of the Lower Realms far below. Who knew Viviane had such power? And what did that say about the person controlling her?

Gareth was somehow making Viviane float behind him, which—while impressive—was also a little spooky.

"Is she going to be all right?" I asked.

"Yes," Du Lac said, glancing at me over his shoulder, "With time."

Why did I keep hearing buzzing sounds in my head? I paused, suddenly light-headed.

"Are you alright?" Alexander asked, gripping my arm.

"I think so," I said. "You?"

"I've been better," he smiled.

"If you hadn't done that, what you did. You saved us all."

I bit my lip, shaking my head.

"It wasn't me," I said quietly.

"Your demon?" he asked, eyes widening.

THE SOURCE OF MAGIC

I nodded, and he squeezed my hand.

"Tell him thanks. For me."

We continued towards the exit. There was a nail-thin crack in the floor beneath me. Everyone else had walked over it without difficulty; the floor seemed intact. It was only towards the center that it started to shift like breaking ice.

"Wynter?" Alexander turned back.

"Sorry," I said. "I just felt like—"

There was no warning. I didn't know if it was a lingering remnant of Viviane's spells, or something else entirely, but the ground gave way beneath me. The Lower Realms were spread out below me, and my mind was slow to catch up to what that meant.

Alexander grabbed my hand as I fell, pulling him with me through the gap in the floor as it opened to swallow us both.

***

A woman screamed, and that sound was so shrill and panicked that at first I couldn't even believe it was mine. I was falling, and Alexander was falling. And we were going to die.

Wynter!

There was a note of panic in Lucian's voice, and I felt that panic in my own beating heart. Wind rushed up against us as we tumbled through the clouds. And I didn't want to die. And—

You need to release me.

I looked over at Alexander, he was shouting something. He drew sigils on his cloak, trying to hold it out like a parachute, but the wind tore it away from him. Then he grabbed my arm in terror, his face white.

Alexander was still wearing his fancy suit, clutching my hand, and now I was the story, my blue dress fluttering behind me like a billowing tail. I was the mage-lady falling from the skies. A piece of broken mage tech, discarded into the refuse piles.

It's the only way.

"Can you save us?" I asked. Alexander's face fell, and he shook his head.

"I'm sorry," he said.

But I wasn't asking him.

"If I free you, will you save him, too?"

I swear I will, Lucian promised.

I wasn't sure I believed him, but what difference did it make now? I'd messed up so many things, but this one was important. Lucian was right, I was just like the other mages at Reverie, using magic without caring where it came from. This was my only chance to prove that I could've been something more.

"I don't know how!" I shouted.

Yes, you do.

I racked my brain. Was it a spell, a sigil? Something else?

Then it dawned on me. Of course, it all made sense now. It was the sigil that Lucian taught me, the one that let you pass through objects. I marveled at the simplicity. Lucian had given me the key to his prison weeks ago.

My hand shook as I unsheathed the rapier, holding it in a death grip. The ground was rushing up to meet us far too quickly. I swiped my hand across the fresh cuts in my arm. My fingers came away sticky with blood.

We were falling so, so fast. I couldn't do this, but I had to try.

I lifted my fingers towards the blade. I could see my own terrified expression in the reflection. My hands shook as I painted the symbol on carefully. I had to get it right. I needed this to work.

"What are you doing?" Alexander screamed.

"Trying to save Lucian."

"Are you insane? You're letting him out? He'll kill us!"

I laughed darkly.

"We're dead already. At least one of us has a chance of surviving."

"You can't trust him."

"It's the right thing to do."

I prayed silently as I closed the last line of the sigil. The blade turned blinding white, and sizzled in my hand. A victorious shout split the air as Lucian launched himself from the blade. For a moment, nothing happened, and all I could hear was the rushing of wind and my heart pounding in my ears as the ground flew towards us. We were close enough now to make out individual buildings, and I recognized a few spots in the Scraps from my childhood. The lone tree where we'd built a tire-swing to play on during my eighth summer. The house where the woman baked apple pie and sometimes gave us a sliver in exchange for the wildflowers Sterling gathered in the forest. My life had begun here, and it would end here. I took a deep breath, and waited to die.

I'd grab your princeling, Wynter.

I didn't ask. I just grabbed Alexander's arm and pulled him towards me, squeezing my arms around him in a tight embrace. And then—pain burst beneath my shoulder blades, so intense that spots danced in my vision.

Dark, smoky tendrils of magic surrounded us like soft feathers. I heard the rustle of wings, like being in the middle of a flock of birds. It felt like my body was moving on its own, pumping muscles I'd never used before. And then, our fall slowed.

When I looked over my shoulder, I had wings. They were large and black, like a raven's. Alexander and I descended lightly. The moment Alexander's feet touched the ground, he stumbled away from me in horror.

"What have you done?" he asked.

THE END

URBAN EPICS

What Happens Next?
FIND OUT NOW

Sign up for new release updates and get a sneak
peek of the next book in this series.

You'll also get access to our starter library (ten free chapters from our
most popular series), discounts, previews, giveaways and more.

YOUR OPINION MATTERS

Here at Urban Epics, we're dedicated to writing books that *you* want to read, so your feedback is important to us! If you liked this book, let us know by posting a review on Amazon. Every review counts (we know, because we count them), and sometimes our readers have the best ideas.

Let us know what you loved, what you hope happens next, and we'll take your feedback to heart. We also use reviews to determine what types of books we should write next, so make sure to "vote" for your favorites by posting a review. You can also join the Urban Epics Facebook group and tell us what you think directly.

Sincerely,
The Authors

Printed in Great Britain
by Amazon